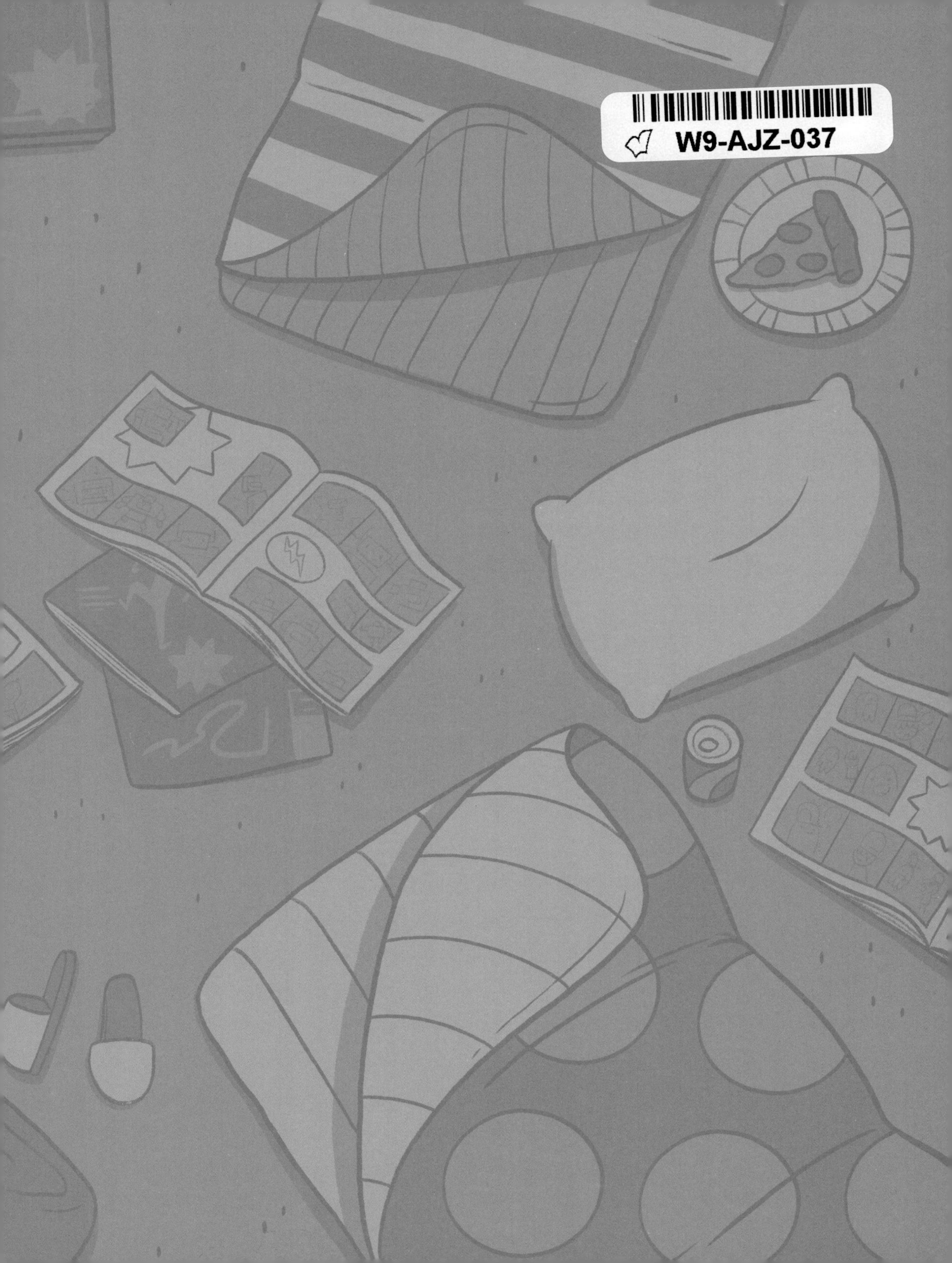

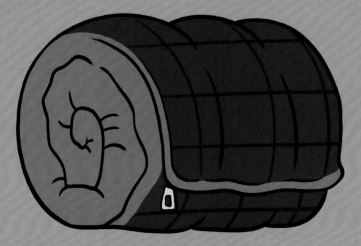

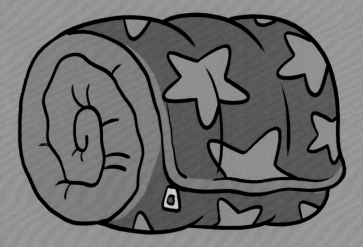

Dedicated to any friends helping each other
navigate the ins and outs of life (and afterlife)

Tundra Books, an imprint of Penguin Random House Canada Young Readers,
a division of Penguin Random House of Canada Limited

Library and Archives Canada Cataloguing in Publication

Title: Super sleepover / Cale Atkinson.
Names: Atkinson, Cale, author, illustrator.
Description: Series statement: Simon and Chester
Identifiers: Canadiana (print) 2020039004X | Canadiana (ebook) 20200390058
ISBN 9780735267442 (hardcover) | ISBN 9780735267459 (EPUB)
Subjects: LCGFT: Graphic novels.
Classification: LCC PN6733.A85 S877 2021 | DDC j741.5/971—dc23

Published simultaneously in the United States of America by Tundra Books of
Northern New York, an imprint of Penguin Random House Canada Young Readers,
a division of Penguin Random House of Canada Limited

Library of Congress Control Number: 2020950281

Edited by Samantha Swenson
Designed by Andrew Roberts
The artwork in this book was created with ecto-plazm,
haunted pencils and Photoshop.
The text was set in Silver Age BB.

Printed in China

www.penguinrandomhouse.ca

1 2 3 4 5   25 24 23 22 21

tundra | Penguin
        | Random House
        | TUNDRA BOOKS

Simon AND Chester
Super Sleepover!

by Cale Atkinson

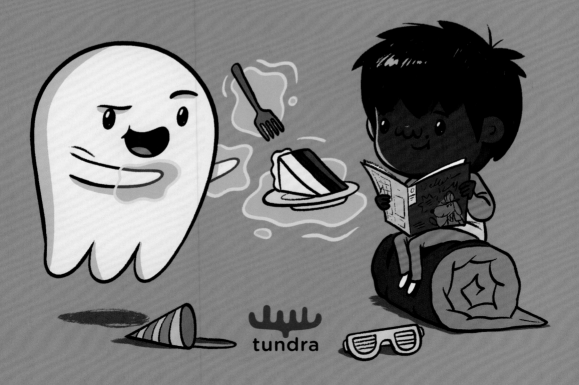

tundra

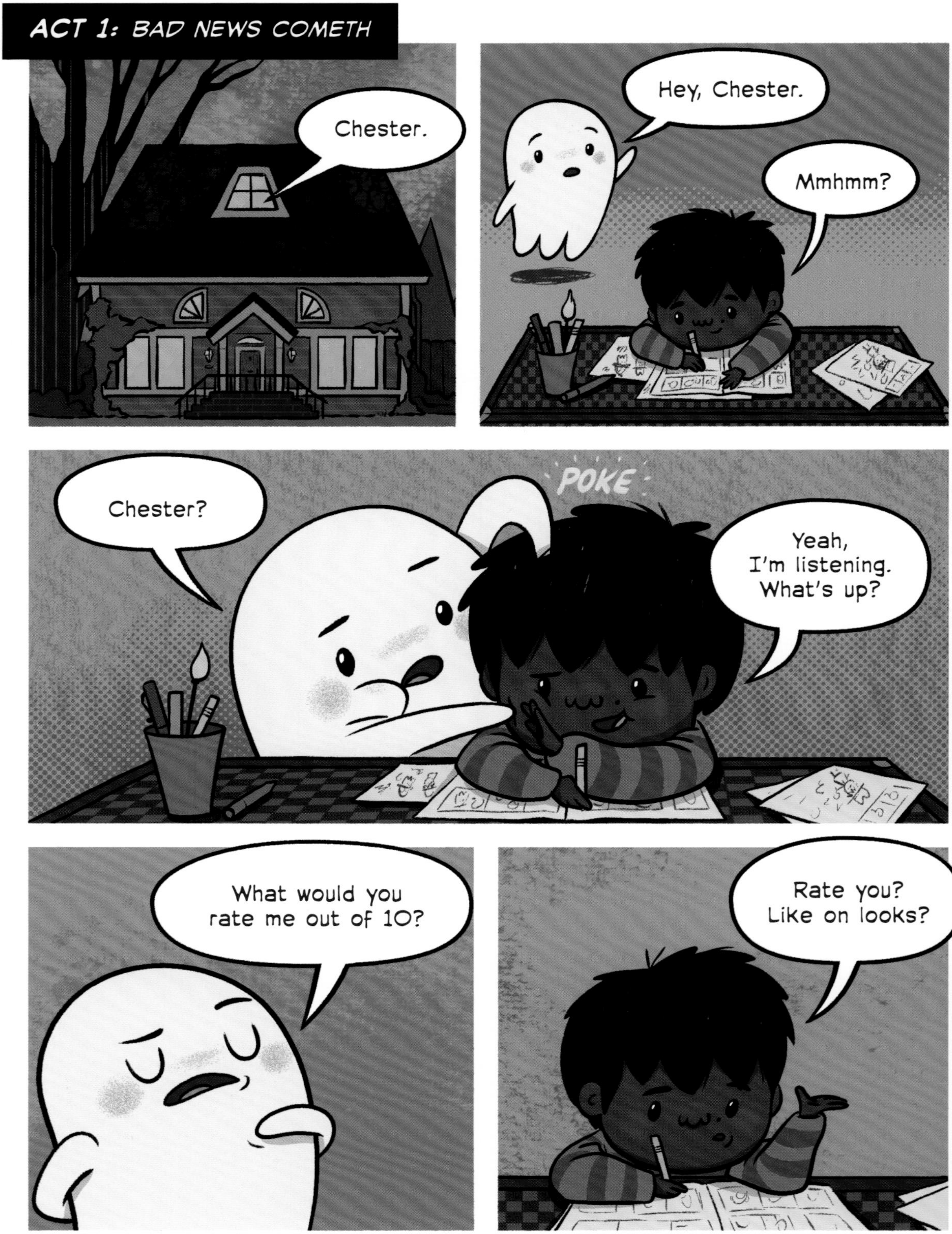
ACT 1: BAD NEWS COMETH
Chester.
Hey, Chester.
Mmhmm?
Chester?
POKE
Yeah, I'm listening. What's up?
What would you rate me out of 10?
Rate you? Like on looks?

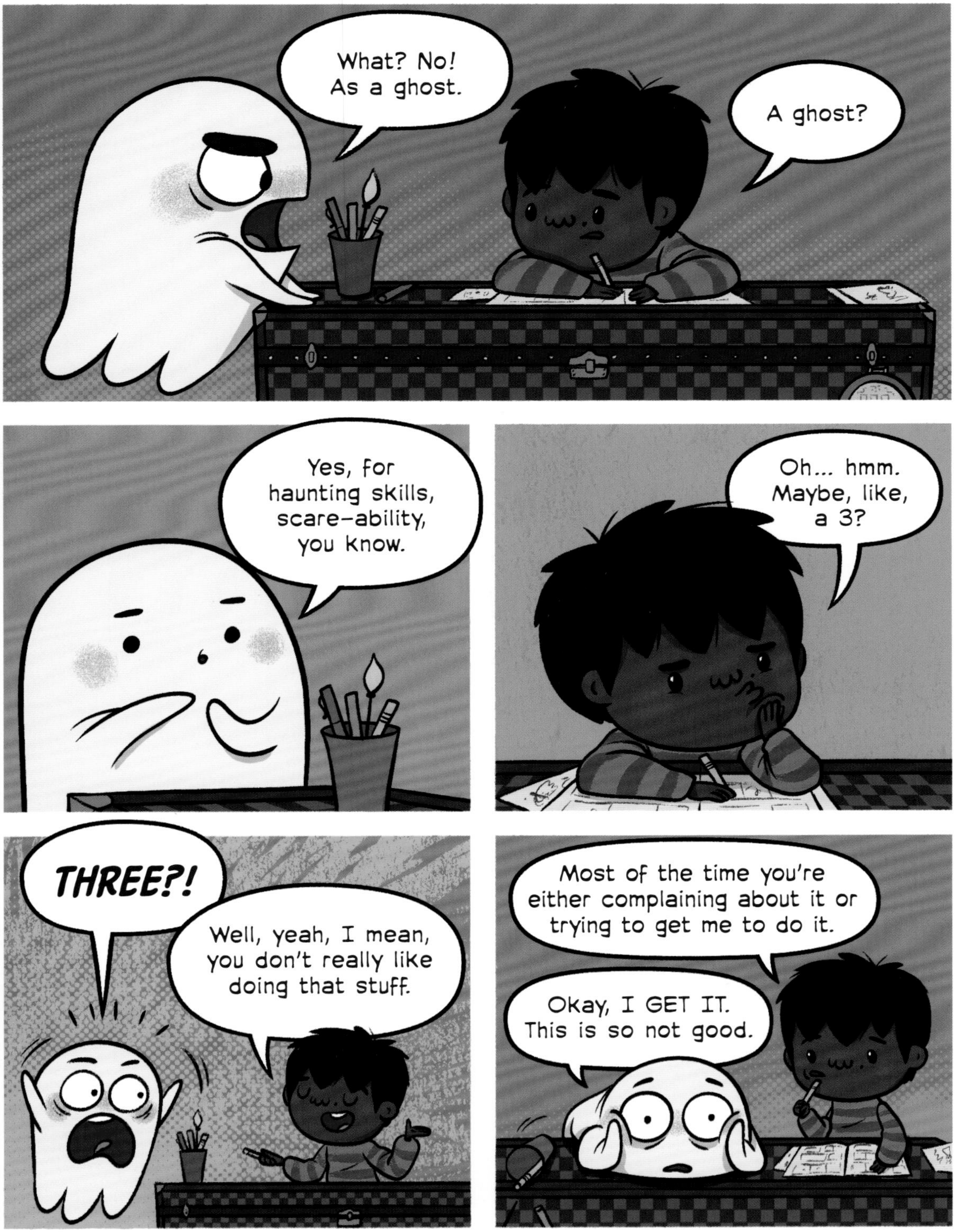

What? No! As a ghost.
A ghost?
Yes, for haunting skills, scare-ability, you know.
Oh... hmm. Maybe, like, a 3?
THREE?!
Well, yeah, I mean, you don't really like doing that stuff.
Most of the time you're either complaining about it or trying to get me to do it.
Okay, I GET IT. This is so not good.

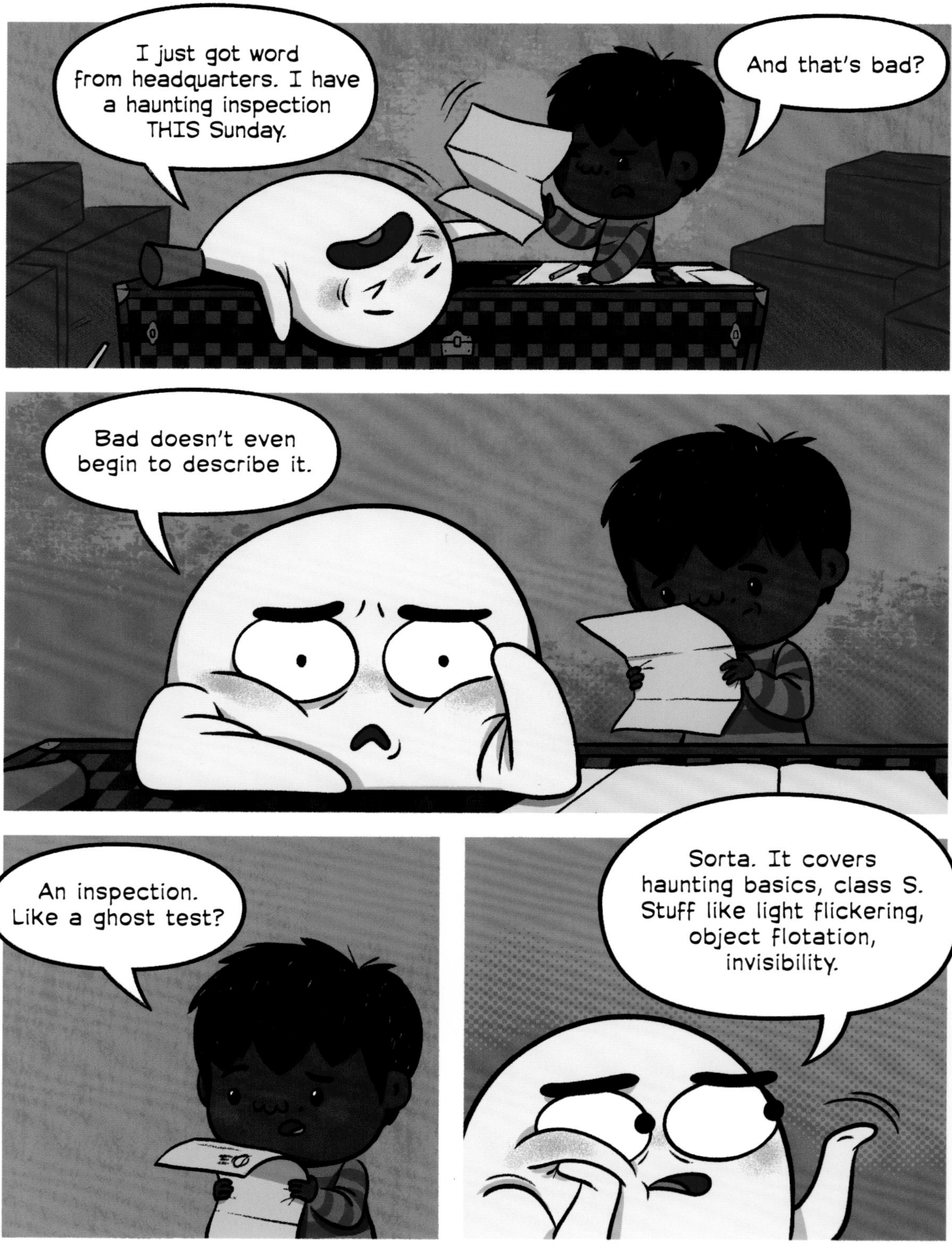
I just got word from headquarters. I have a haunting inspection THIS Sunday.
And that's bad?
Bad doesn't even begin to describe it.
An inspection. Like a ghost test?
Sorta. It covers haunting basics, class S. Stuff like light flickering, object flotation, invisibility.

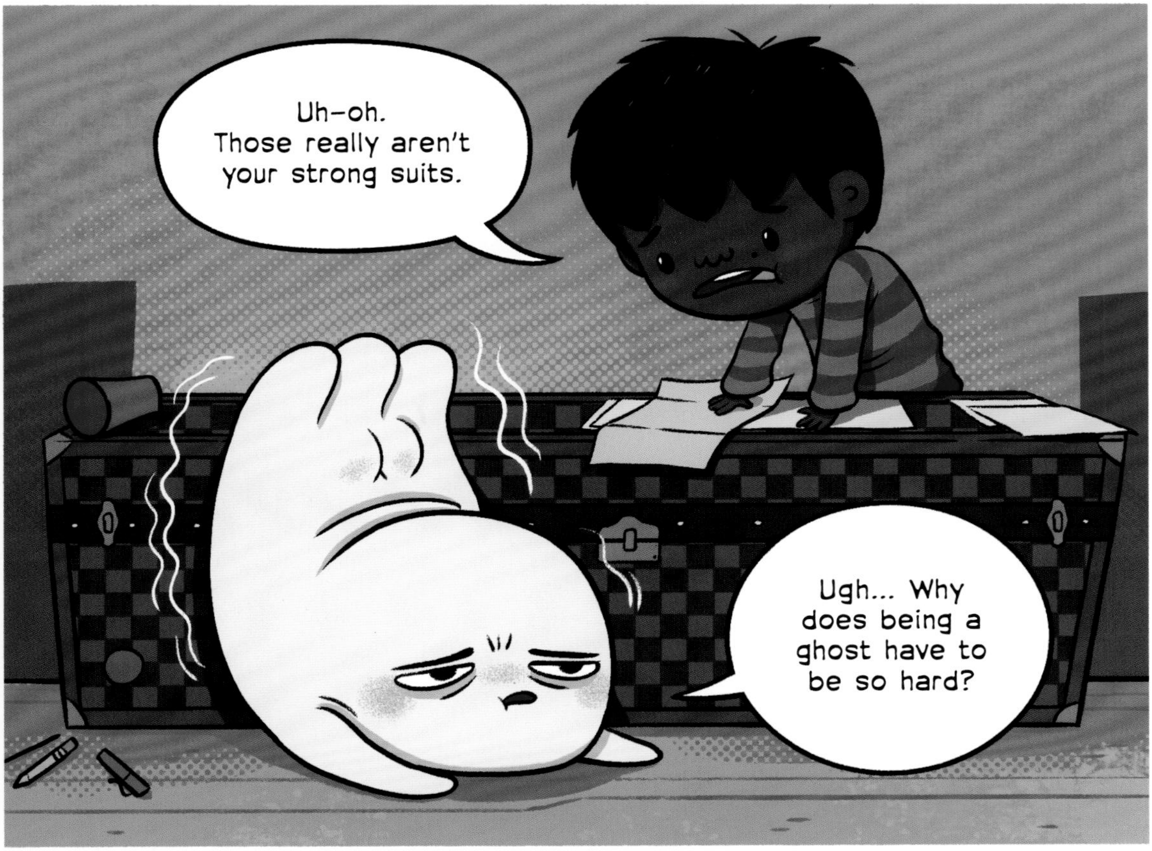
Uh-oh. Those really aren't your strong suits.
Ugh... Why does being a ghost have to be so hard?

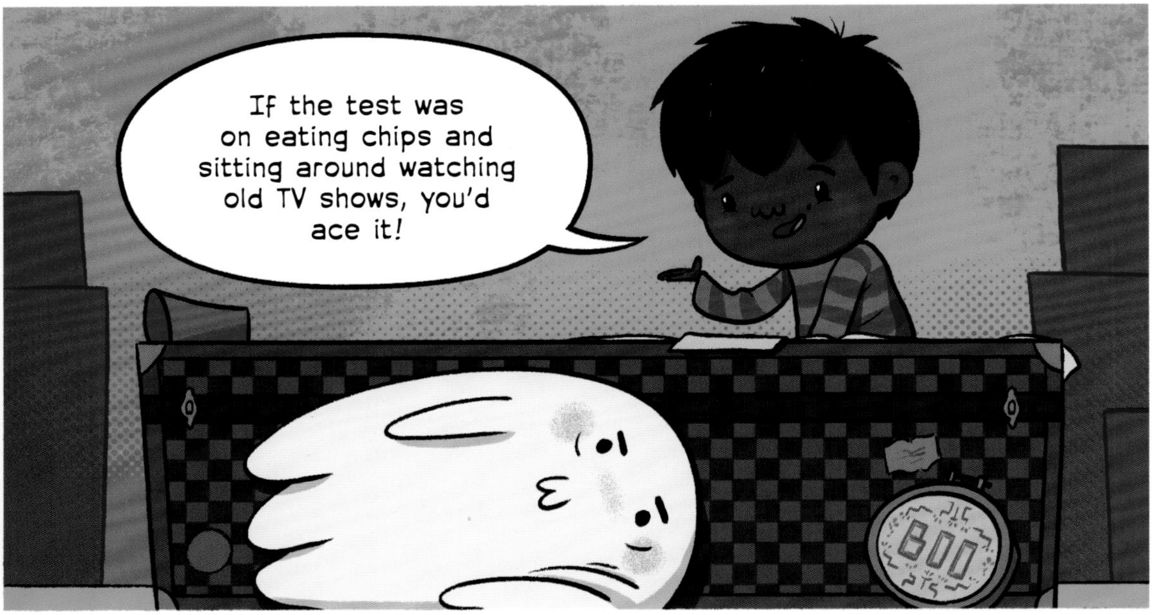
If the test was on eating chips and sitting around watching old TV shows, you'd ace it!
800

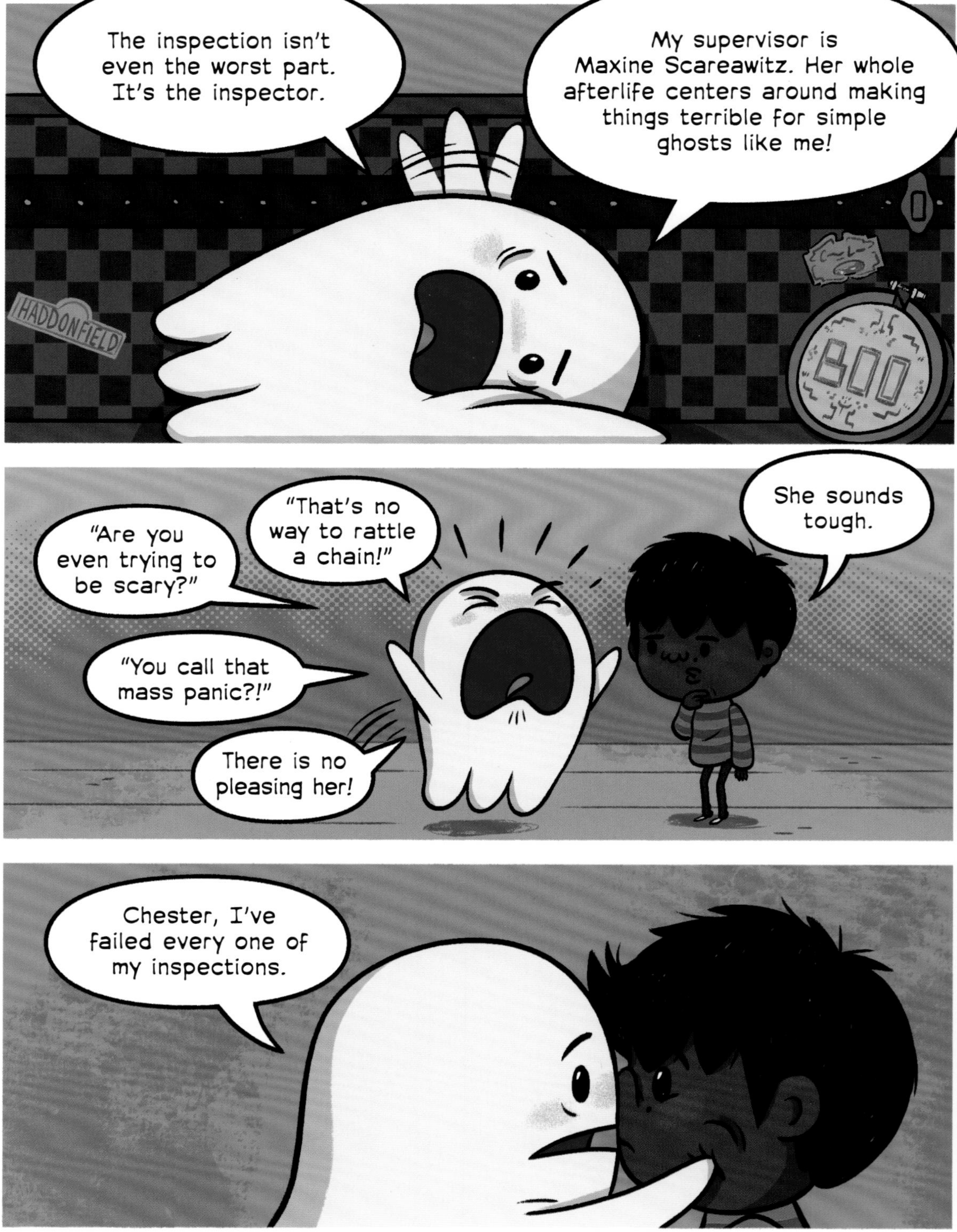
The inspection isn't even the worst part. It's the inspector.
My supervisor is Maxine Scareawitz. Her whole afterlife centers around making things terrible for simple ghosts like me!
HADDONFIELD
BOO
"Are you even trying to be scary?"
"That's no way to rattle a chain!"
She sounds tough.
"You call that mass panic?!"
There is no pleasing her!
Chester, I've failed every one of my inspections.

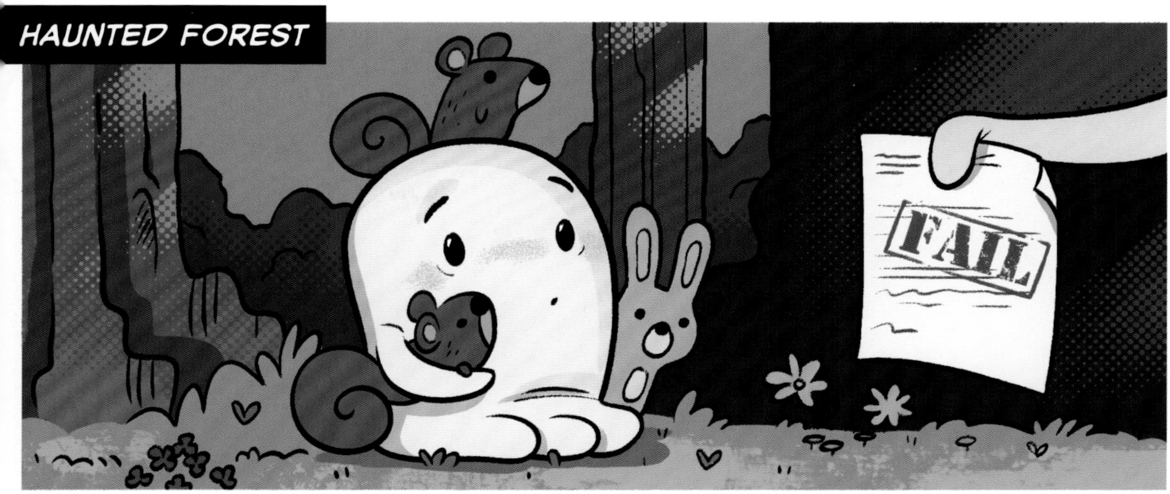
HAUNTED FOREST
FAIL

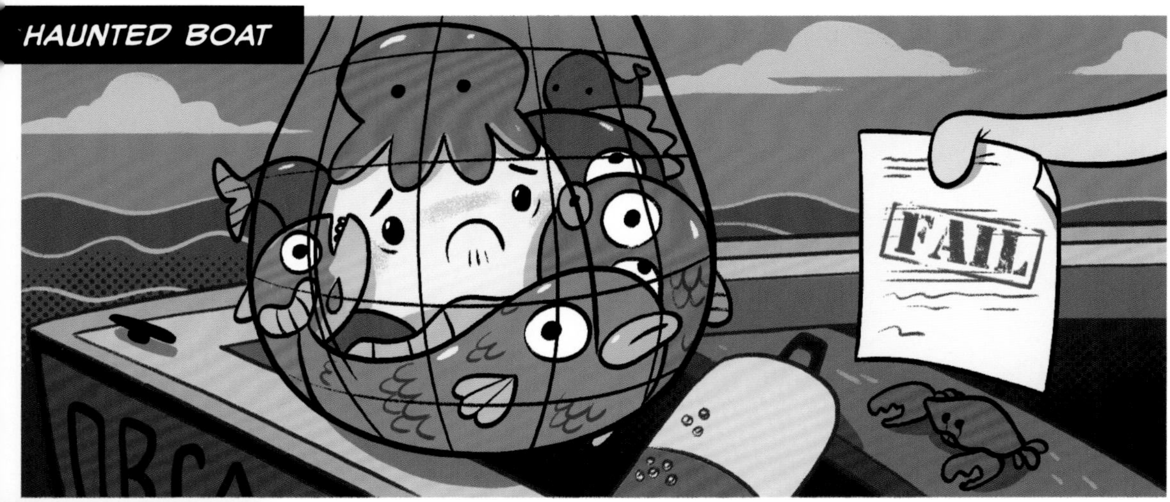
HAUNTED BOAT
FAIL

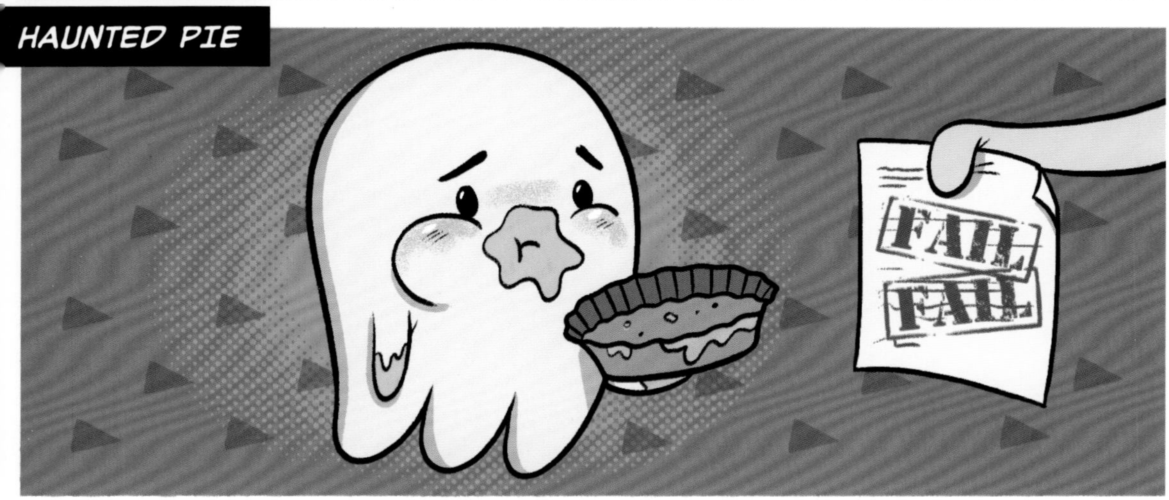
HAUNTED PIE
FAIL
FAIL

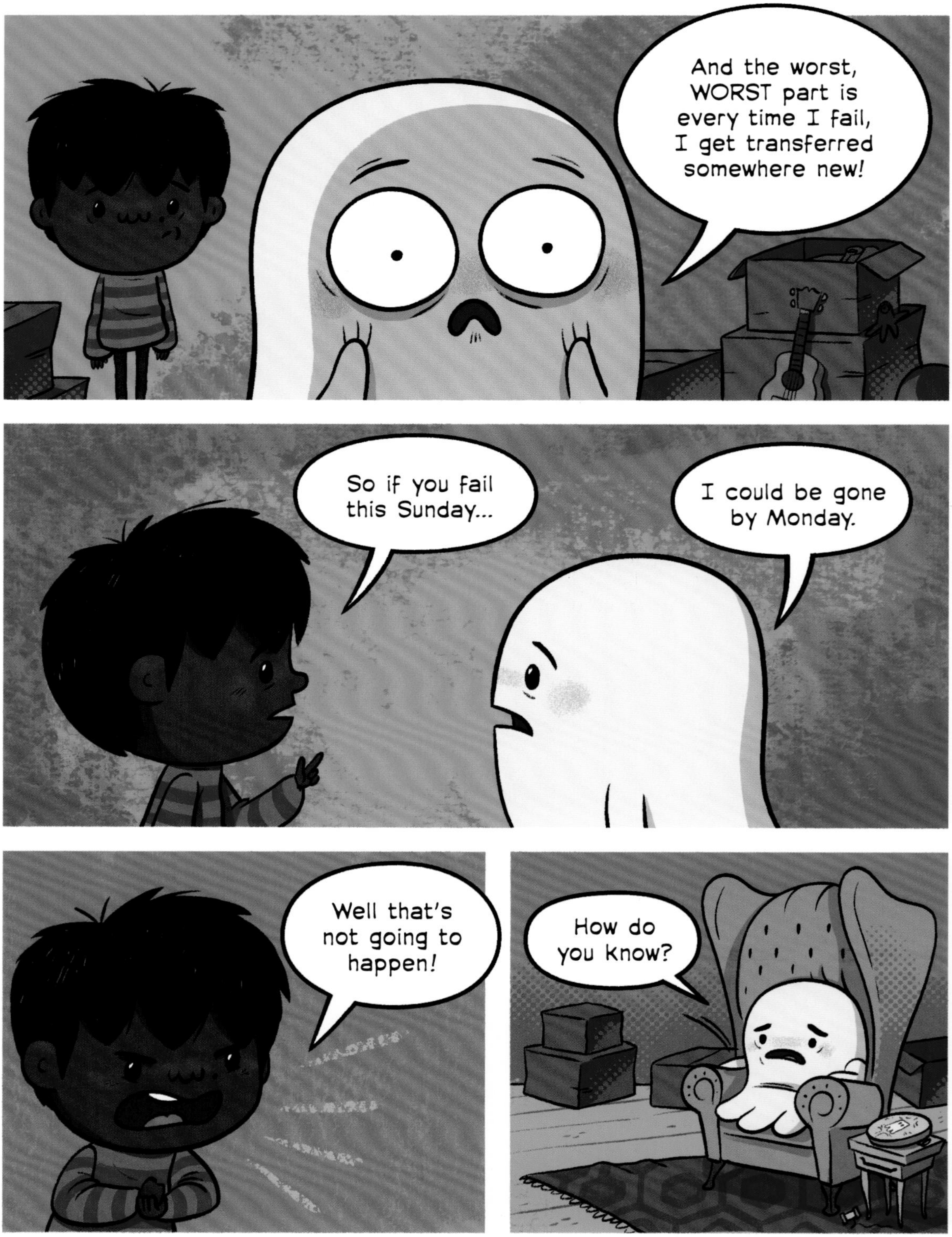
And the worst, WORST part is every time I fail, I get transferred somewhere new!
So if you fail this Sunday...
I could be gone by Monday.
Well that's not going to happen!
How do you know?

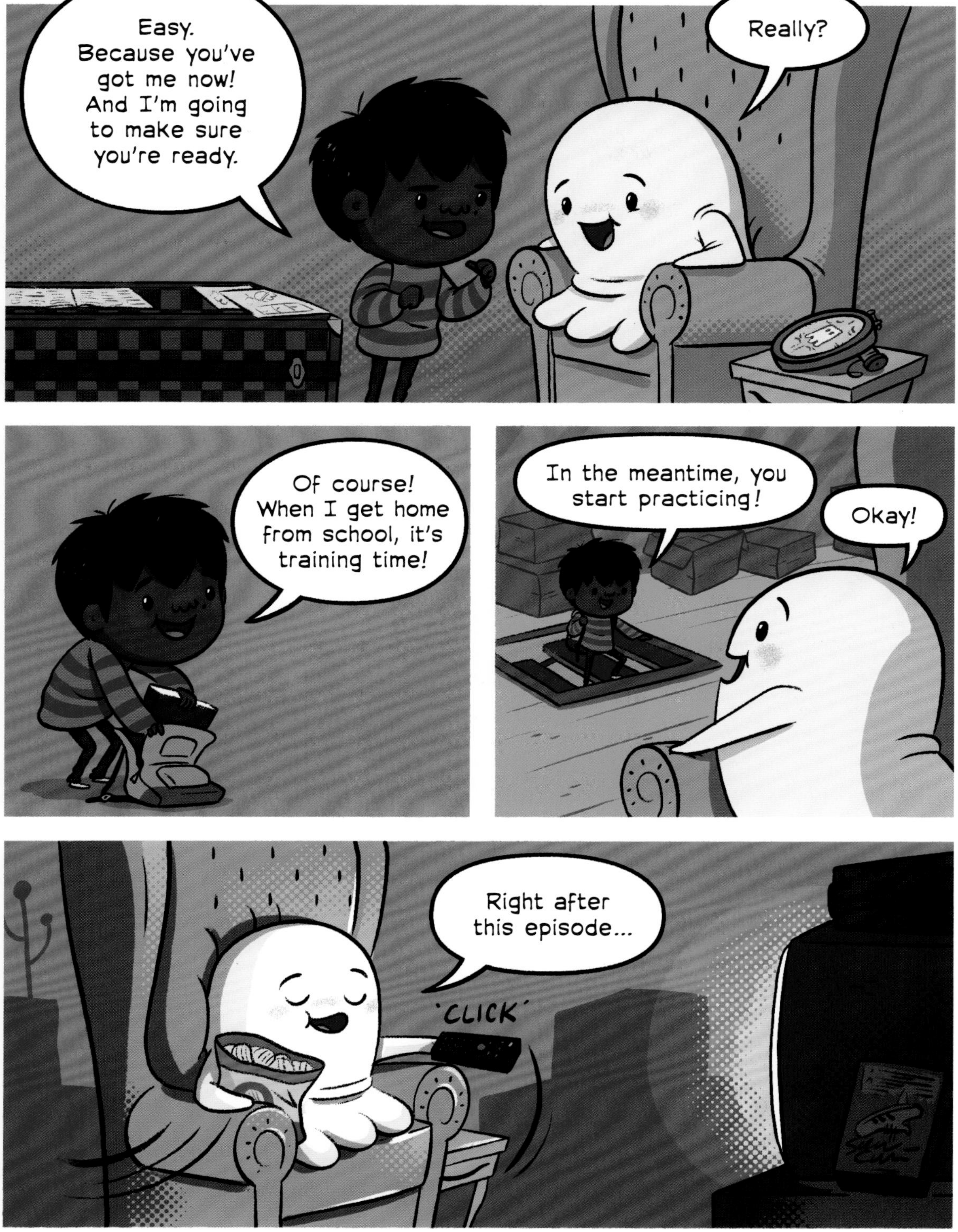
Easy. Because you've got me now! And I'm going to make sure you're ready.
Really?
Of course! When I get home from school, it's training time!
In the meantime, you start practicing!
Okay!
Right after this episode...
'CLICK'

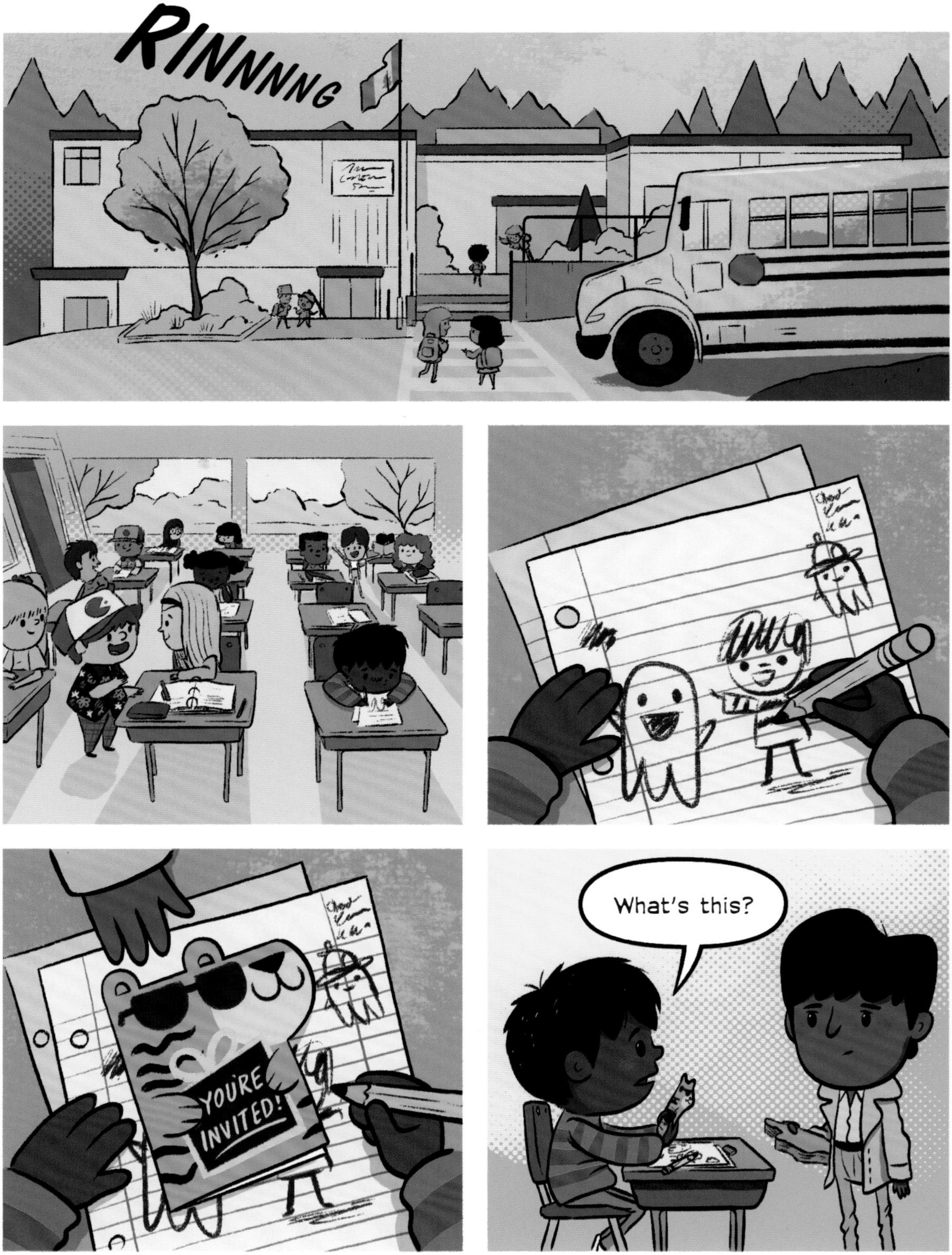
RINNNNG
YOU'RE INVITED!
What's this?

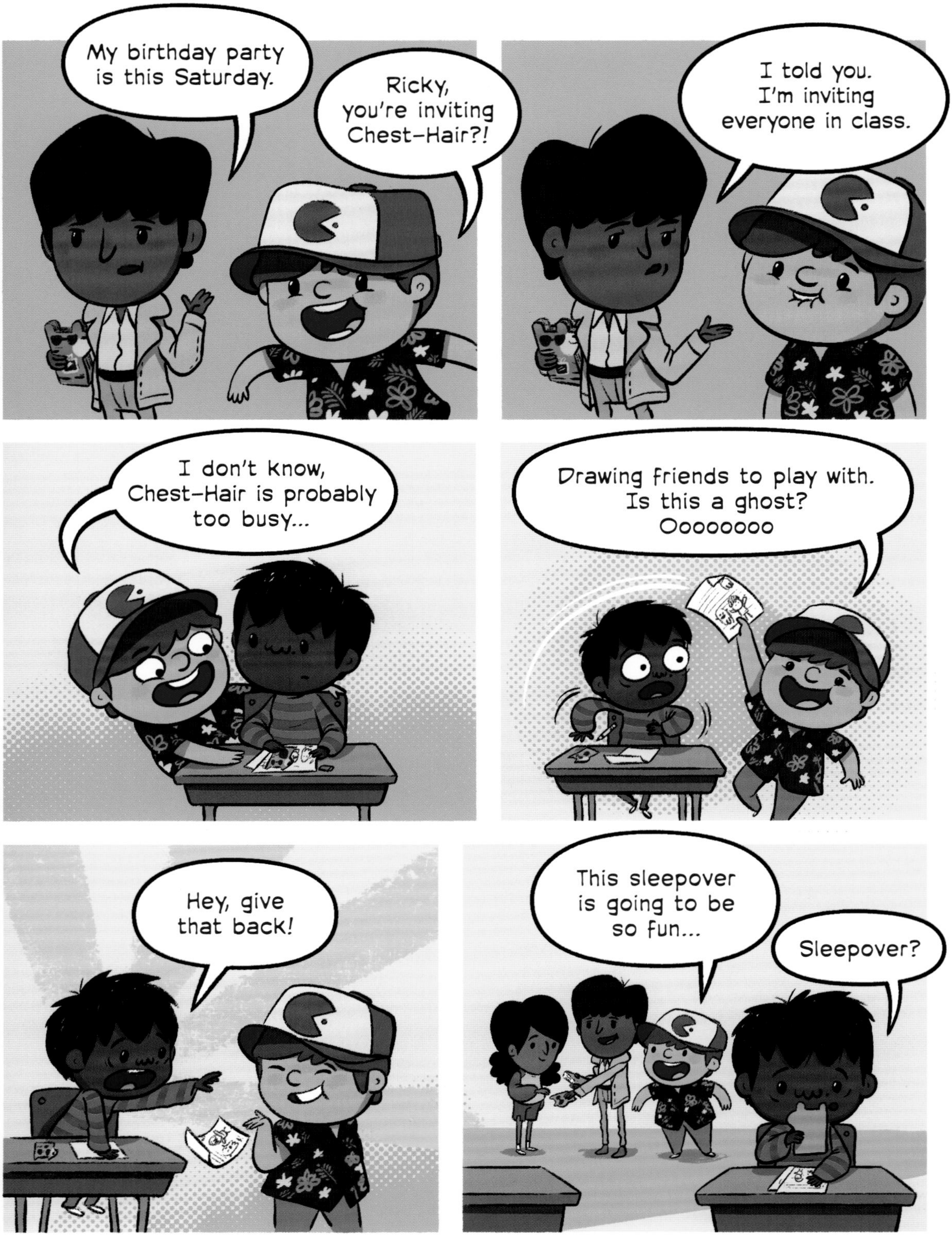
My birthday party is this Saturday.
Ricky, you're inviting Chest-Hair?!
I told you. I'm inviting everyone in class.
I don't know, Chest-Hair is probably too busy...
Drawing friends to play with. Is this a ghost? Ooooooo
Hey, give that back!
This sleepover is going to be so fun...
Sleepover?

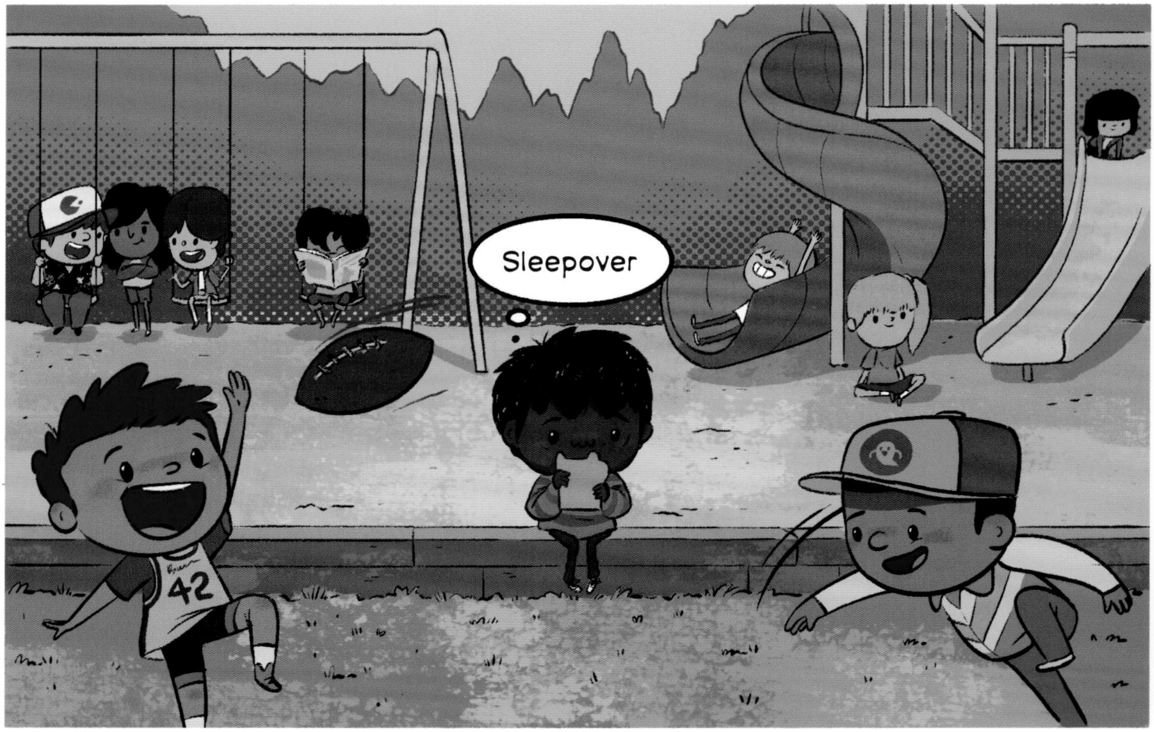
Sleepover
42

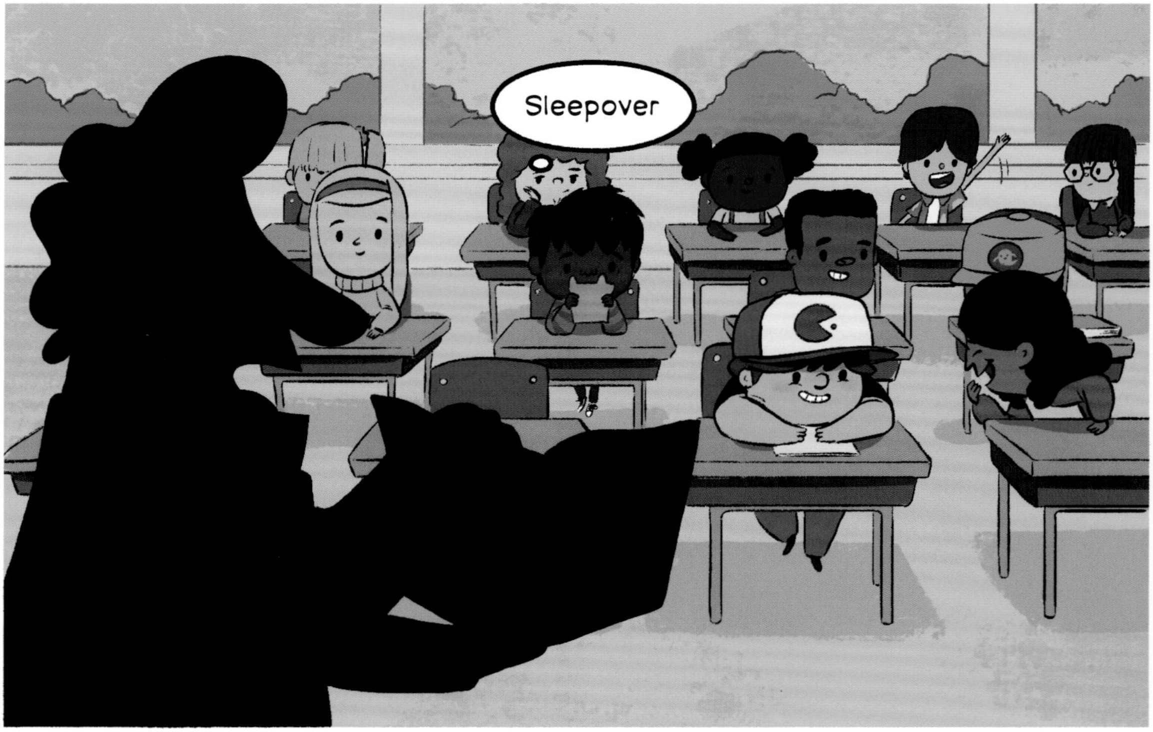
Sleepover

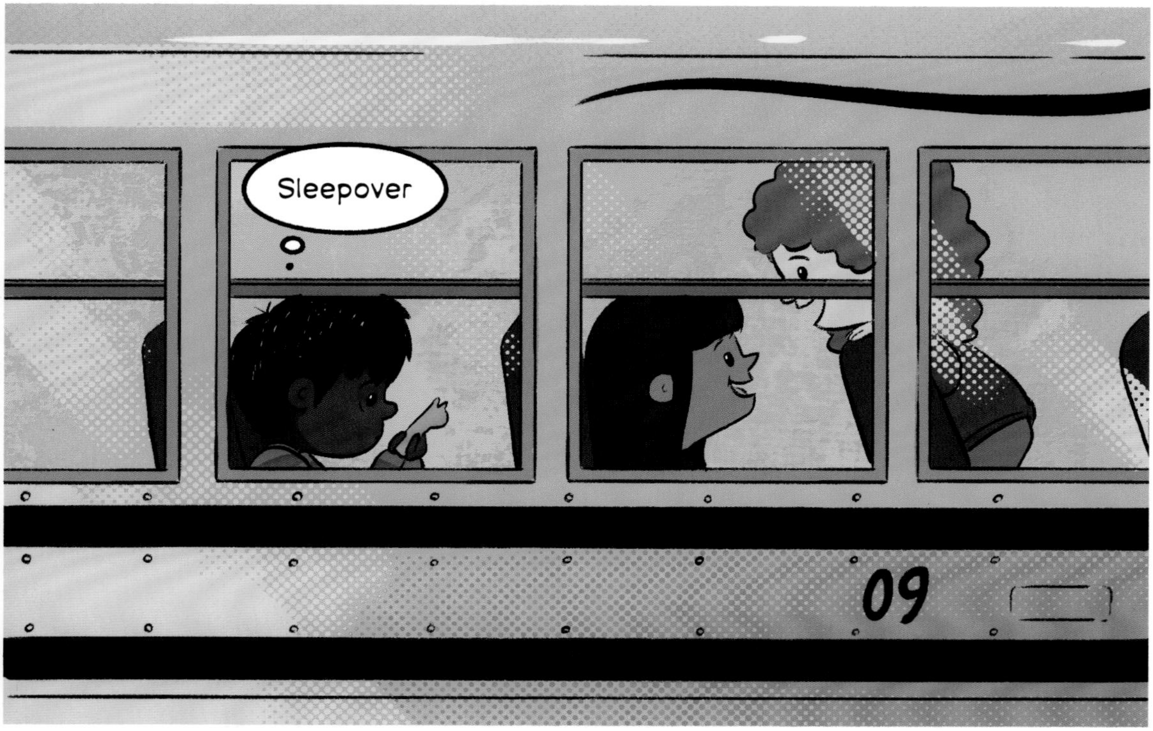
Sleepover
09

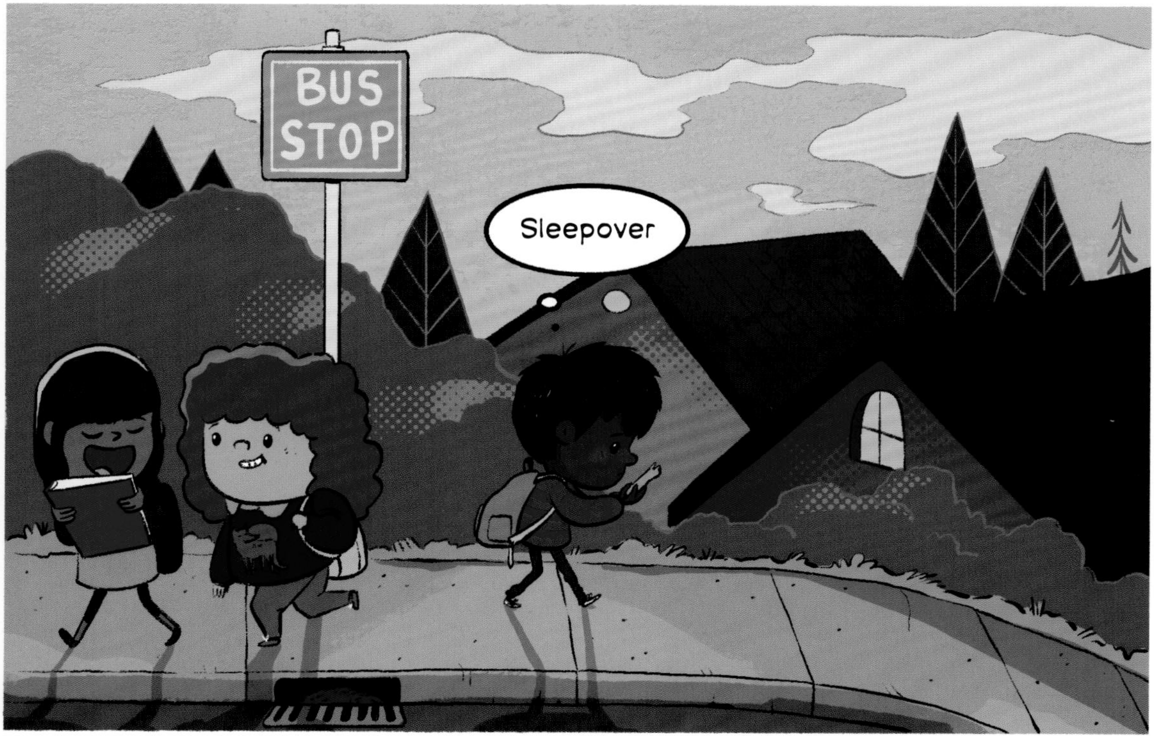
BUS STOP
Sleepover

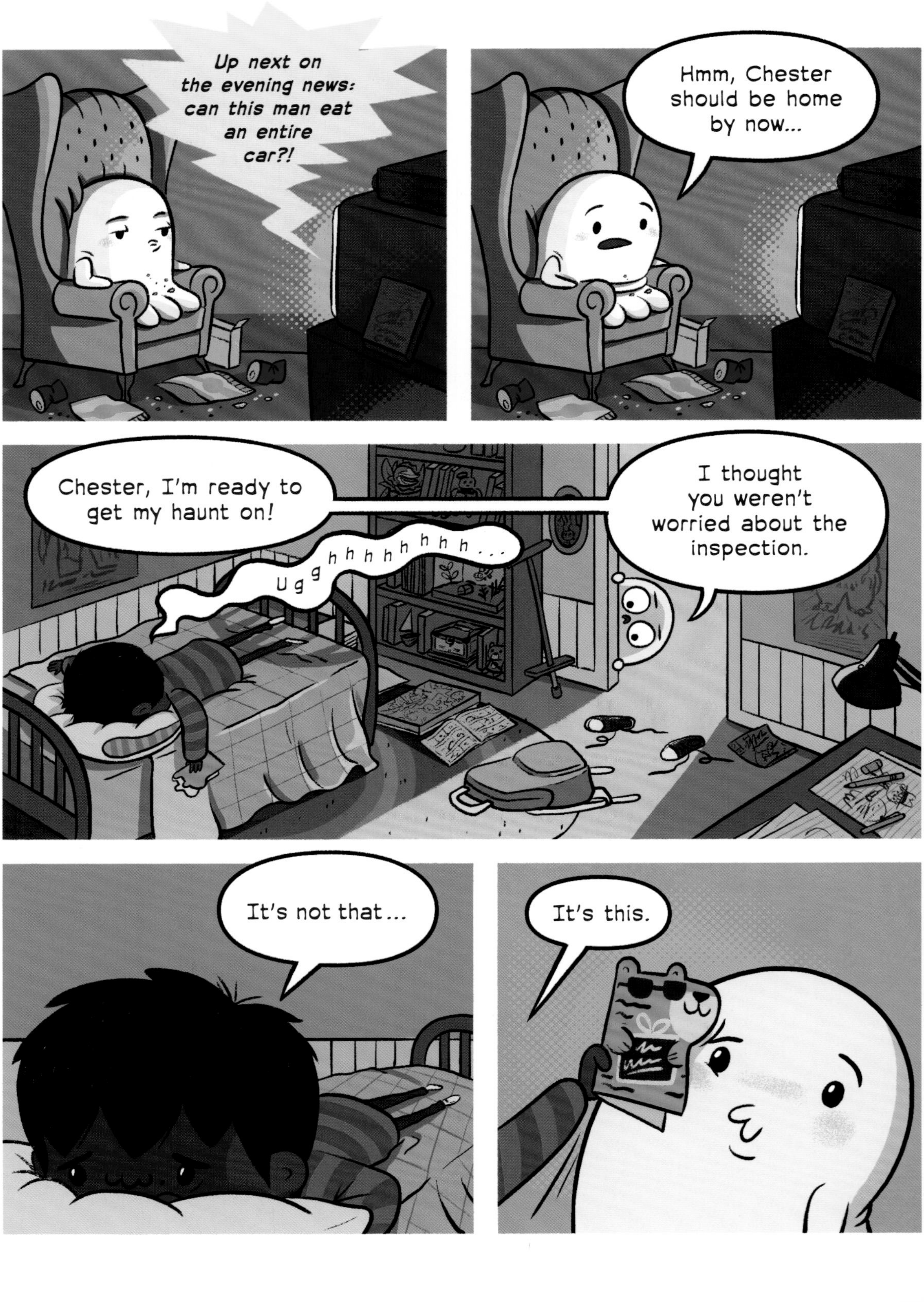

Up next on the evening news: can this man eat an entire car?!
Hmm, Chester should be home by now...
Chester, I'm ready to get my haunt on!
Uggghhhhhhhh...
I thought you weren't worried about the inspection.
It's not that...
It's this.

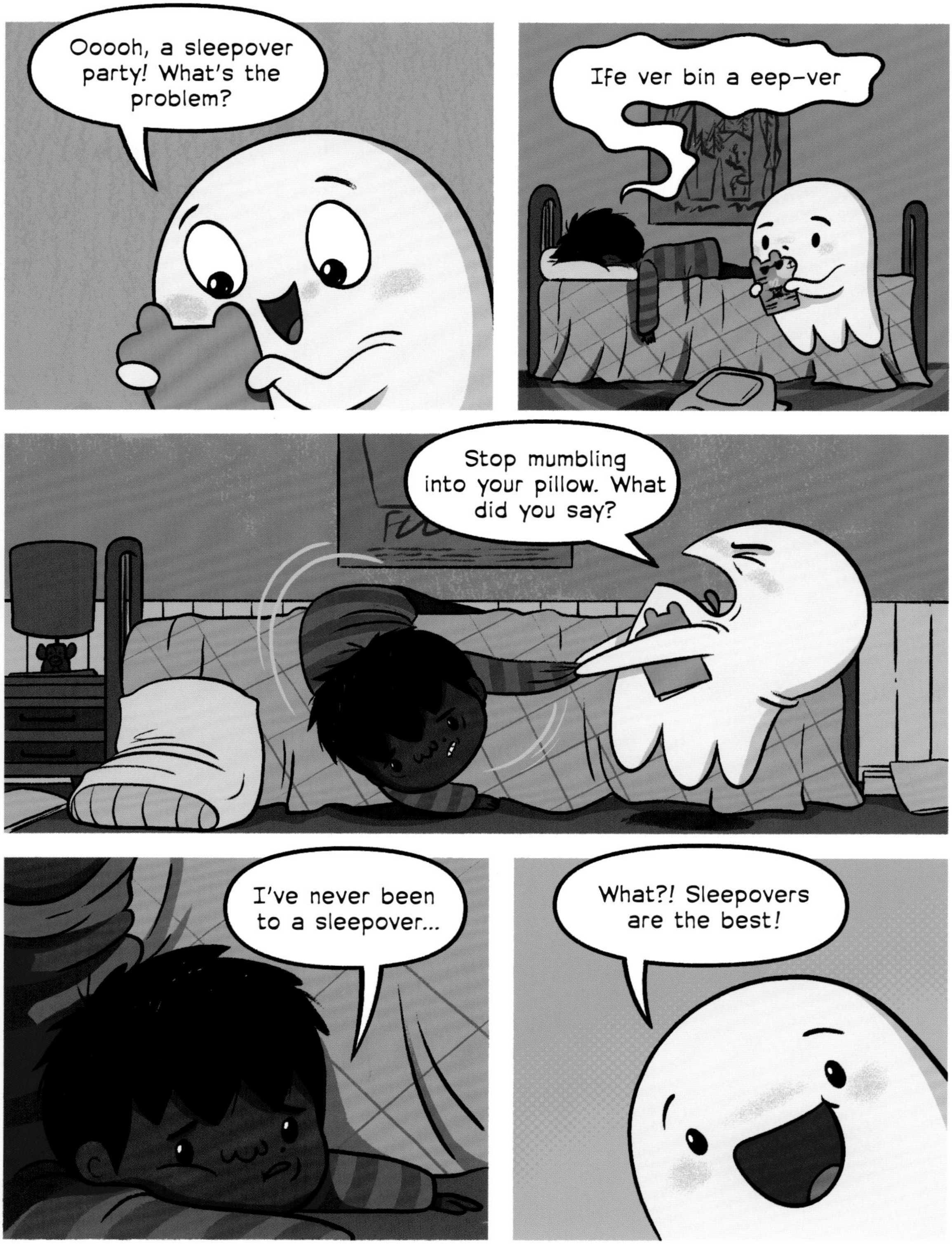

Ooooh, a sleepover party! What's the problem?
Ife ver bin a eep-ver
Stop mumbling into your pillow. What did you say?
I've never been to a sleepover...
What?! Sleepovers are the best!

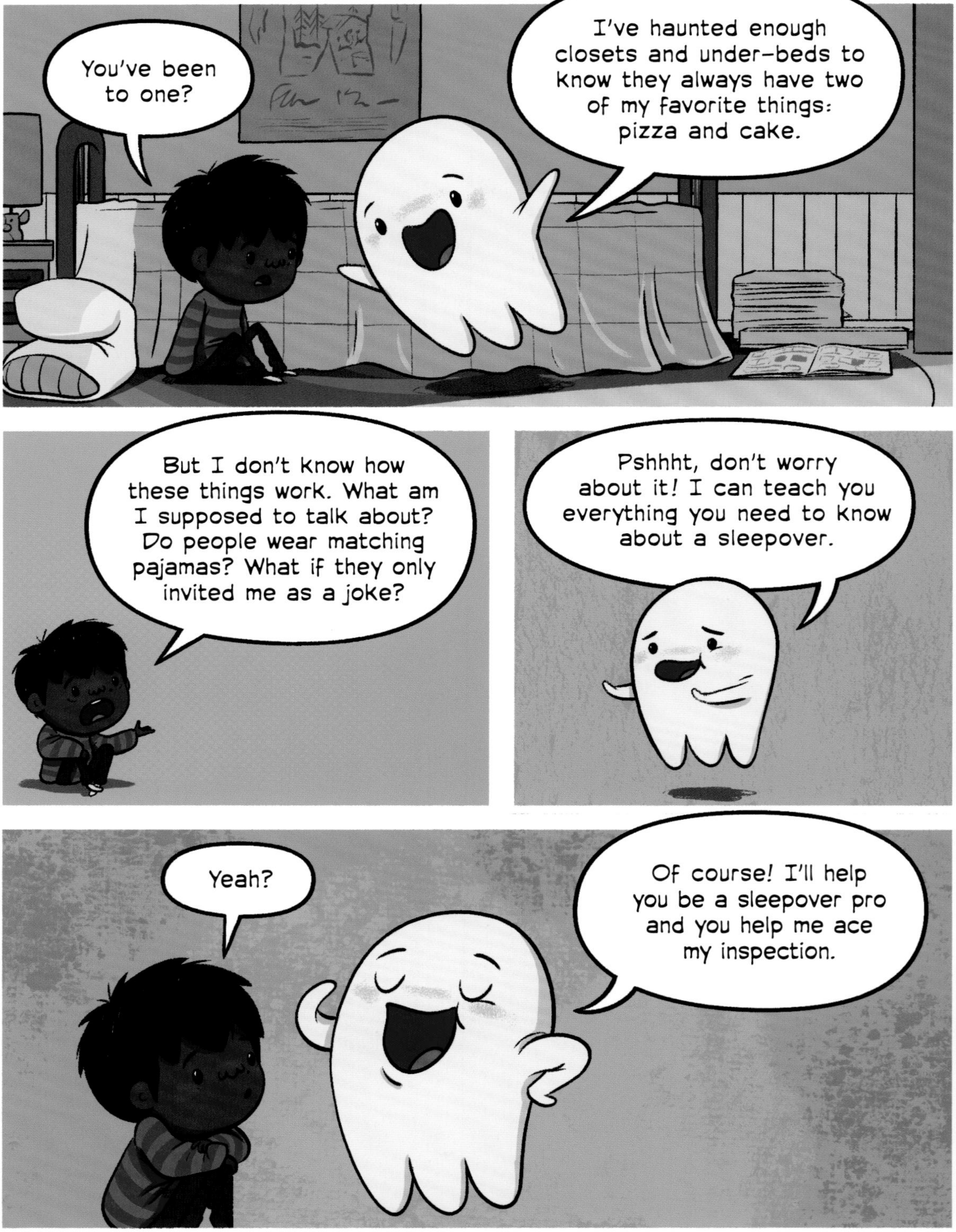

You've been to one?
I've haunted enough closets and under-beds to know they always have two of my favorite things: pizza and cake.
But I don't know how these things work. What am I supposed to talk about? Do people wear matching pajamas? What if they only invited me as a joke?
Pshhht, don't worry about it! I can teach you everything you need to know about a sleepover.
Yeah?
Of course! I'll help you be a sleepover pro and you help me ace my inspection.

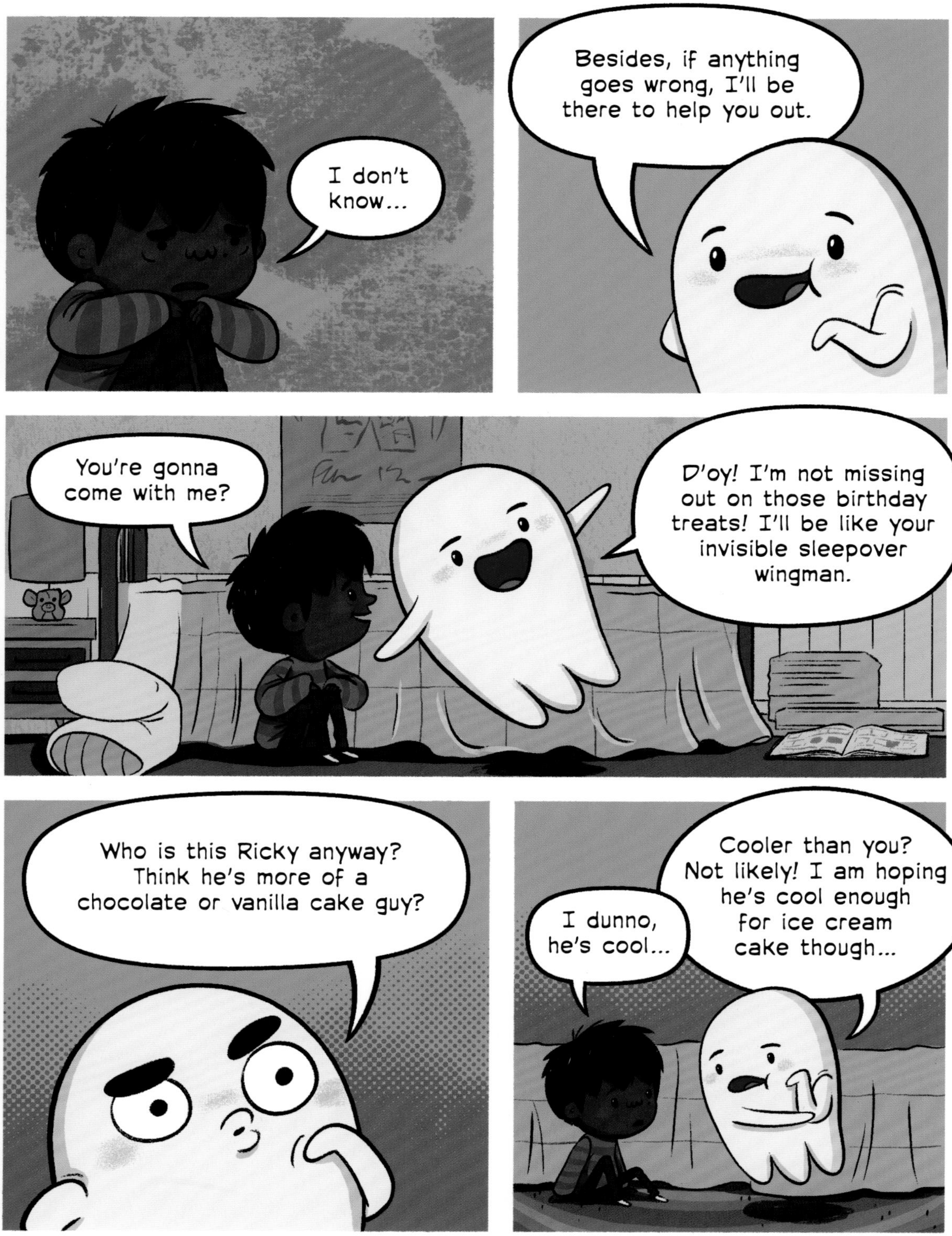
I don't know...
Besides, if anything goes wrong, I'll be there to help you out.
You're gonna come with me?
D'oy! I'm not missing out on those birthday treats! I'll be like your invisible sleepover wingman.
Who is this Ricky anyway? Think he's more of a chocolate or vanilla cake guy?
I dunno, he's cool...
Cooler than you? Not likely! I am hoping he's cool enough for ice cream cake though...

ACT 2: TRAINING DAY

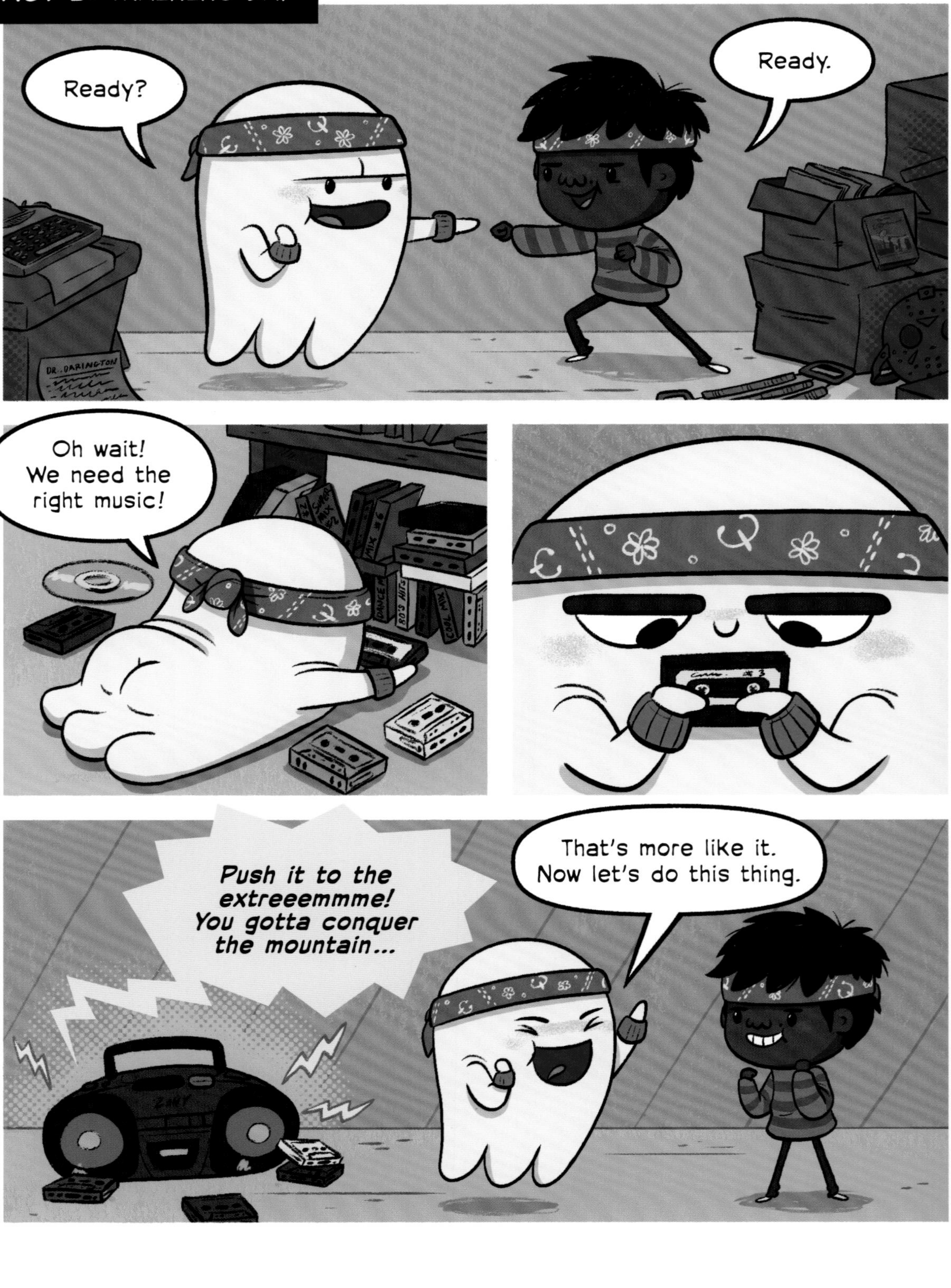

Ready?
Ready.
Oh wait! We need the right music!
Push it to the extreeemmme! You gotta conquer the mountain...
That's more like it. Now let's do this thing.

SIMON

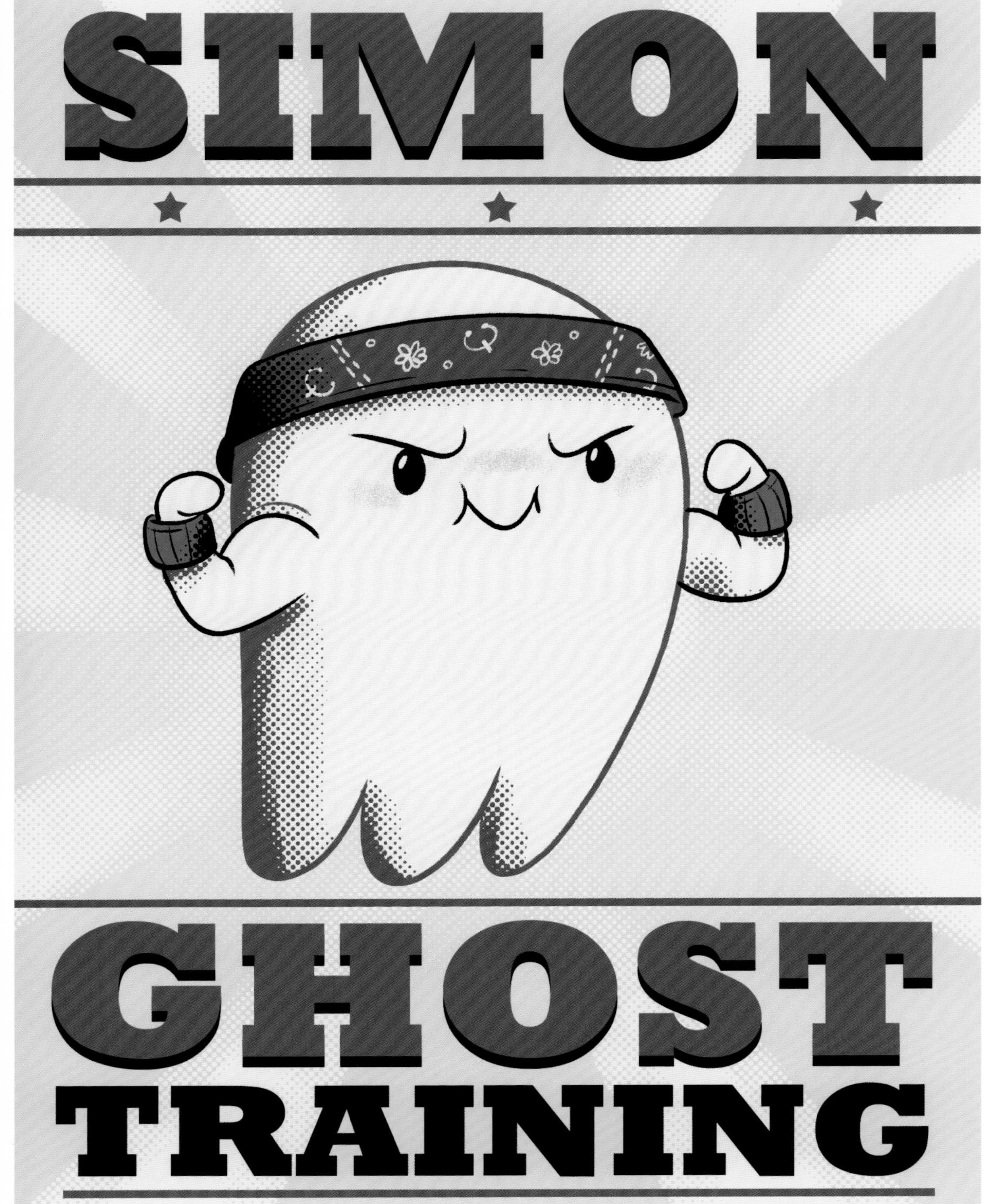

GHOST TRAINING

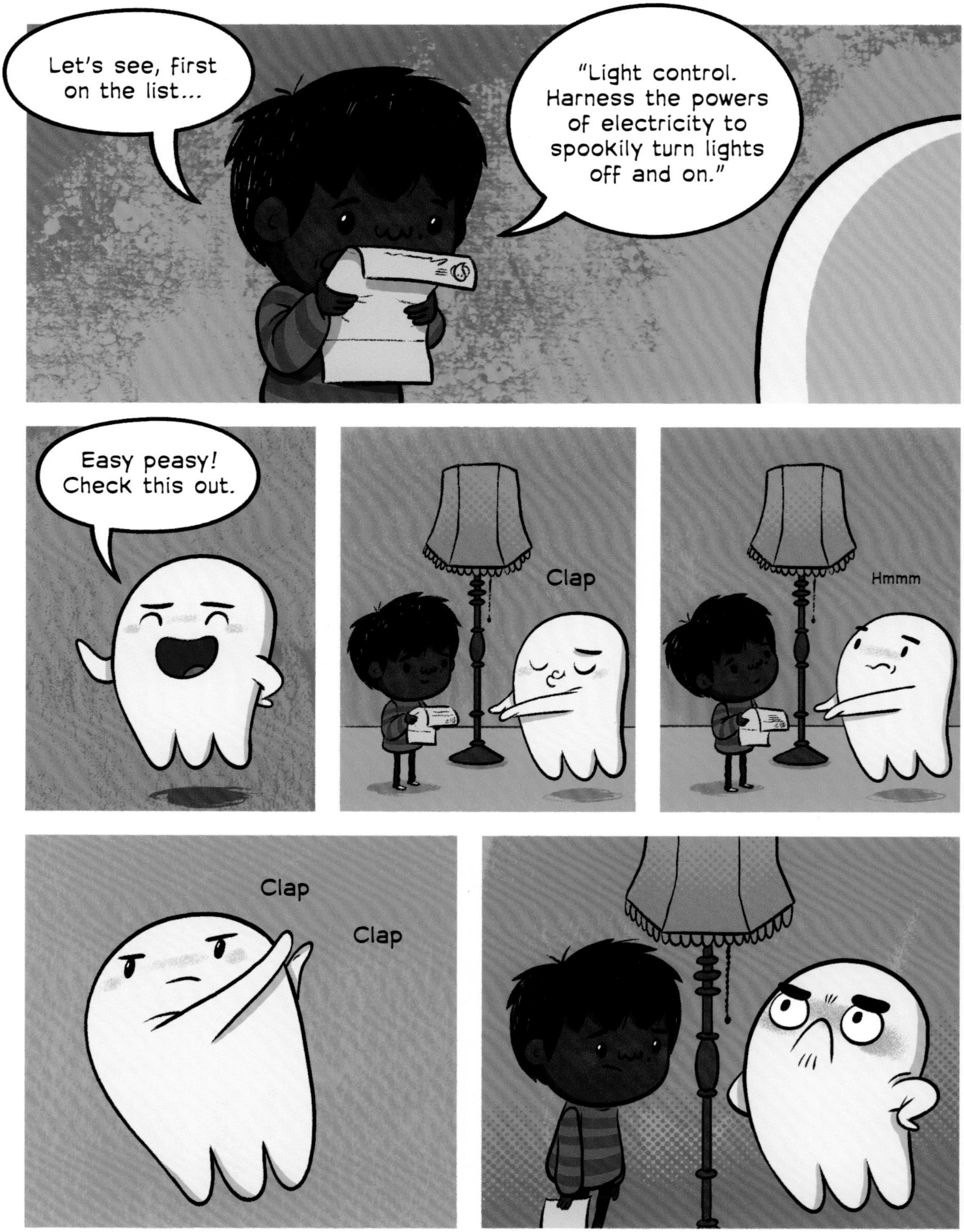
Let's see, first on the list...
"Light control. Harness the powers of electricity to spookily turn lights off and on."
Easy peasy! Check this out.
Clap
Hmmm
Clap
Clap

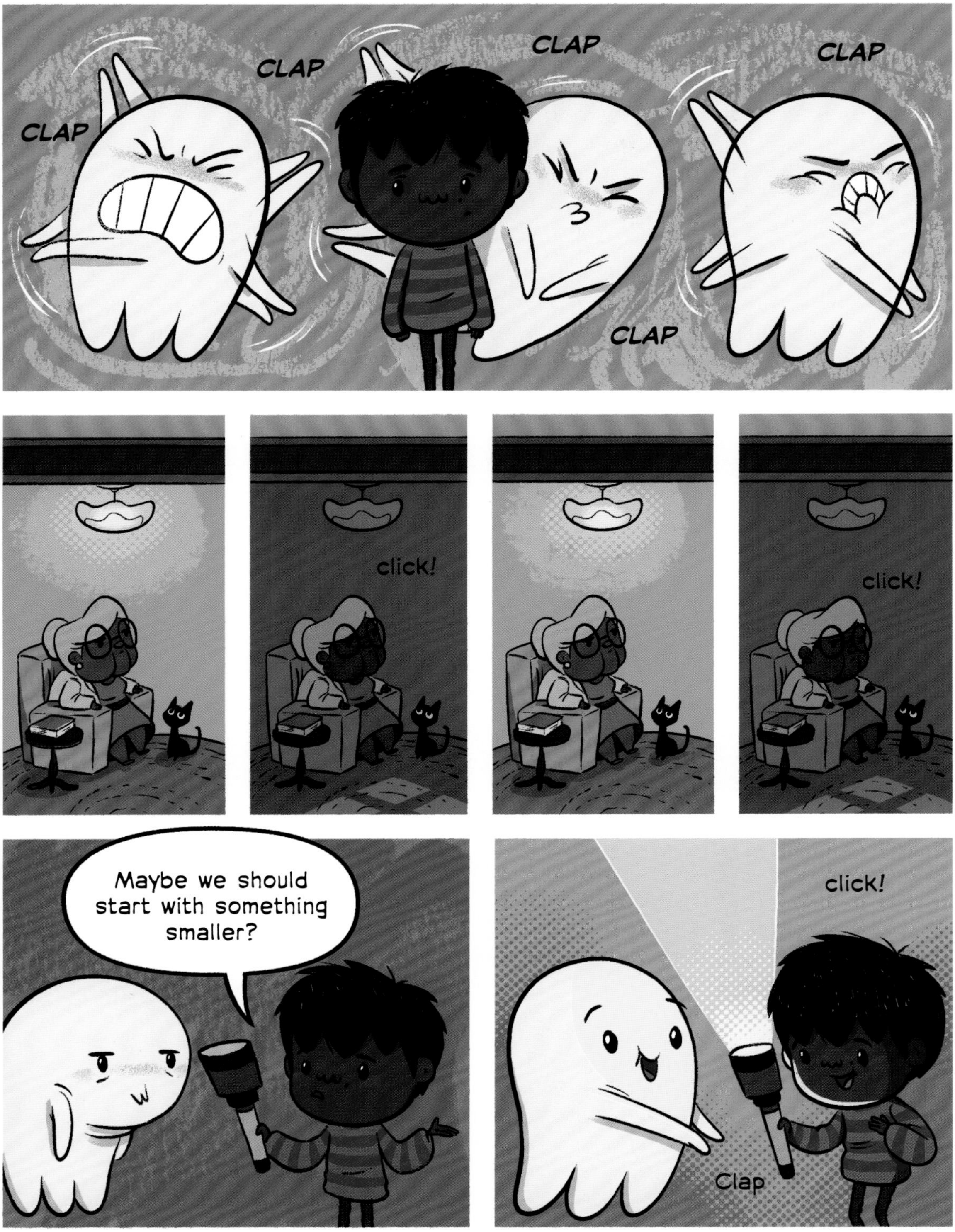
CLAP
CLAP
CLAP
CLAP
CLAP
click!
click!
Maybe we should start with something smaller?
click!
Clap

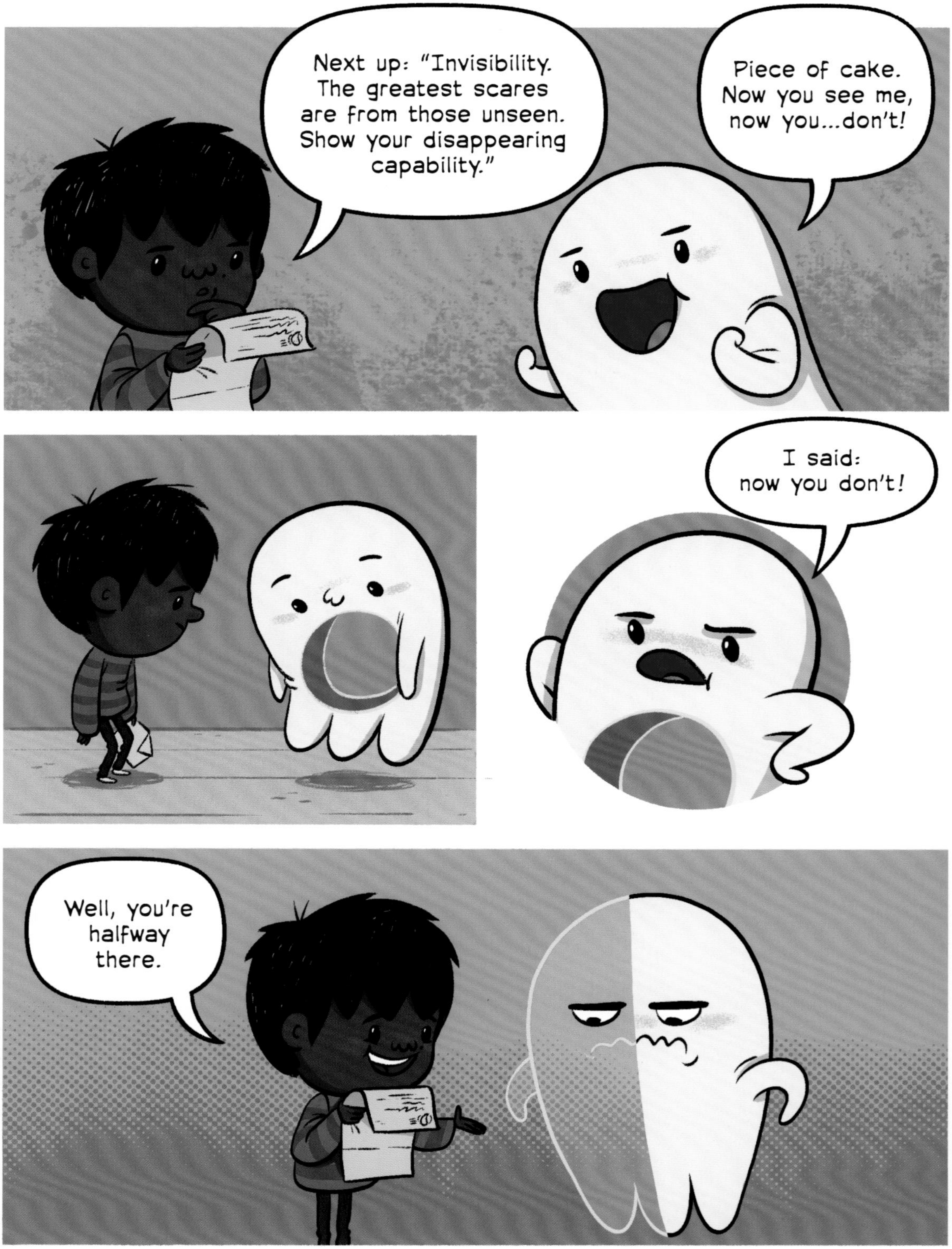
Next up: "Invisibility. The greatest scares are from those unseen. Show your disappearing capability."
Piece of cake. Now you see me, now you...don't!
I said: now you don't!
Well, you're halfway there.

Let's really see what you got.
Here's your mission if you choose to accept it.

Sneak downstairs to the kitchen,

past Grandma and Mr. Pickles
in the living room,

locate the box of cookies
and bring it back, unseen.

Say no more.
Or should I say,
SEE no more.

POOF

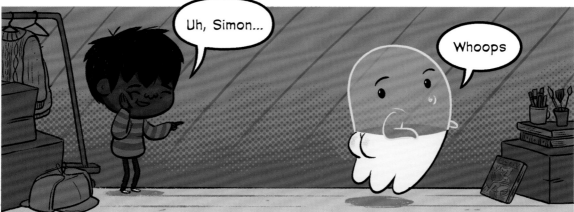

Uh, Simon...

Whoops

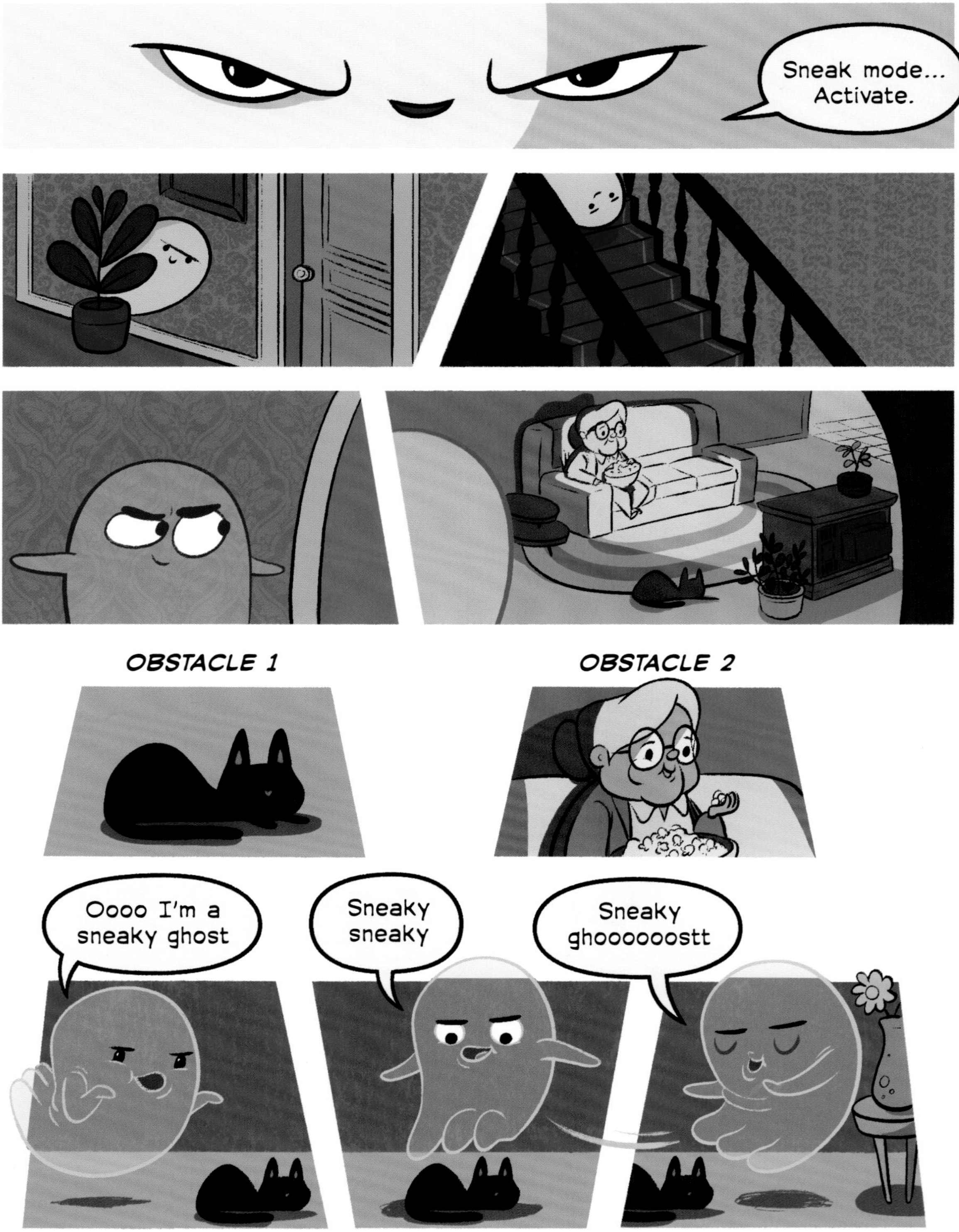
Sneak mode... Activate.
OBSTACLE 1
OBSTACLE 2
Oooo I'm a sneaky ghost
Sneaky sneaky
Sneaky ghoooooostt

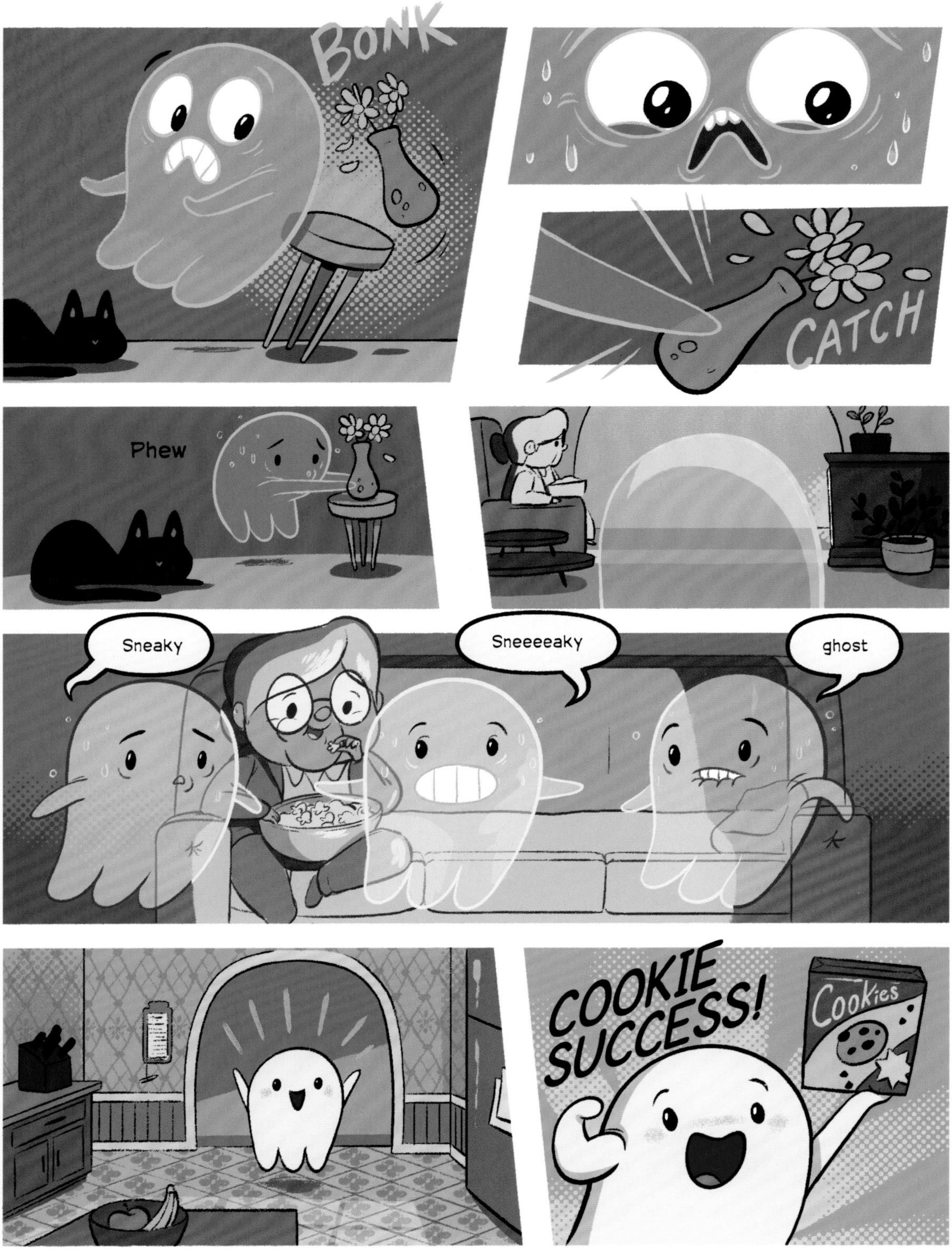
BONK
CATCH
Phew
Sneaky
Sneeeeaky
ghost
COOKIE SUCCESS!
Cookies

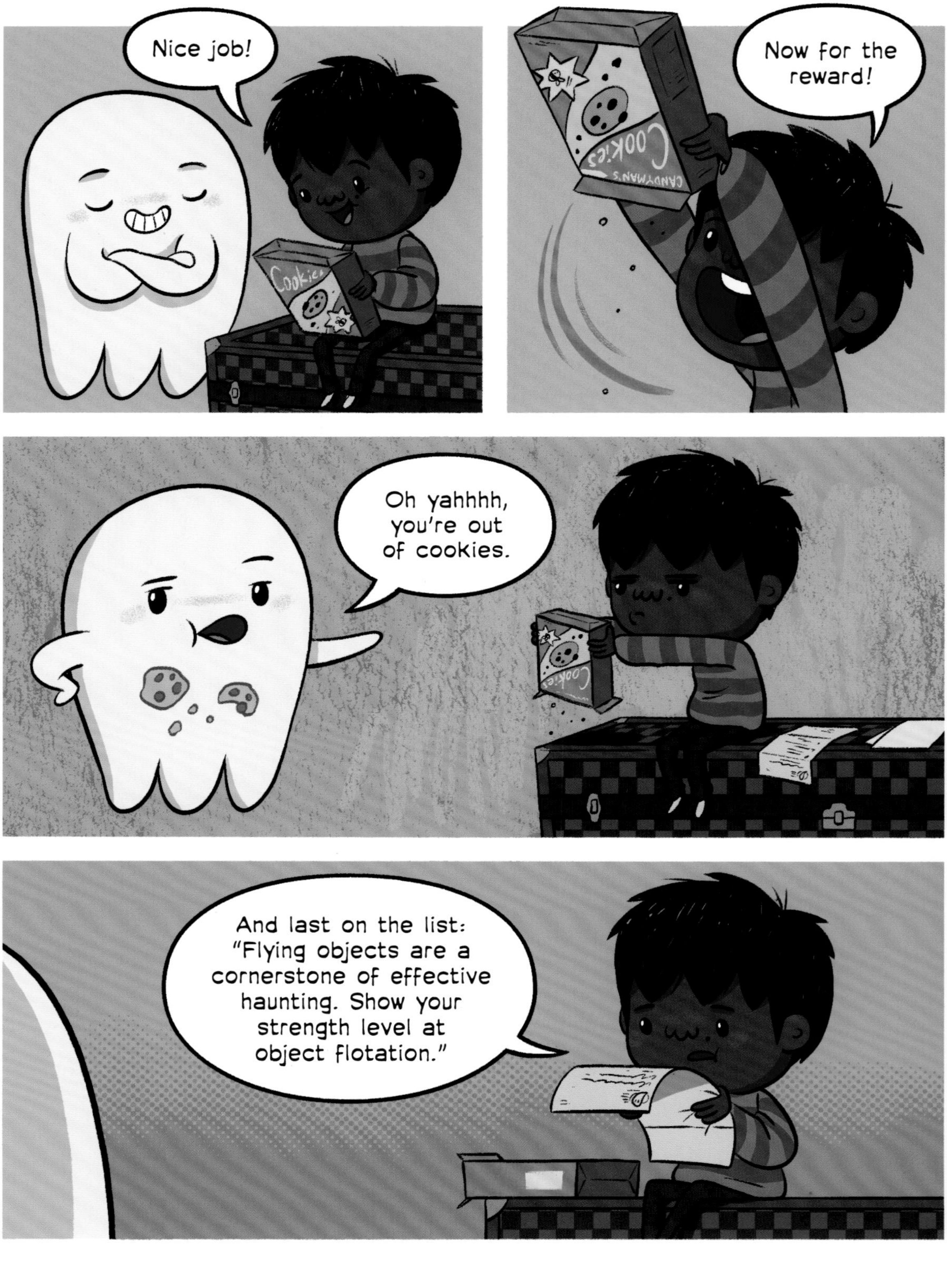
Nice job!
Now for the reward!
Oh yahhhh, you're out of cookies.
And last on the list: "Flying objects are a cornerstone of effective haunting. Show your strength level at object flotation."

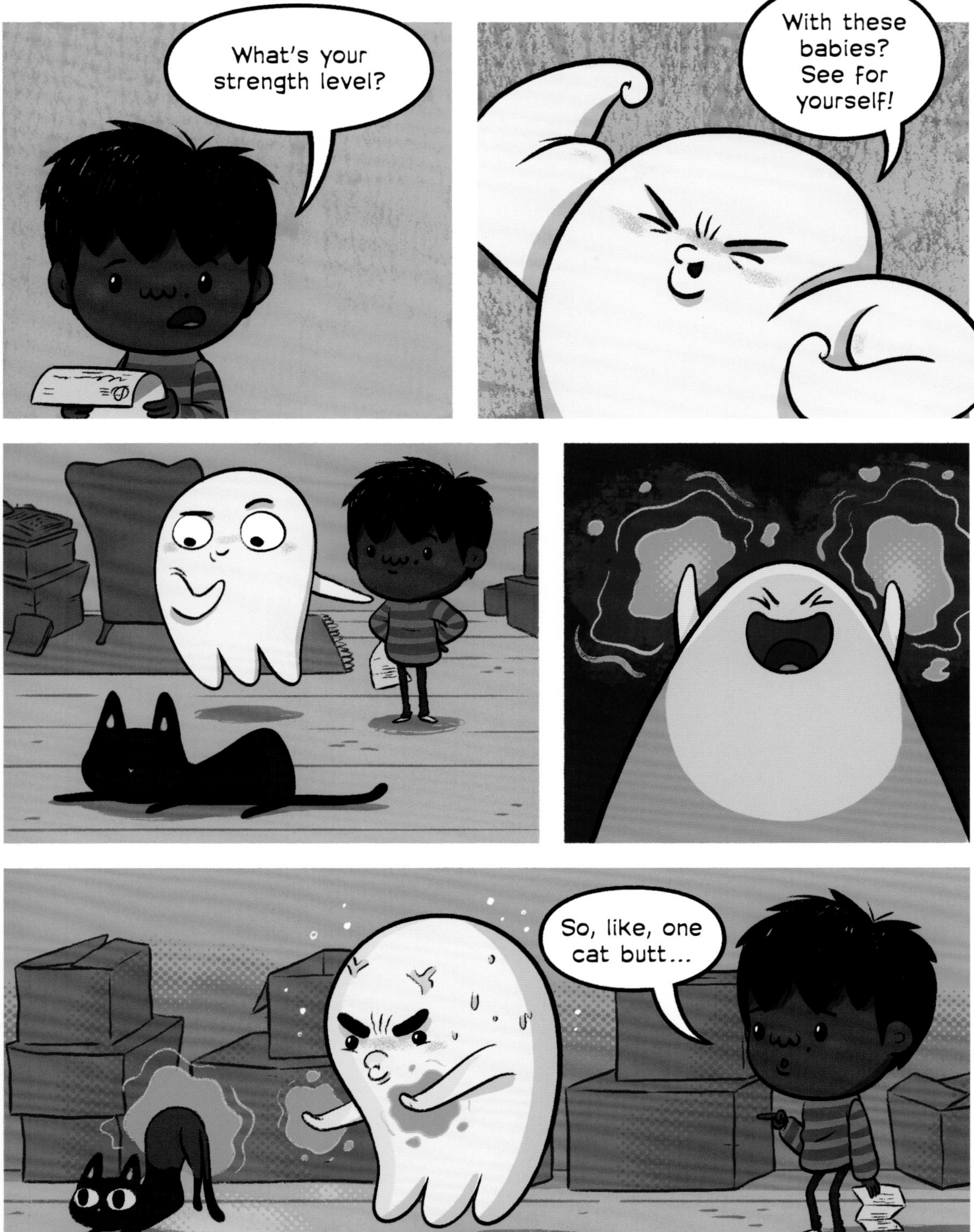
What's your strength level?
With these babies? See for yourself!
So, like, one cat butt...

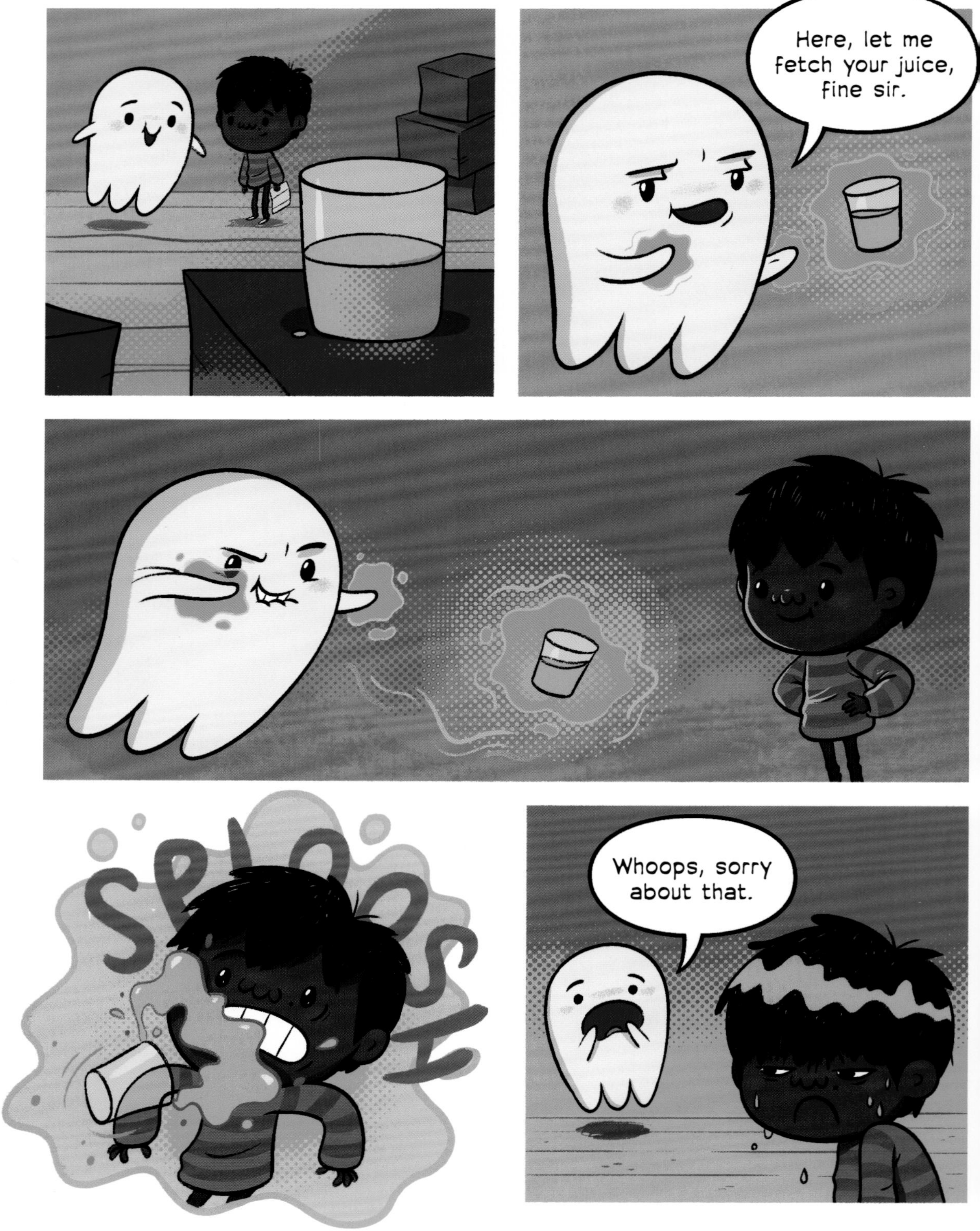
Here, let me fetch your juice, fine sir.
Whoops, sorry about that.

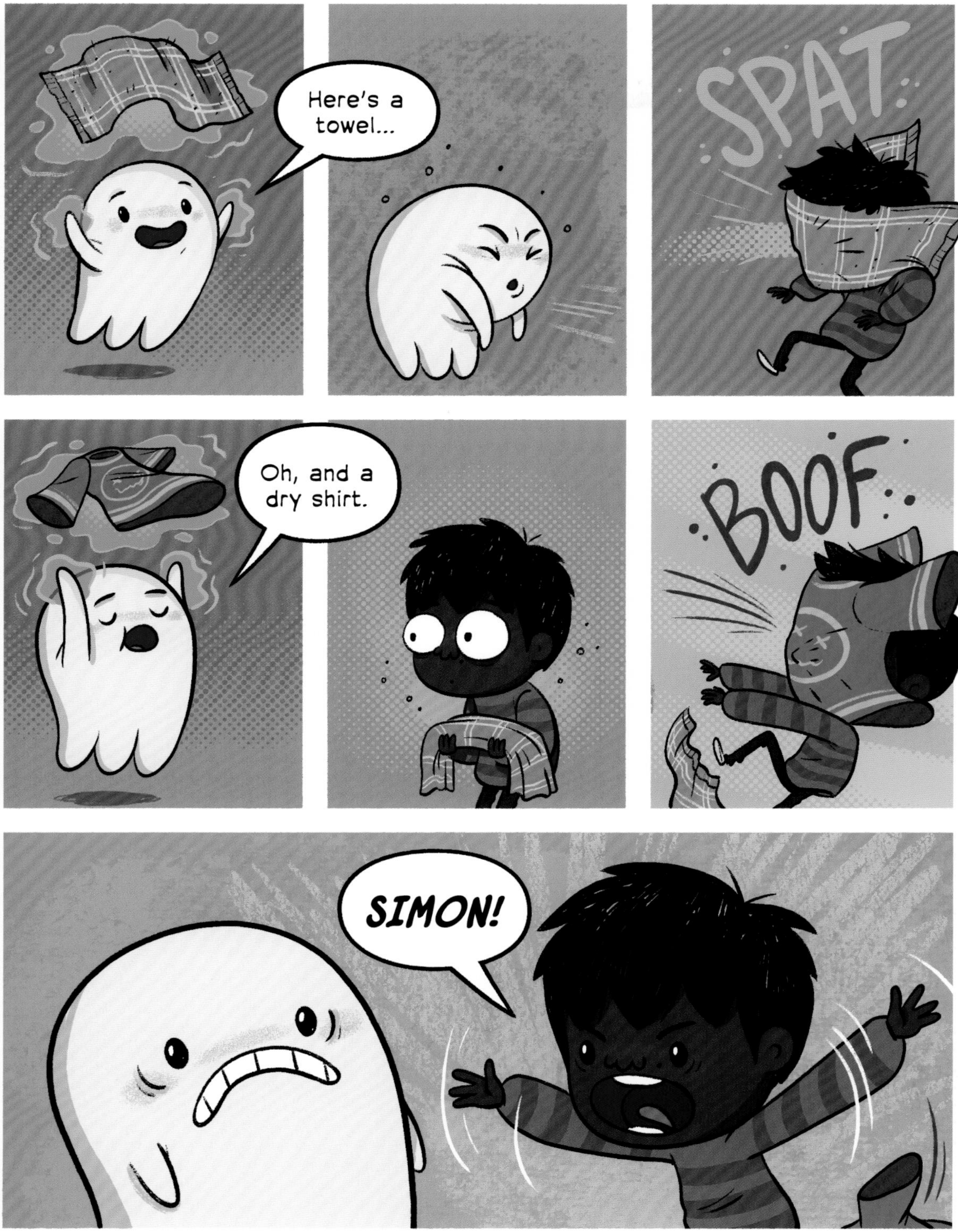
Here's a towel...
SPAT
Oh, and a dry shirt.
BOOF
SIMON!

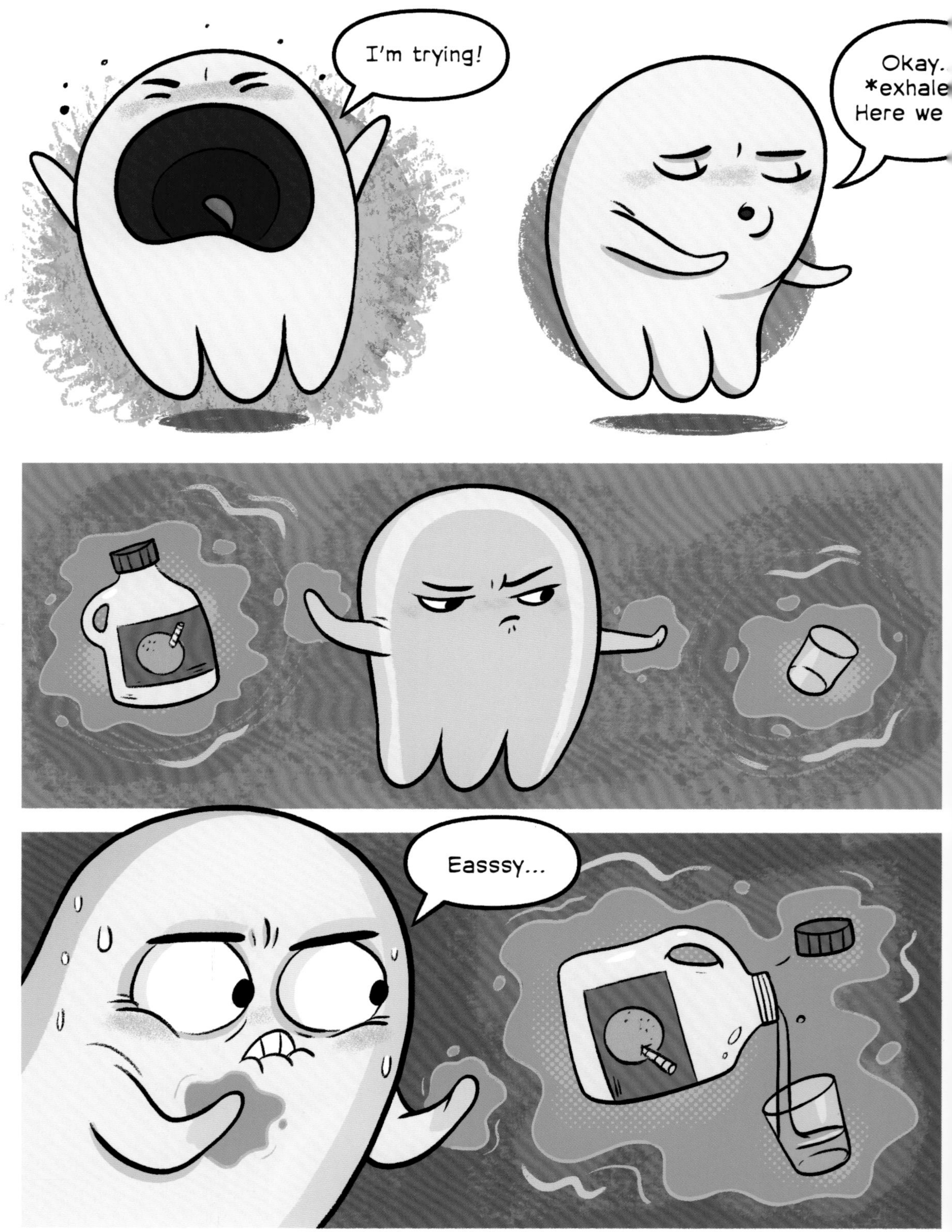
I'm trying!
Okay.
*exhale
Here we
Easssy...

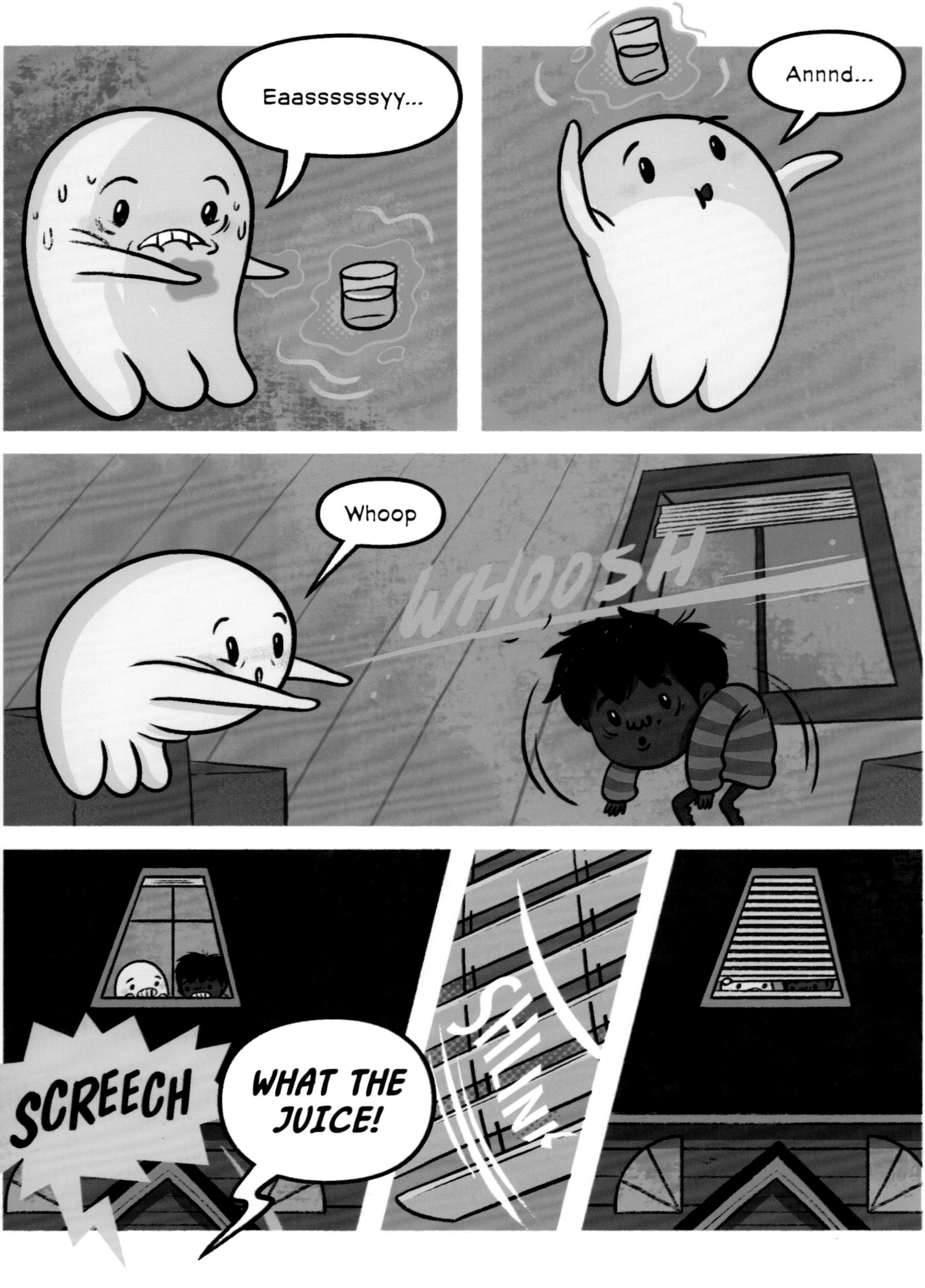
Eaassssssyy...
Annnd...
Whoop
WHOOSH
SCREECH
WHAT THE JUICE!
SHUNK

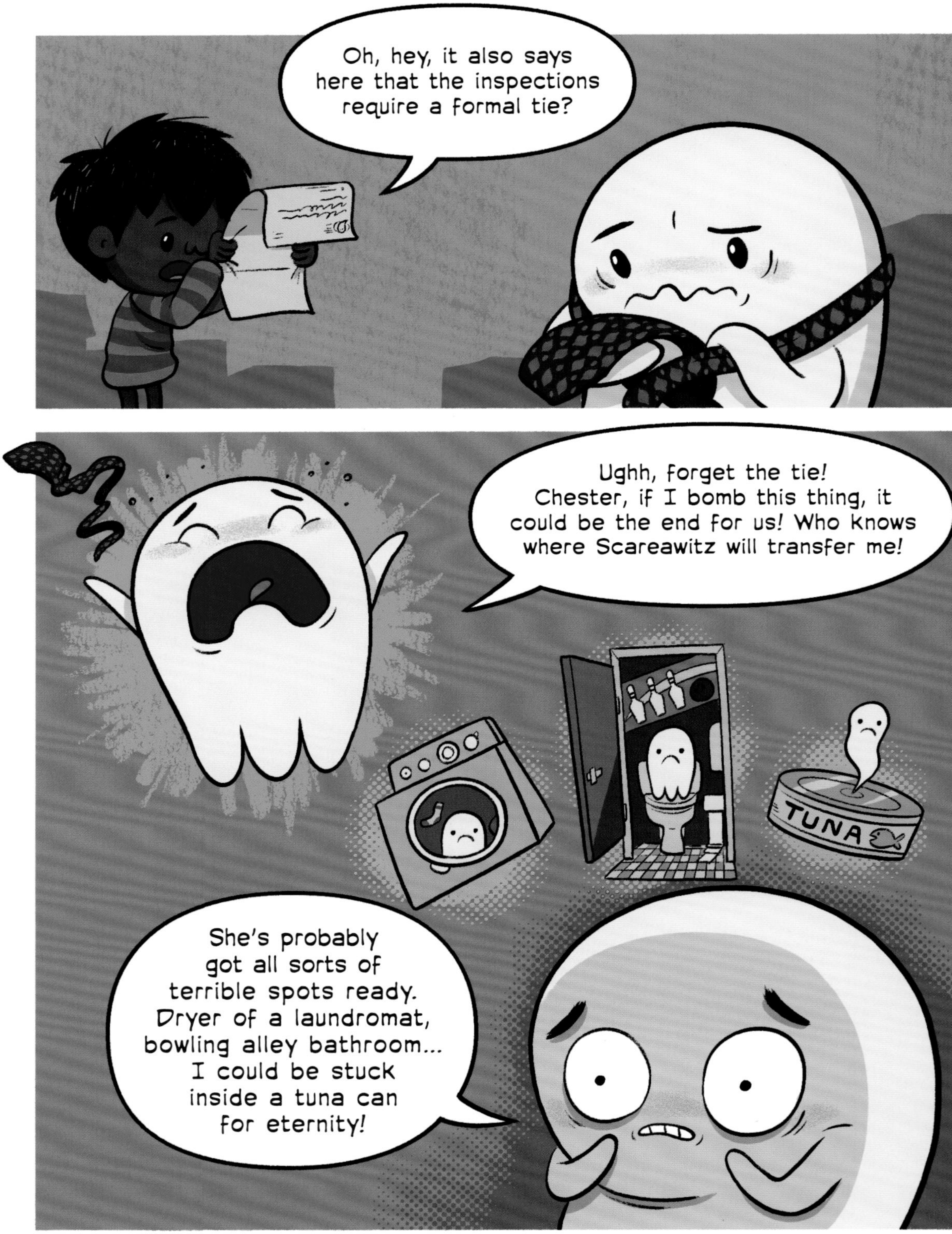
Oh, hey, it also says here that the inspections require a formal tie?
Ughh, forget the tie! Chester, if I bomb this thing, it could be the end for us! Who knows where Scareawitz will transfer me!
TUNA
She's probably got all sorts of terrible spots ready. Dryer of a laundromat, bowling alley bathroom... I could be stuck inside a tuna can for eternity!

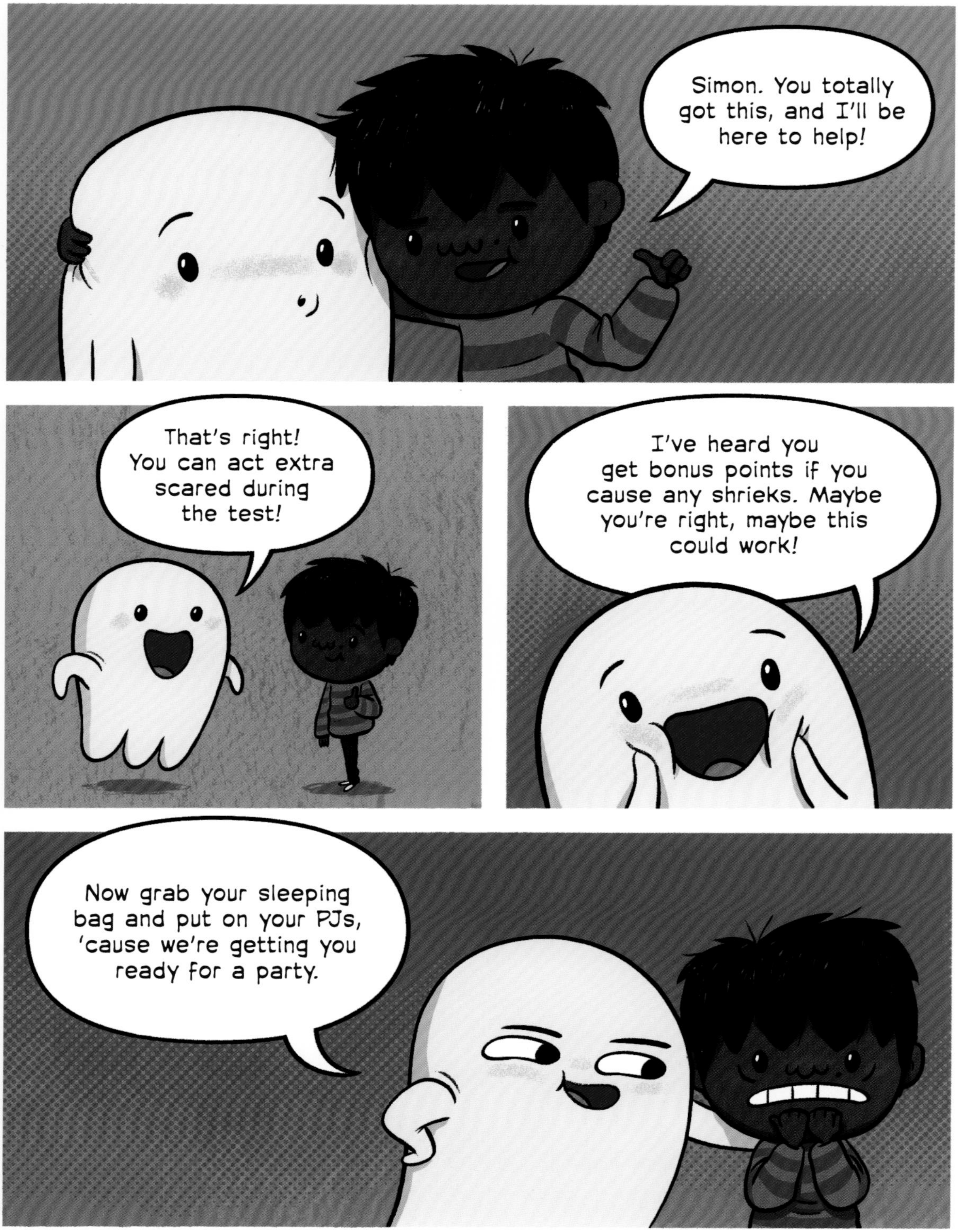
Simon. You totally got this, and I'll be here to help!
That's right! You can act extra scared during the test!
I've heard you get bonus points if you cause any shrieks. Maybe you're right, maybe this could work!
Now grab your sleeping bag and put on your PJs, 'cause we're getting you ready for a party.

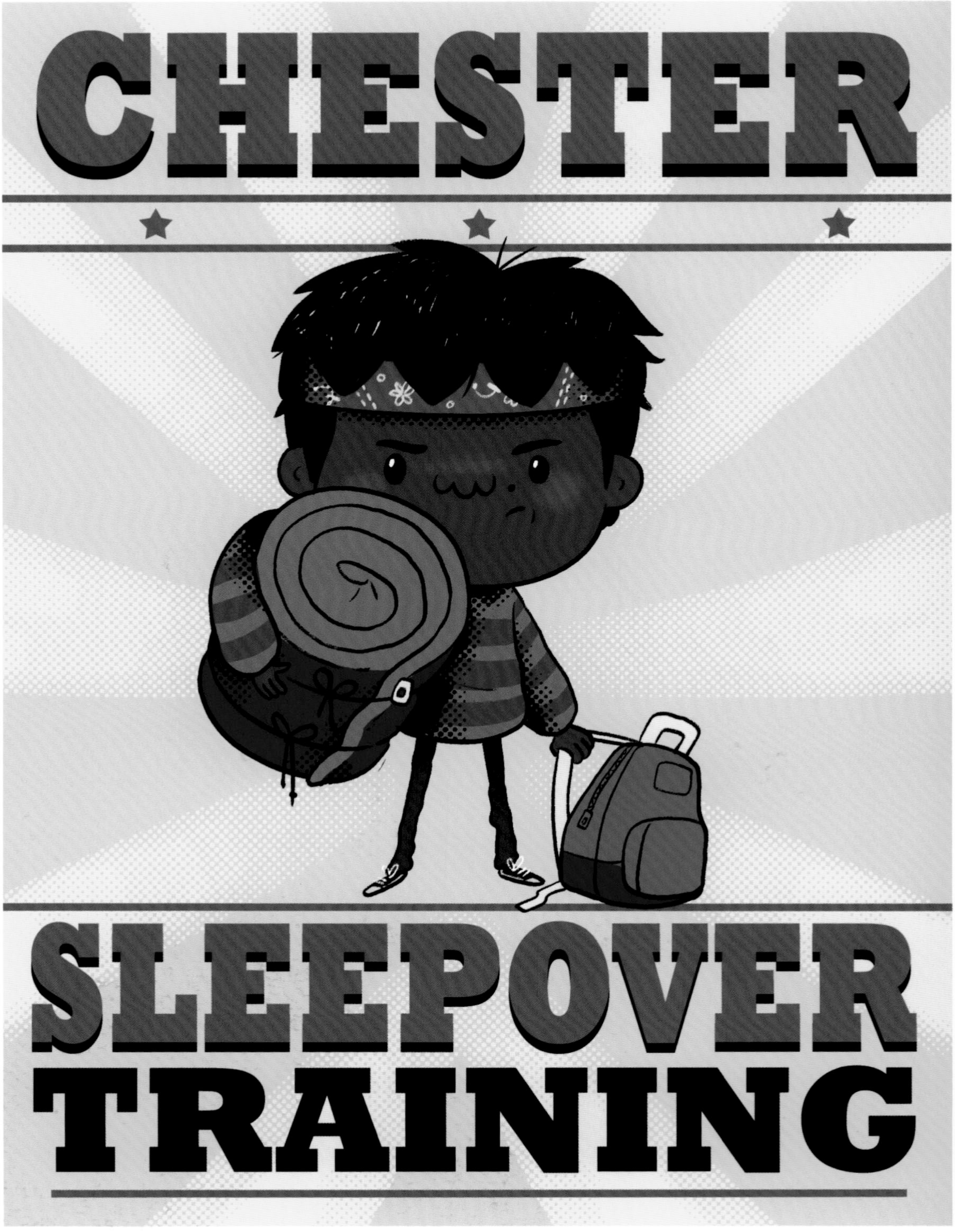
CHESTER
SLEEPOVER
TRAINING

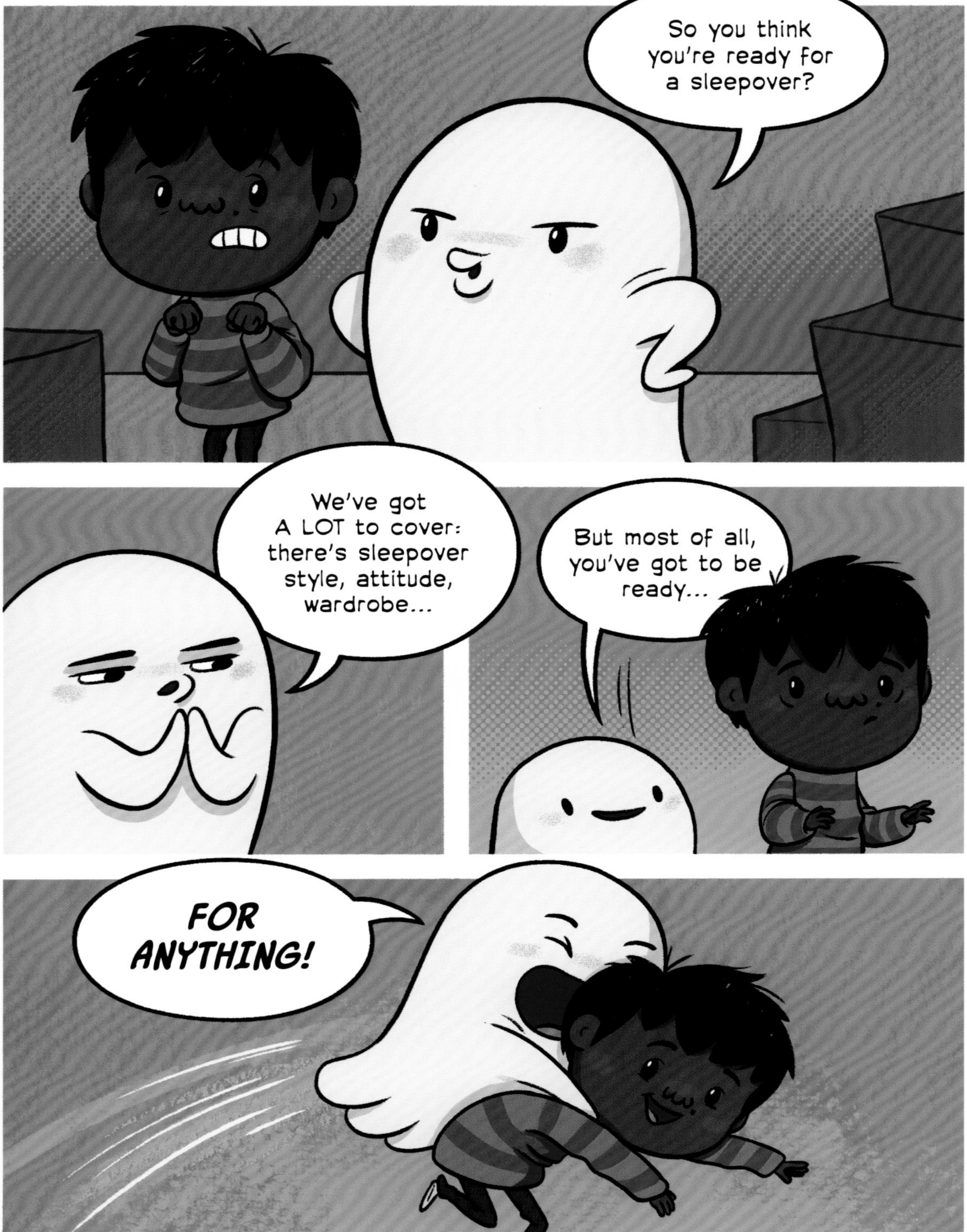
So you think you're ready for a sleepover?
We've got A LOT to cover: there's sleepover style, attitude, wardrobe...
But most of all, you've got to be ready...
FOR ANYTHING!

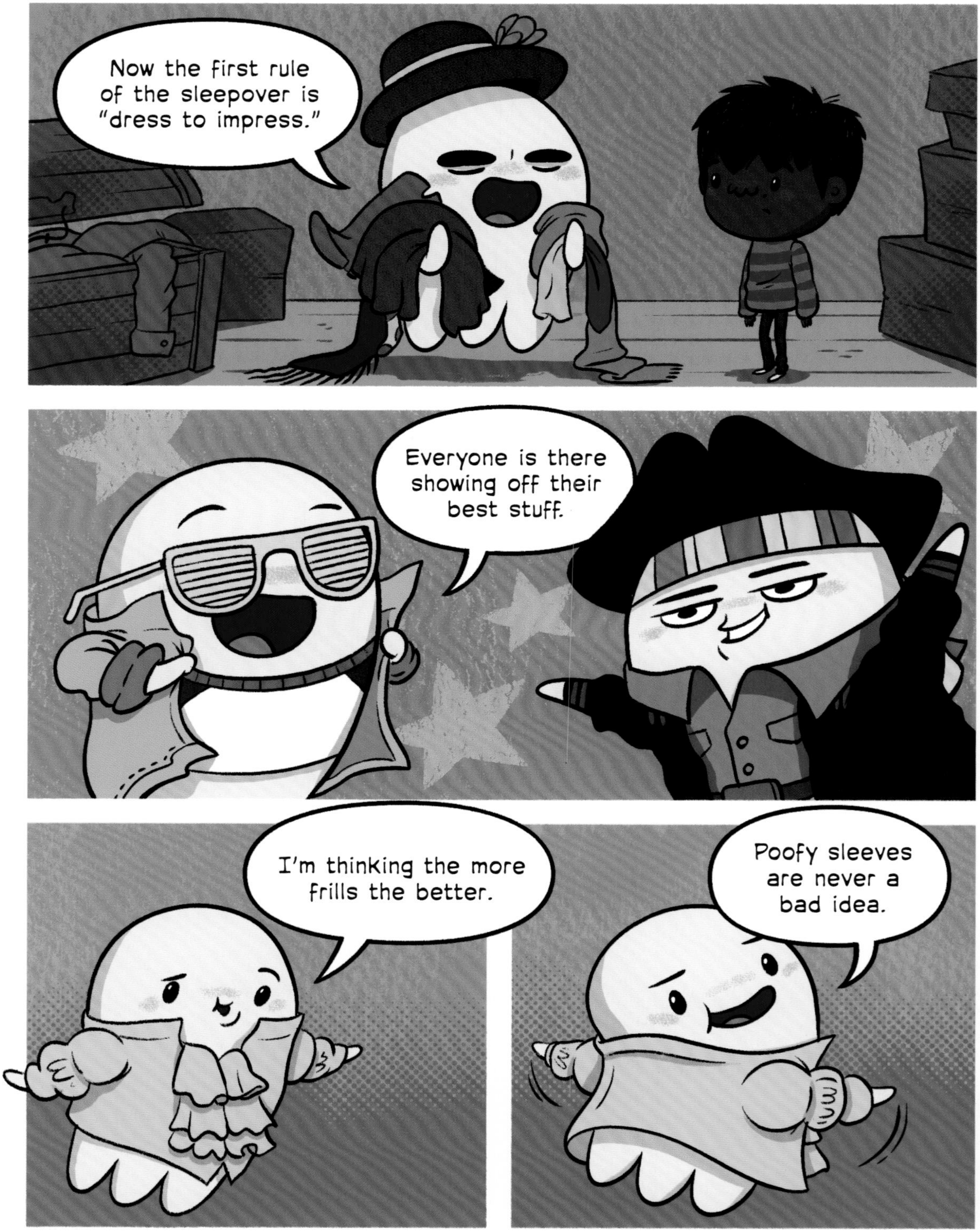
Now the first rule of the sleepover is "dress to impress."
Everyone is there showing off their best stuff.
I'm thinking the more frills the better.
Poofy sleeves are never a bad idea.

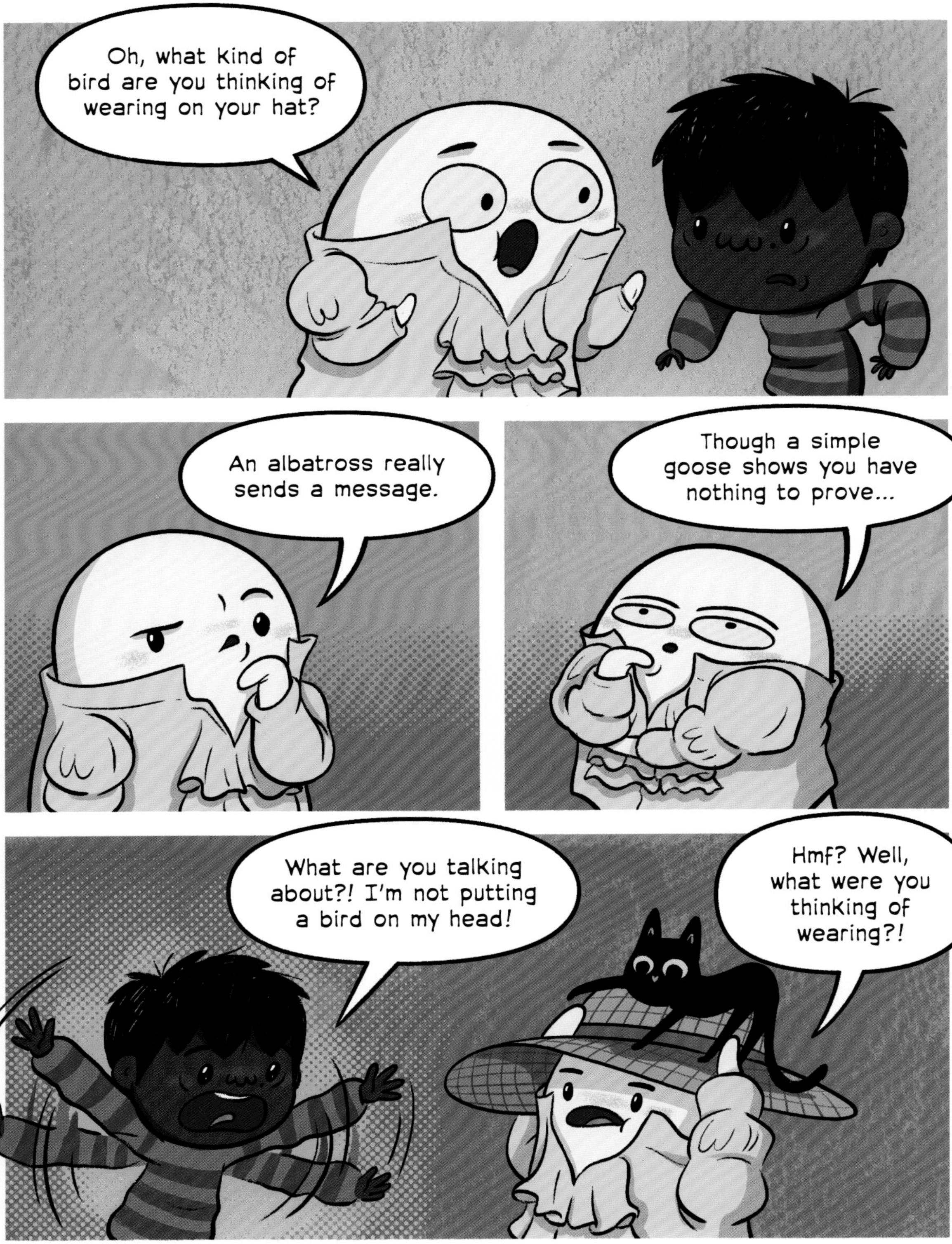
Oh, what kind of bird are you thinking of wearing on your hat?
An albatross really sends a message.
Though a simple goose shows you have nothing to prove...
What are you talking about?! I'm not putting a bird on my head!
Hmf? Well, what were you thinking of wearing?!

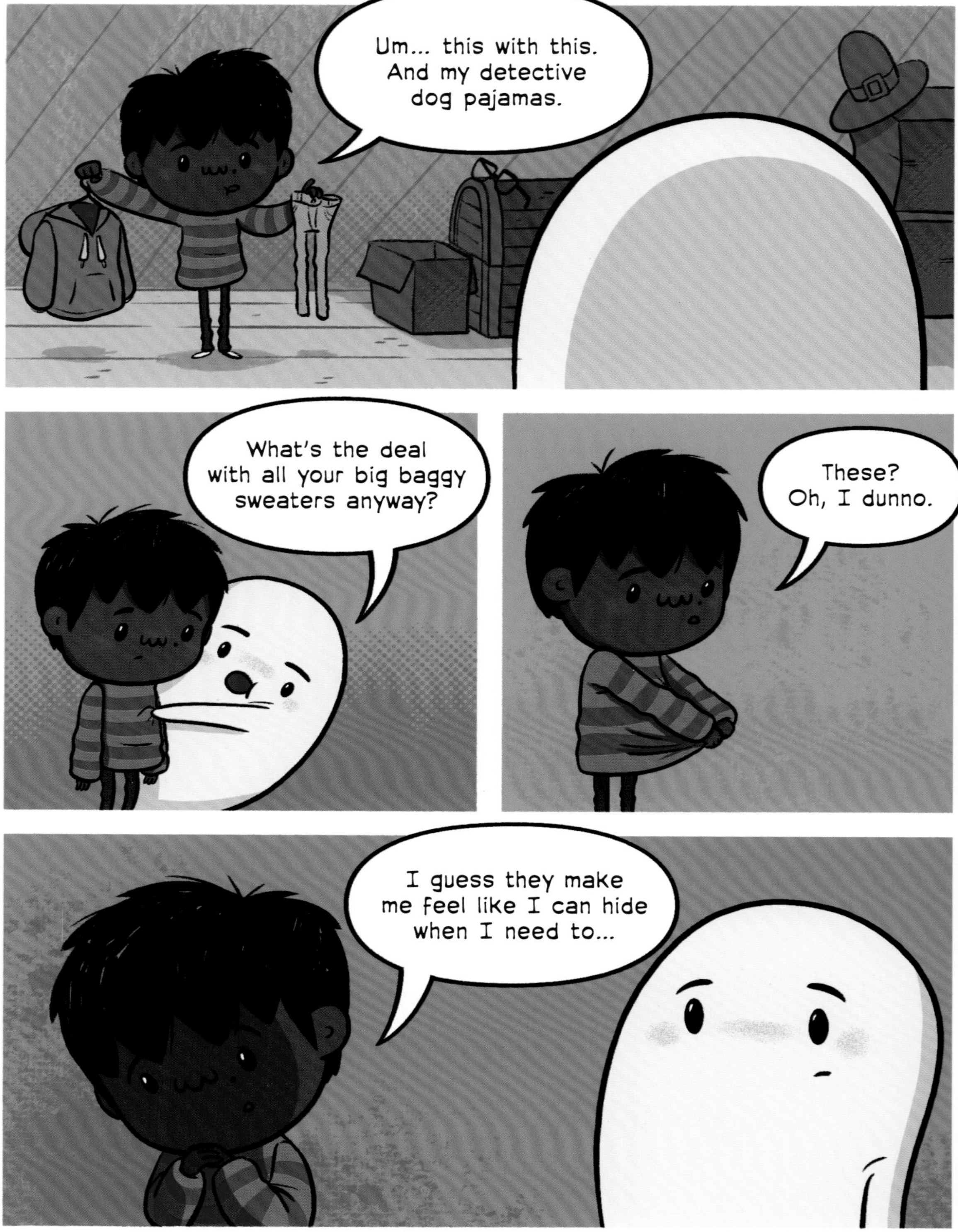

Um... this with this. And my detective dog pajamas.
What's the deal with all your big baggy sweaters anyway?
These? Oh, I dunno.
I guess they make me feel like I can hide when I need to...

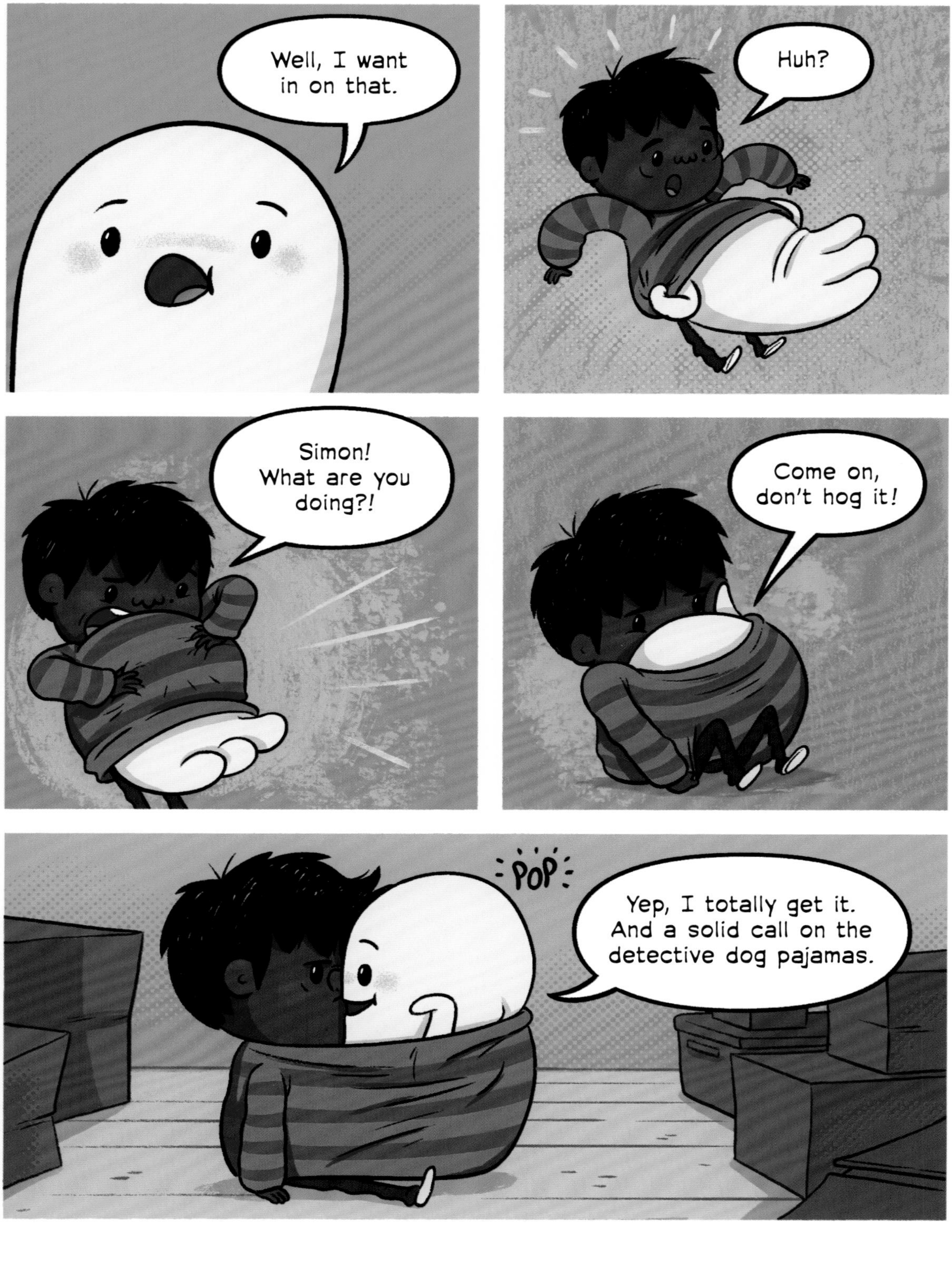
Well, I want in on that.
Huh?
Simon! What are you doing?!
Come on, don't hog it!
POP
Yep, I totally get it. And a solid call on the detective dog pajamas.

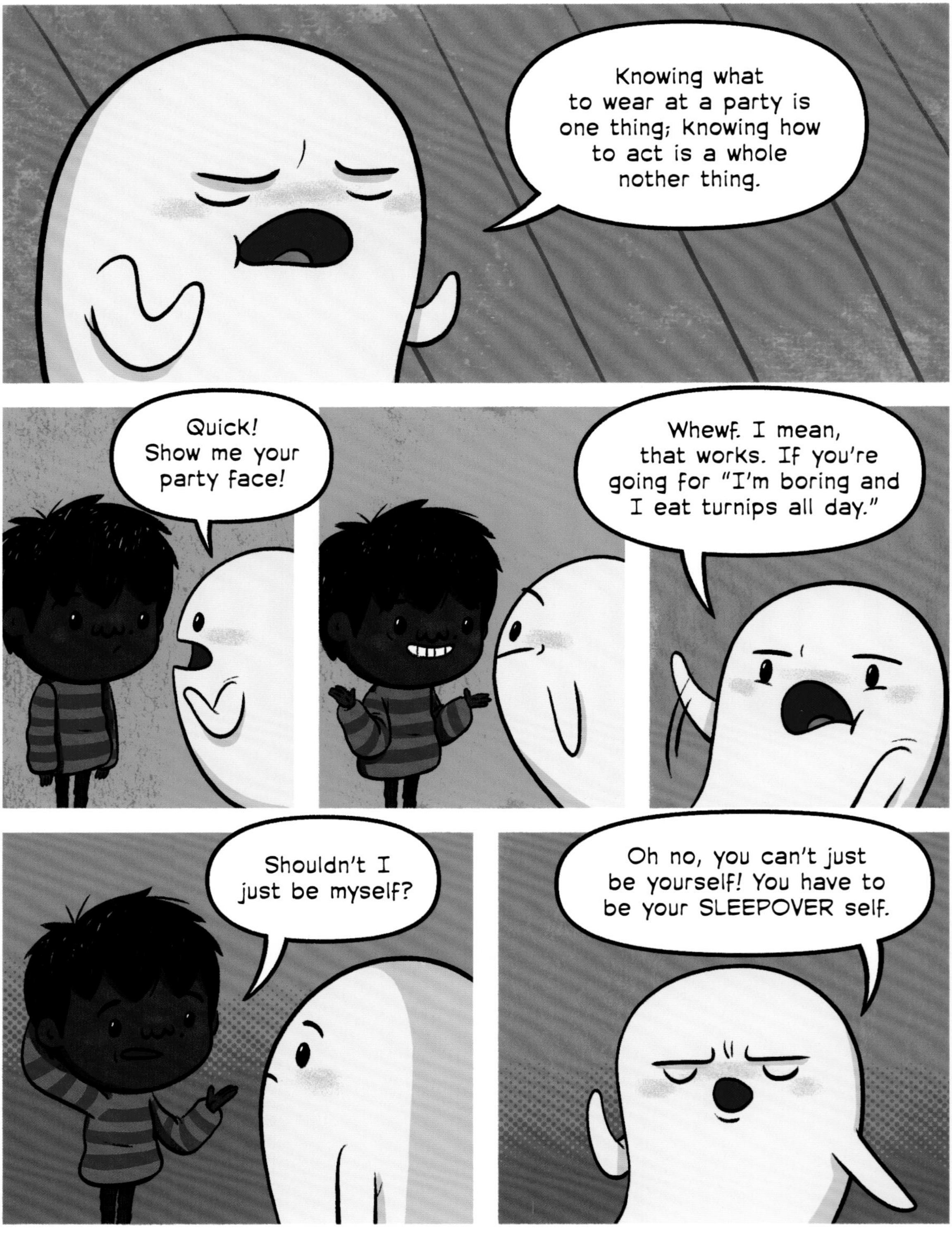
Knowing what to wear at a party is one thing; knowing how to act is a whole nother thing.
Quick! Show me your party face!
Whewf. I mean, that works. If you're going for "I'm boring and I eat turnips all day."
Shouldn't I just be myself?
Oh no, you can't just be yourself! You have to be your SLEEPOVER self.

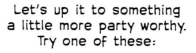
Let's up it to something a little more party worthy. Try one of these:

the I'm Too Cool To Hear What You're Saying look

the I'm Having SO Much Fun look

the I Own A Fancy Boat look

the I'm Dark And Mysterious look

the I Have Avocado In My Eye look

the I'm Smarter Than You look

Come on, now you try.

Simon...

Ooo nice, the Grumpy With A Heart Of Gold look.

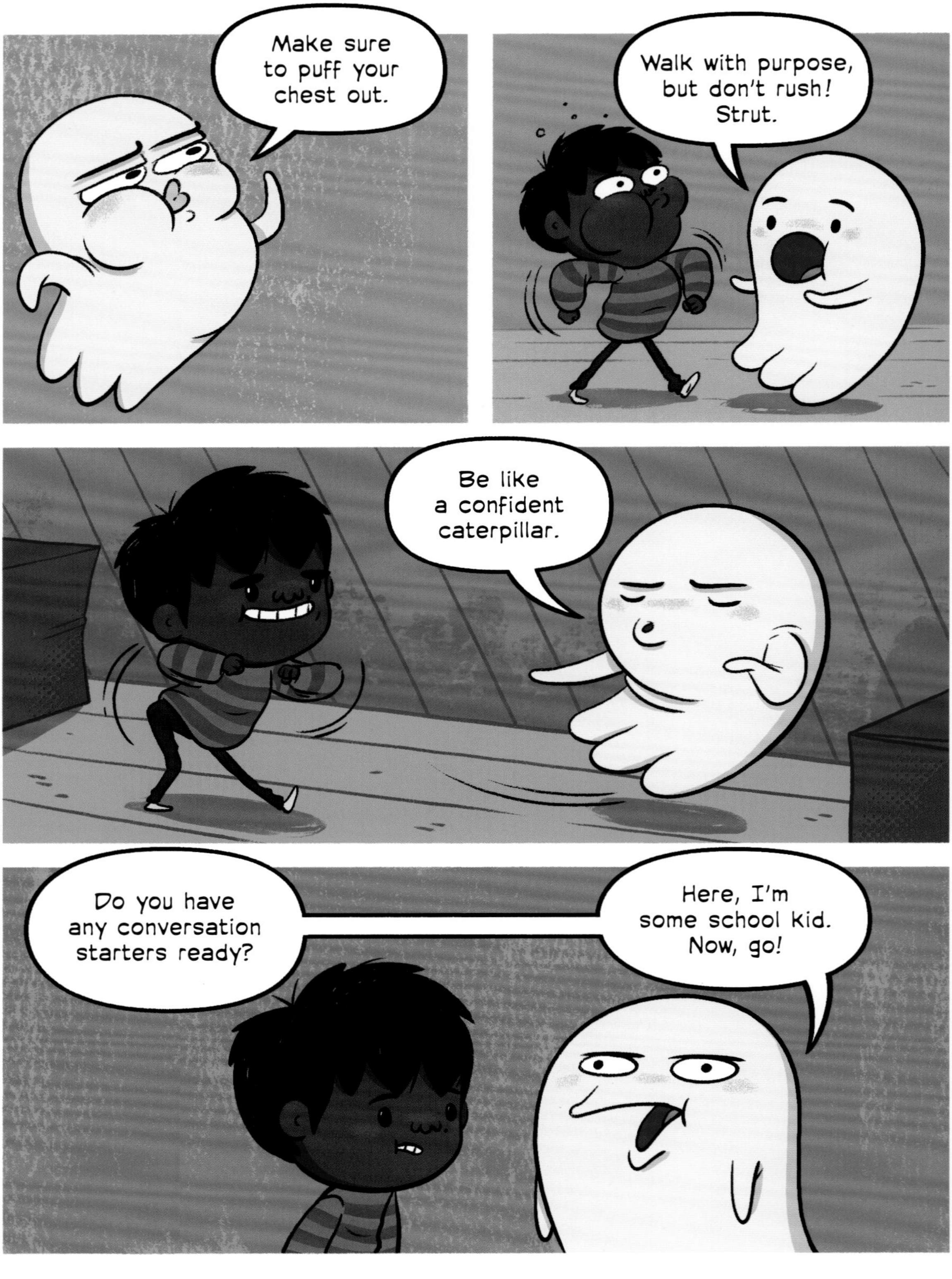
Make sure to puff your chest out.
Walk with purpose, but don't rush! Strut.
Be like a confident caterpillar.
Do you have any conversation starters ready?
Here, I'm some school kid. Now, go!

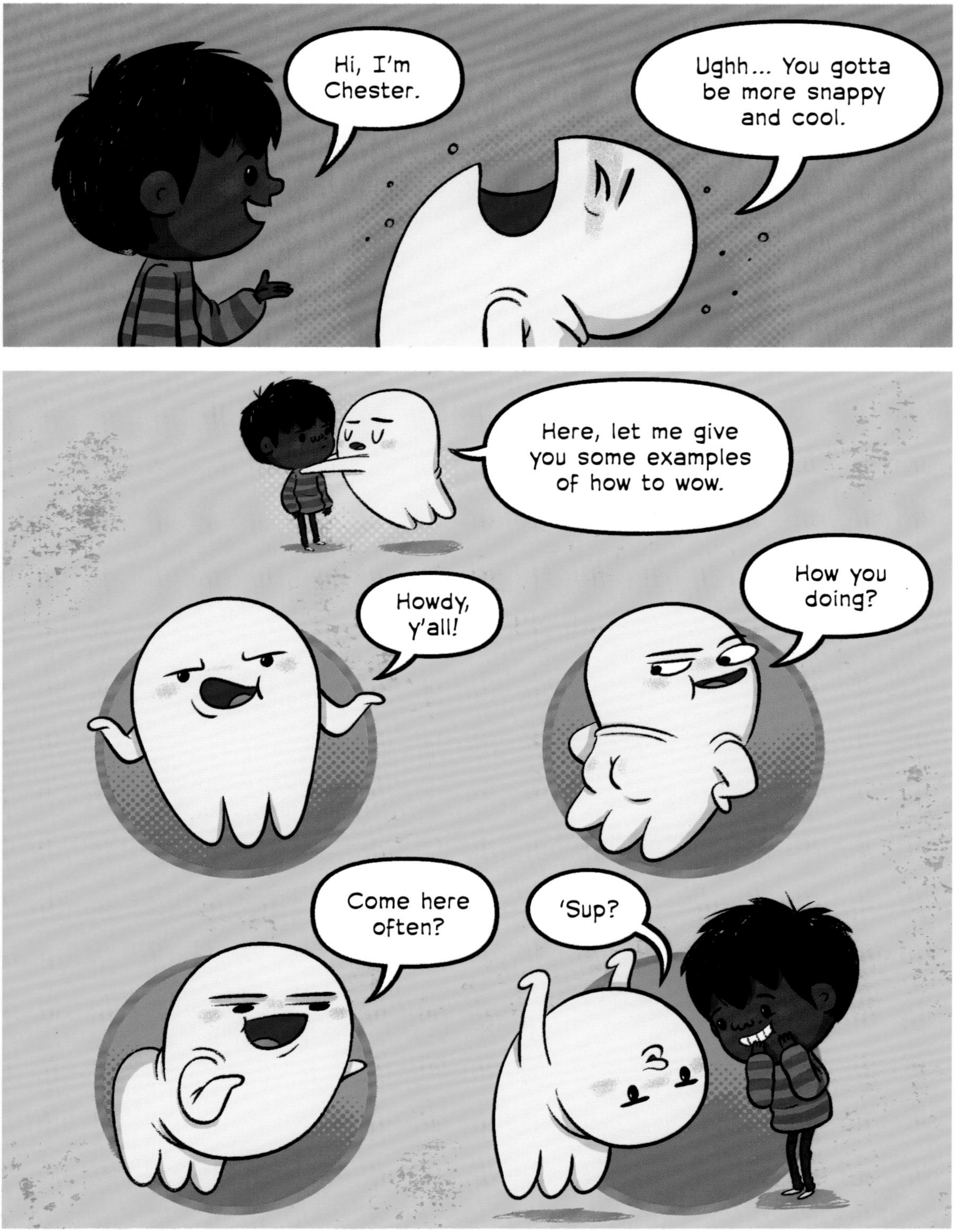
Hi, I'm Chester.
Ughh... You gotta be more snappy and cool.
Here, let me give you some examples of how to wow.
Howdy, y'all!
How you doing?
Come here often?
'Sup?

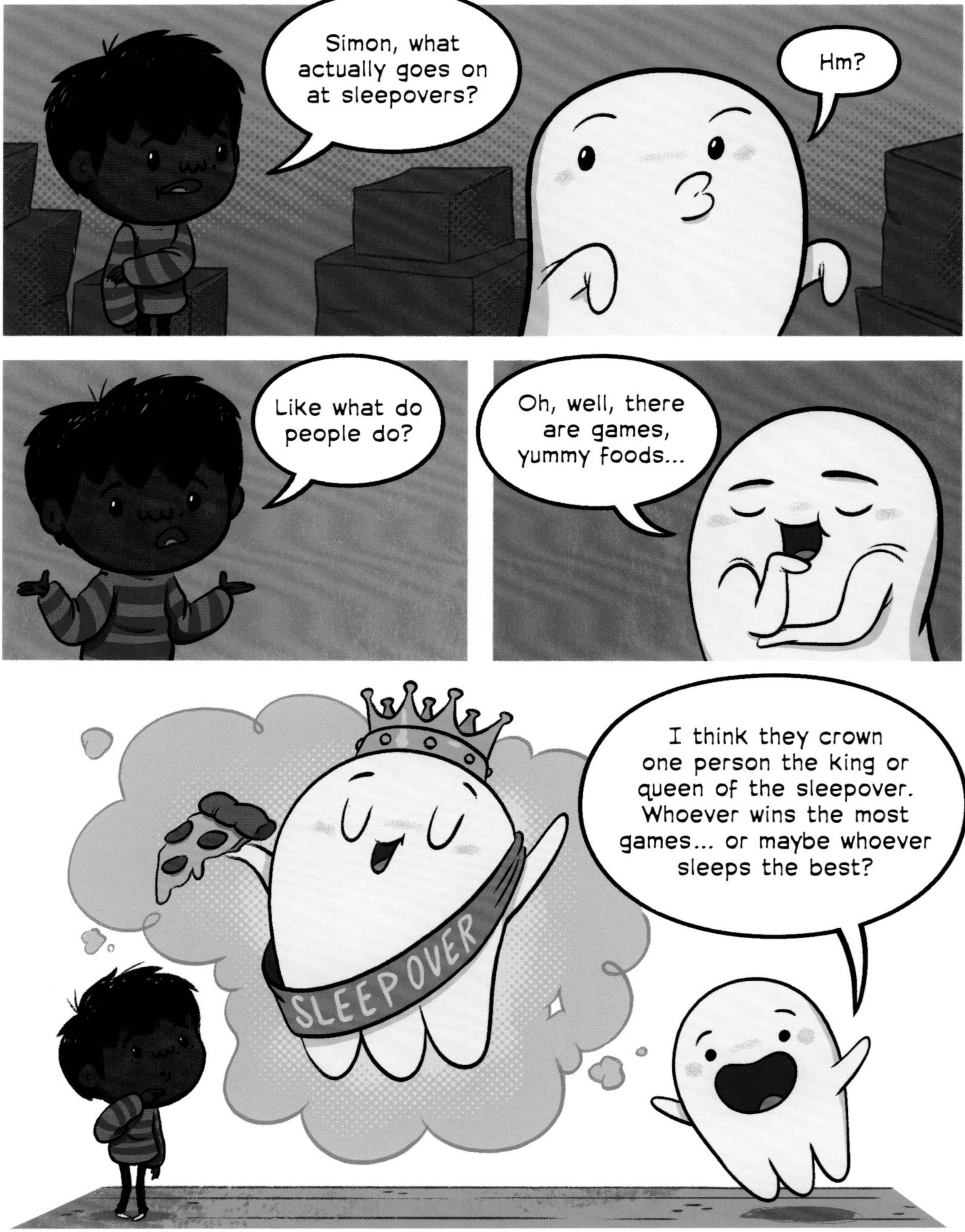
Simon, what actually goes on at sleepovers?
Hm?
Like what do people do?
Oh, well, there are games, yummy foods...
SLEEPOVER
I think they crown one person the king or queen of the sleepover. Whoever wins the most games... or maybe whoever sleeps the best?

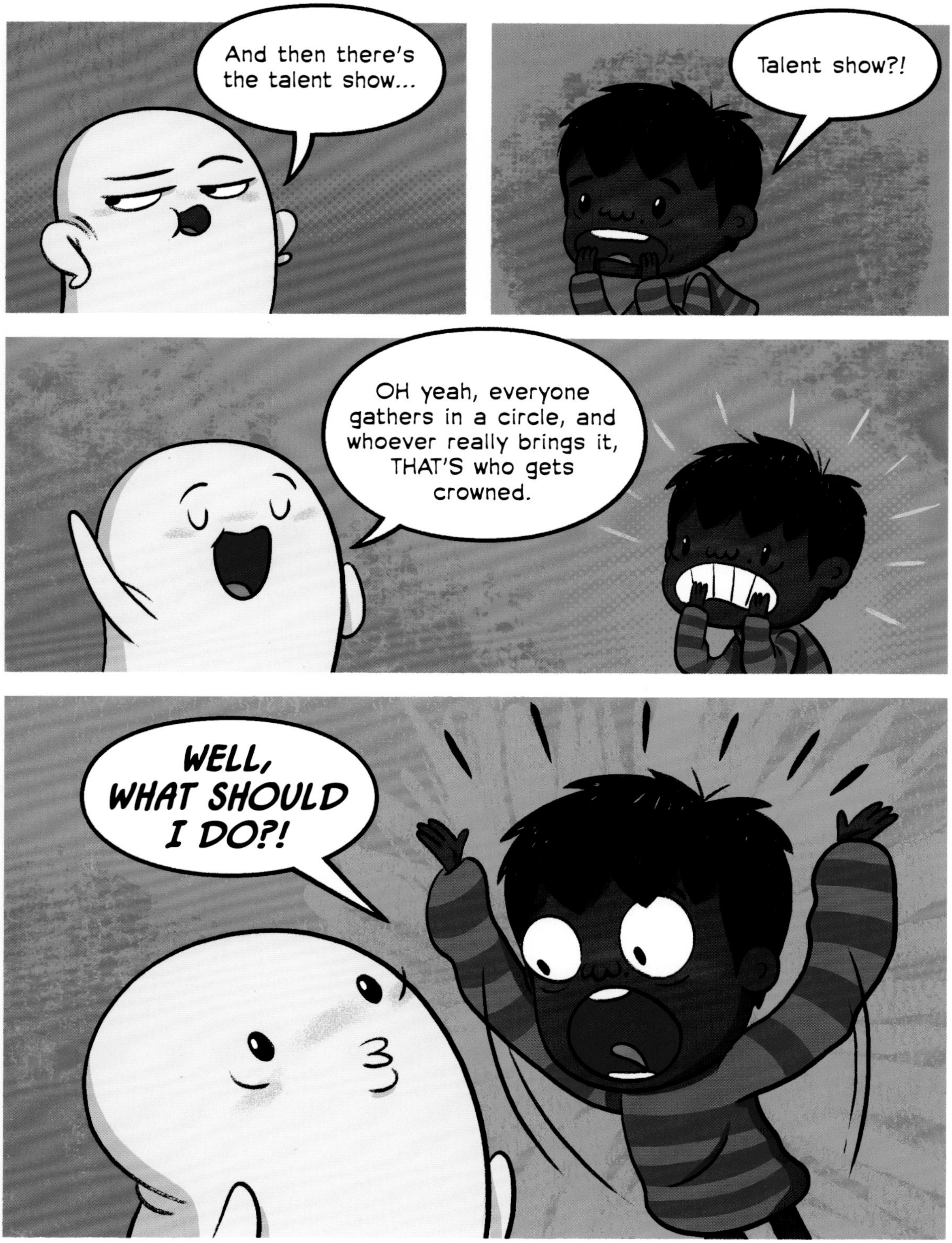
And then there's the talent show...
Talent show?!
OH yeah, everyone gathers in a circle, and whoever really brings it, THAT'S who gets crowned.
WELL, WHAT SHOULD I DO?!

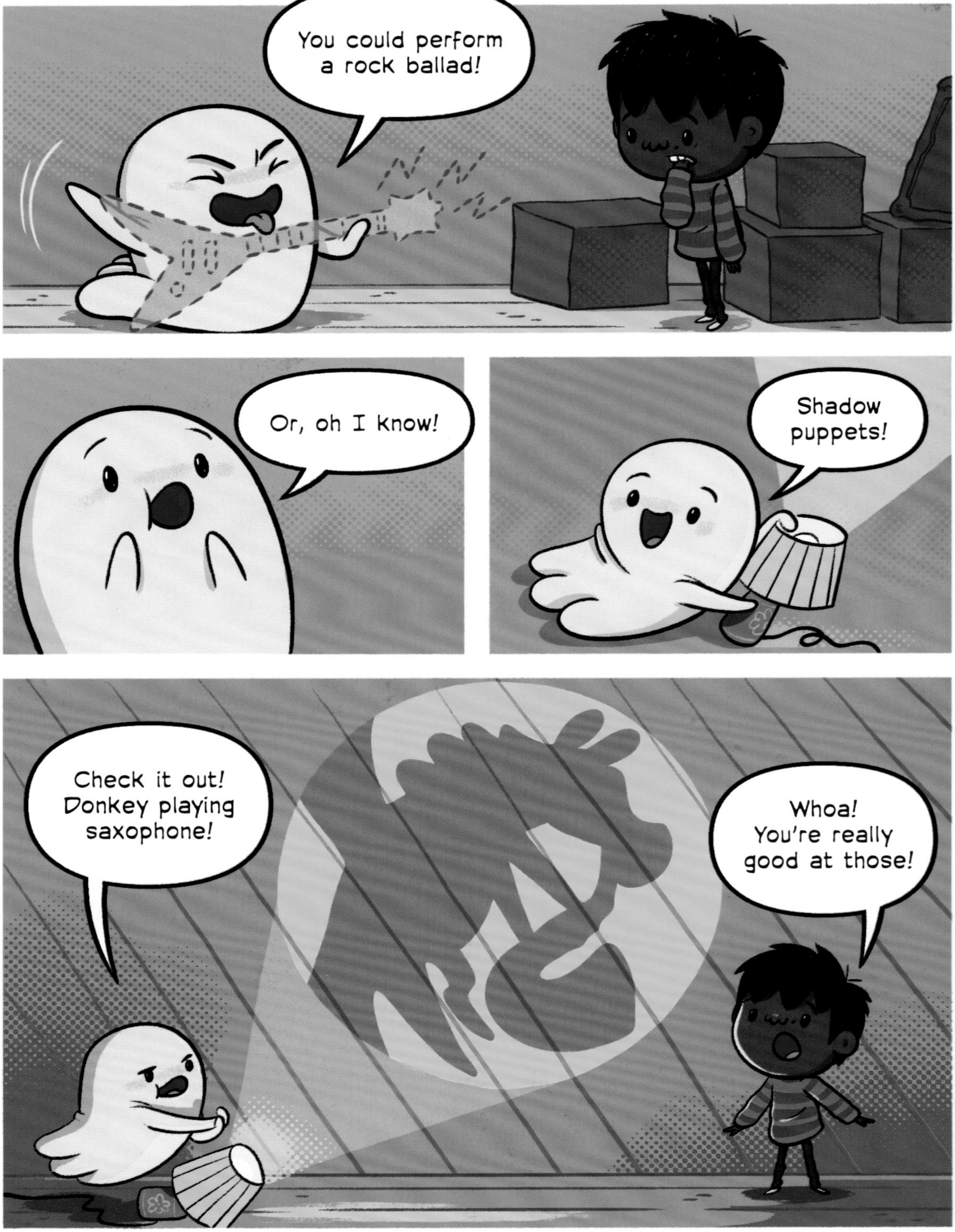

You could perform a rock ballad!
Or, oh I know!
Shadow puppets!
Check it out! Donkey playing saxophone!
Whoa! You're really good at those!

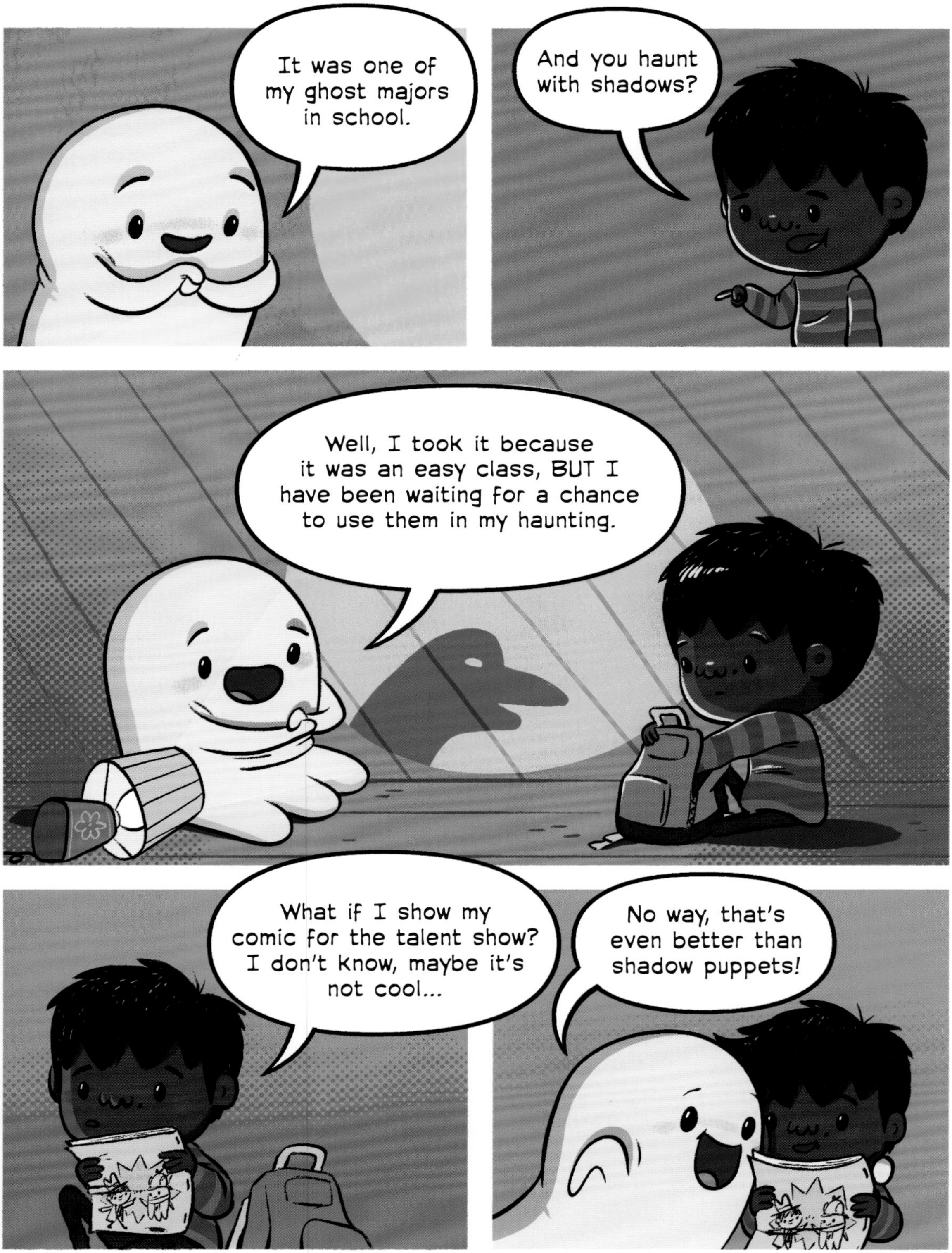
It was one of my ghost majors in school.
And you haunt with shadows?
Well, I took it because it was an easy class, BUT I have been waiting for a chance to use them in my haunting.
What if I show my comic for the talent show? I don't know, maybe it's not cool...
No way, that's even better than shadow puppets!

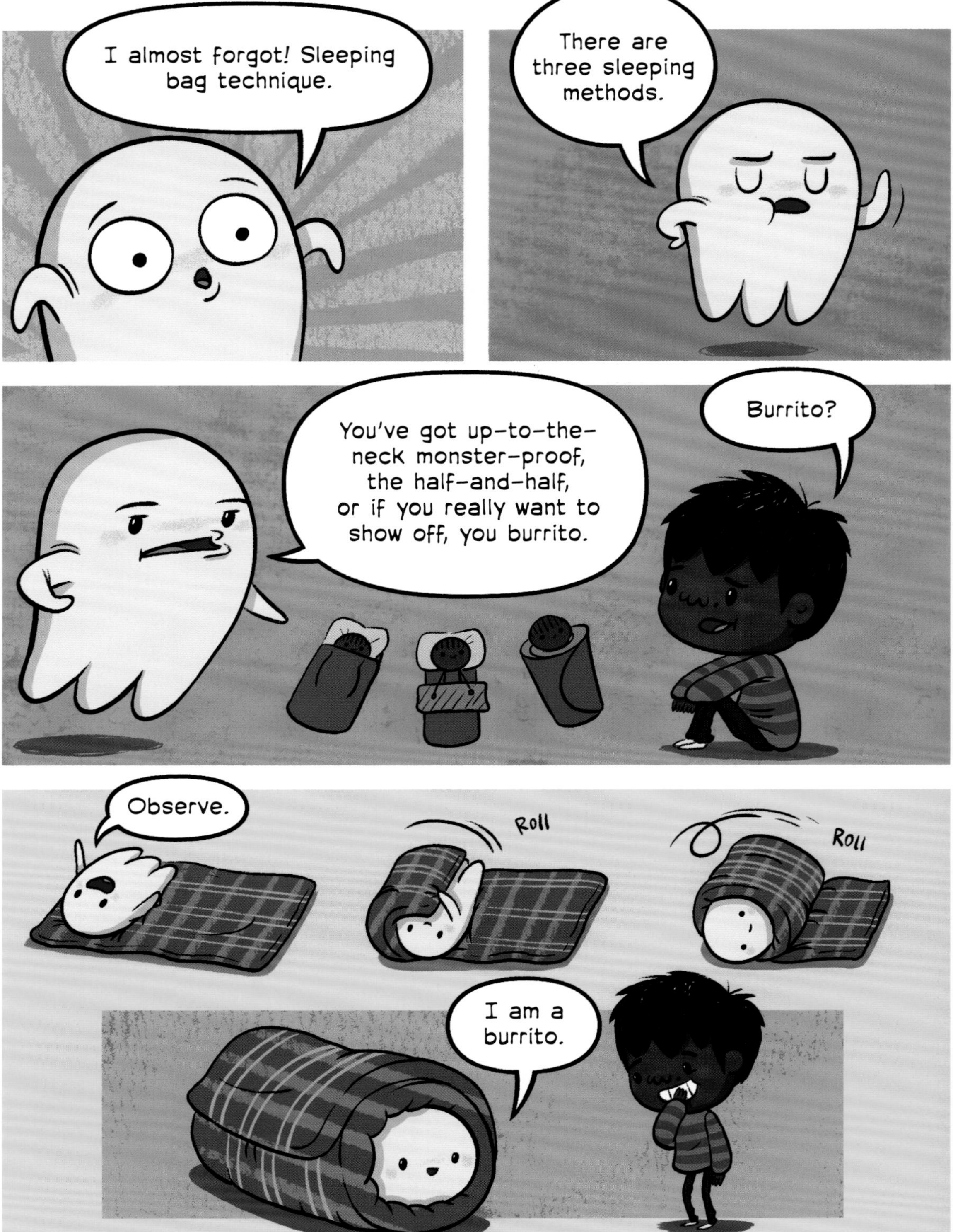
I almost forgot! Sleeping bag technique.
There are three sleeping methods.
You've got up-to-the-neck monster-proof, the half-and-half, or if you really want to show off, you burrito.
Burrito?
Observe.
Roll
Roll
I am a burrito.

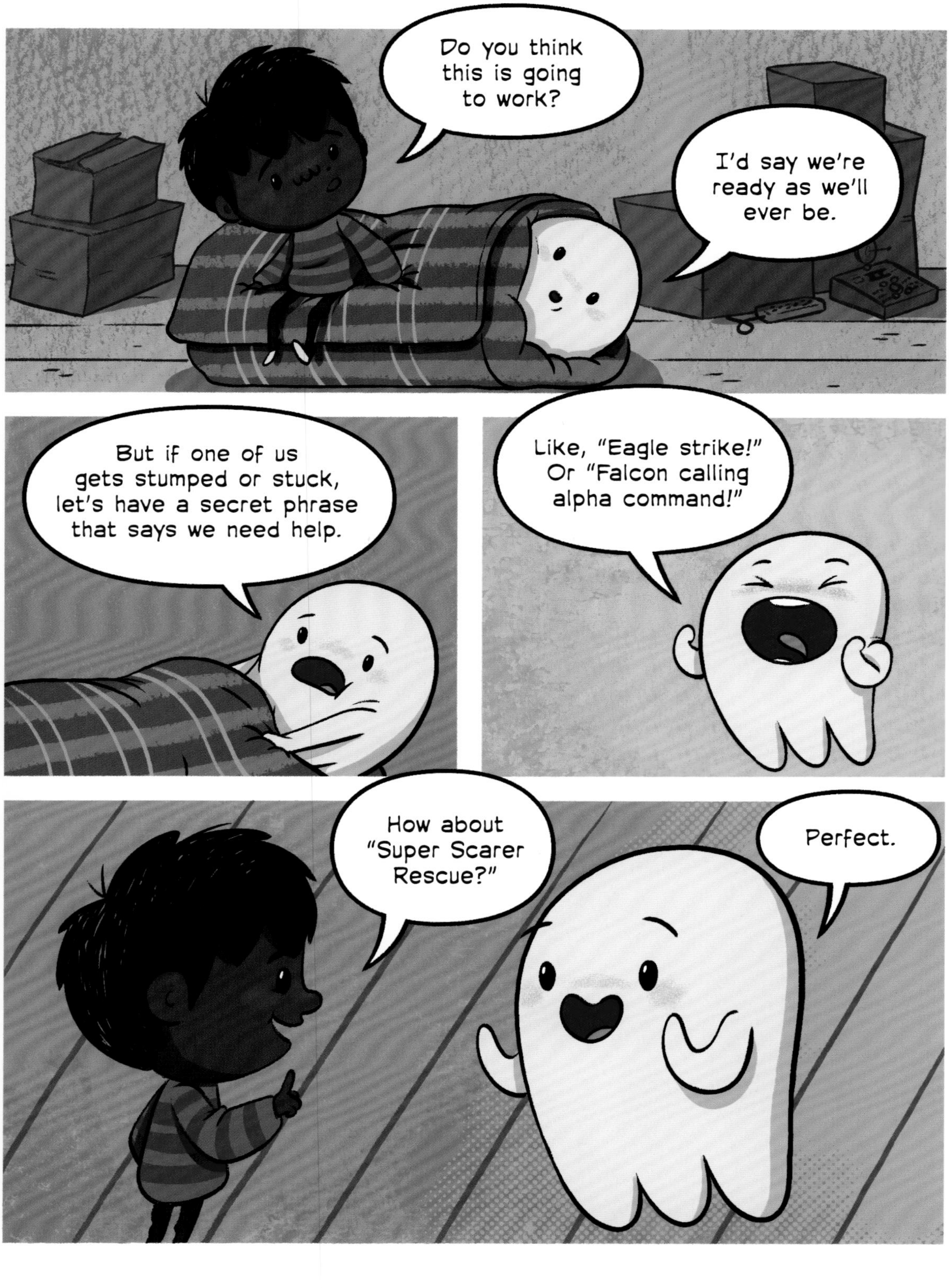
Do you think this is going to work?
I'd say we're ready as we'll ever be.
But if one of us gets stumped or stuck, let's have a secret phrase that says we need help.
Like, "Eagle strike!" Or "Falcon calling alpha command!"
How about "Super Scarer Rescue?"
Perfect.

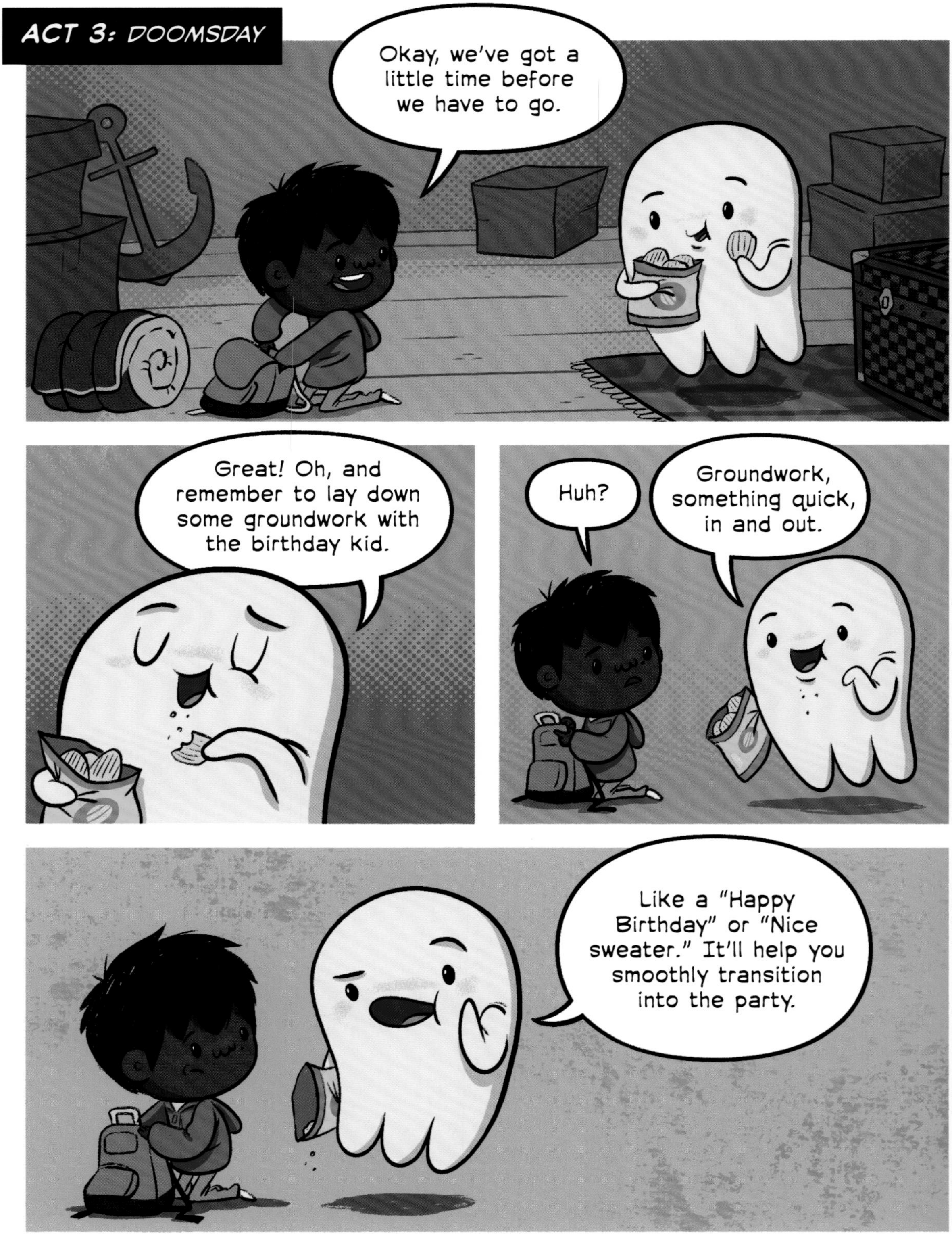
ACT 3: DOOMSDAY
Okay, we've got a little time before we have to go.
Great! Oh, and remember to lay down some groundwork with the birthday kid.
Huh?
Groundwork, something quick, in and out.
Like a "Happy Birthday" or "Nice sweater." It'll help you smoothly transition into the party.

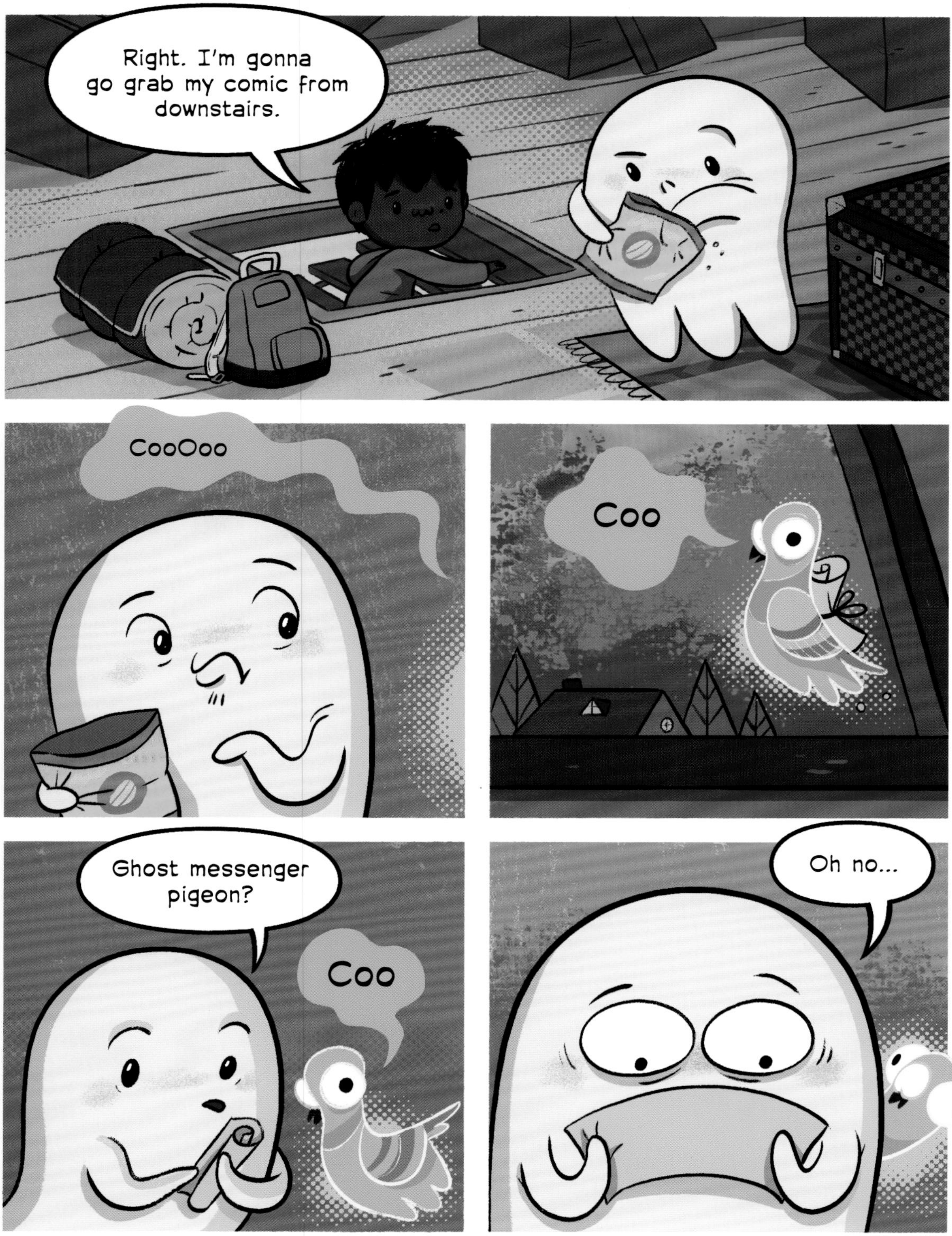
Right. I'm gonna go grab my comic from downstairs.
CooOoo
Coo
Ghost messenger pigeon?
Coo
Oh no...

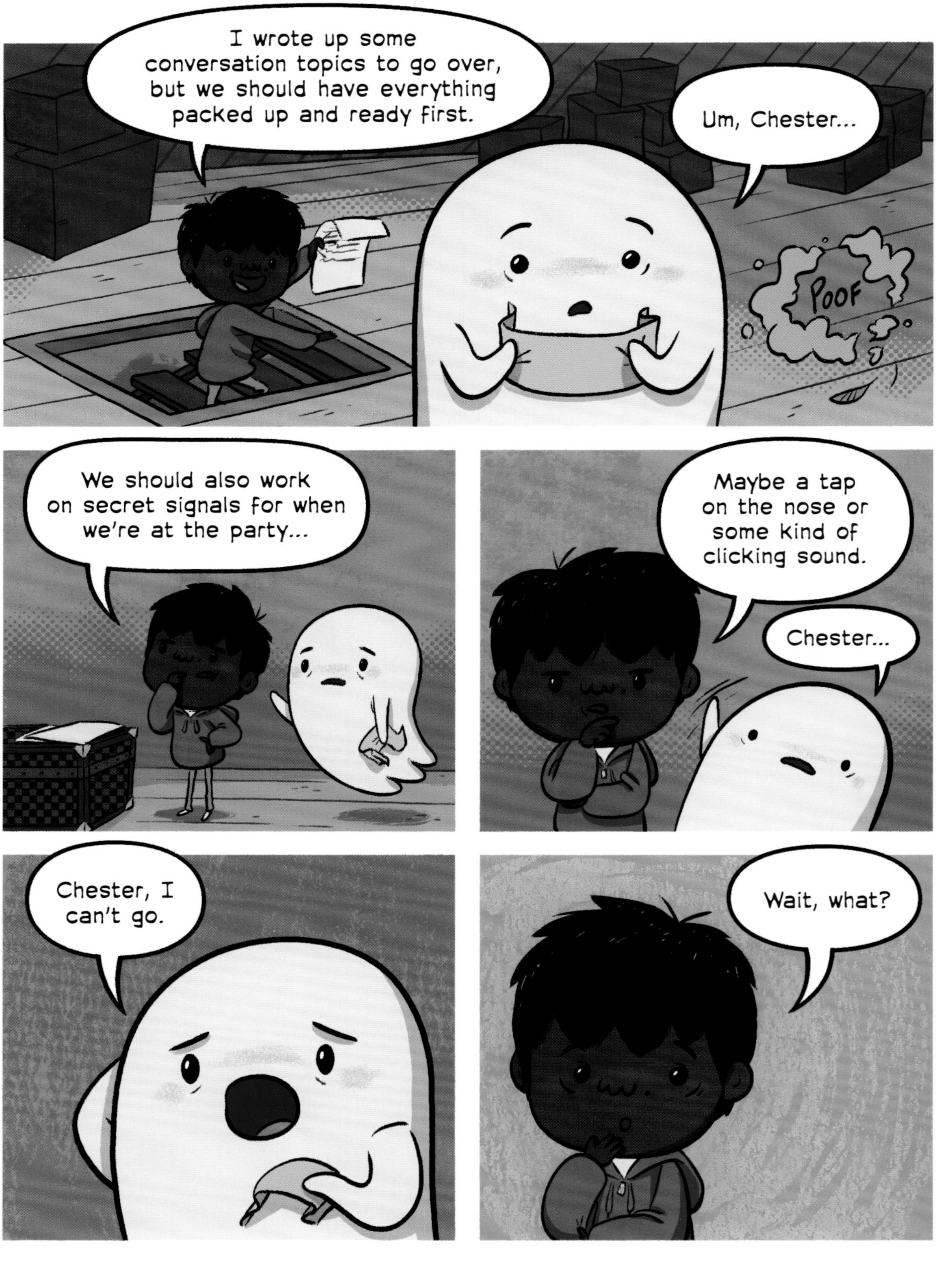
I wrote up some conversation topics to go over, but we should have everything packed up and ready first.
Um, Chester...
POOF
We should also work on secret signals for when we're at the party...
Maybe a tap on the nose or some kind of clicking sound.
Chester...
Chester, I can't go.
Wait, what?

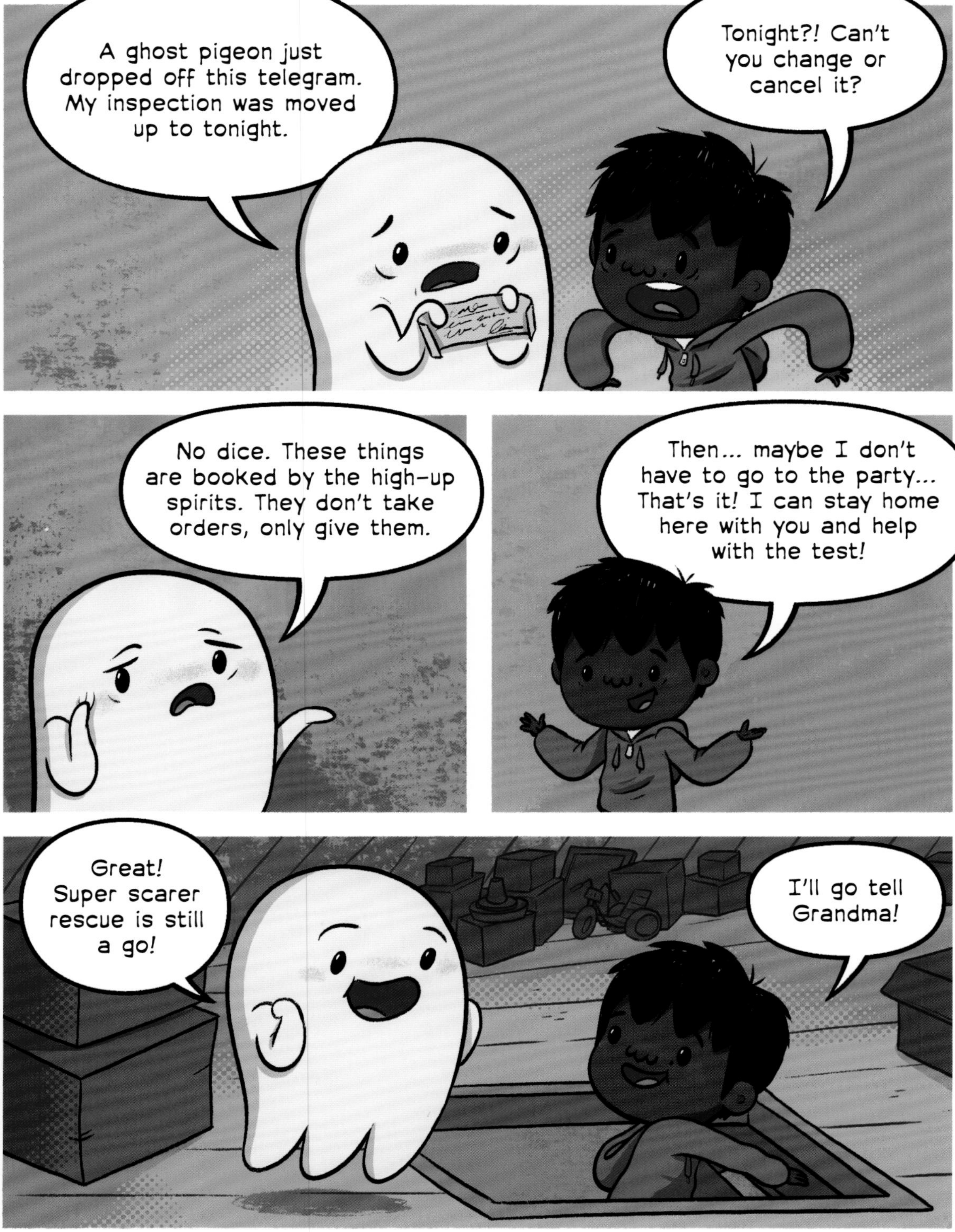
A ghost pigeon just dropped off this telegram. My inspection was moved up to tonight.
Tonight?! Can't you change or cancel it?
No dice. These things are booked by the high-up spirits. They don't take orders, only give them.
Then... maybe I don't have to go to the party... That's it! I can stay home here with you and help with the test!
Great! Super scarer rescue is still a go!
I'll go tell Grandma!

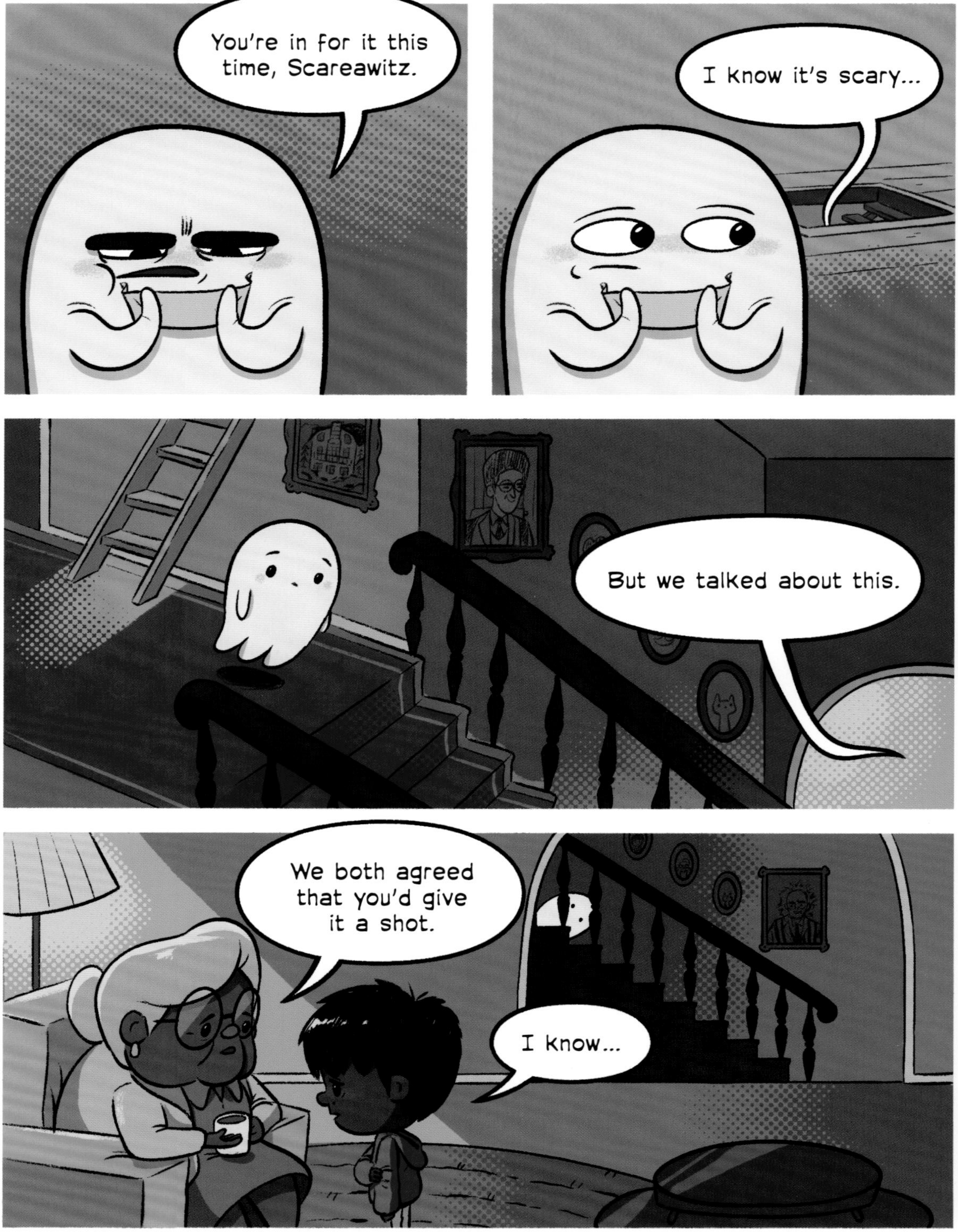
You're in for it this time, Scareawitz.
I know it's scary...
But we talked about this.
We both agreed that you'd give it a shot.
I know...

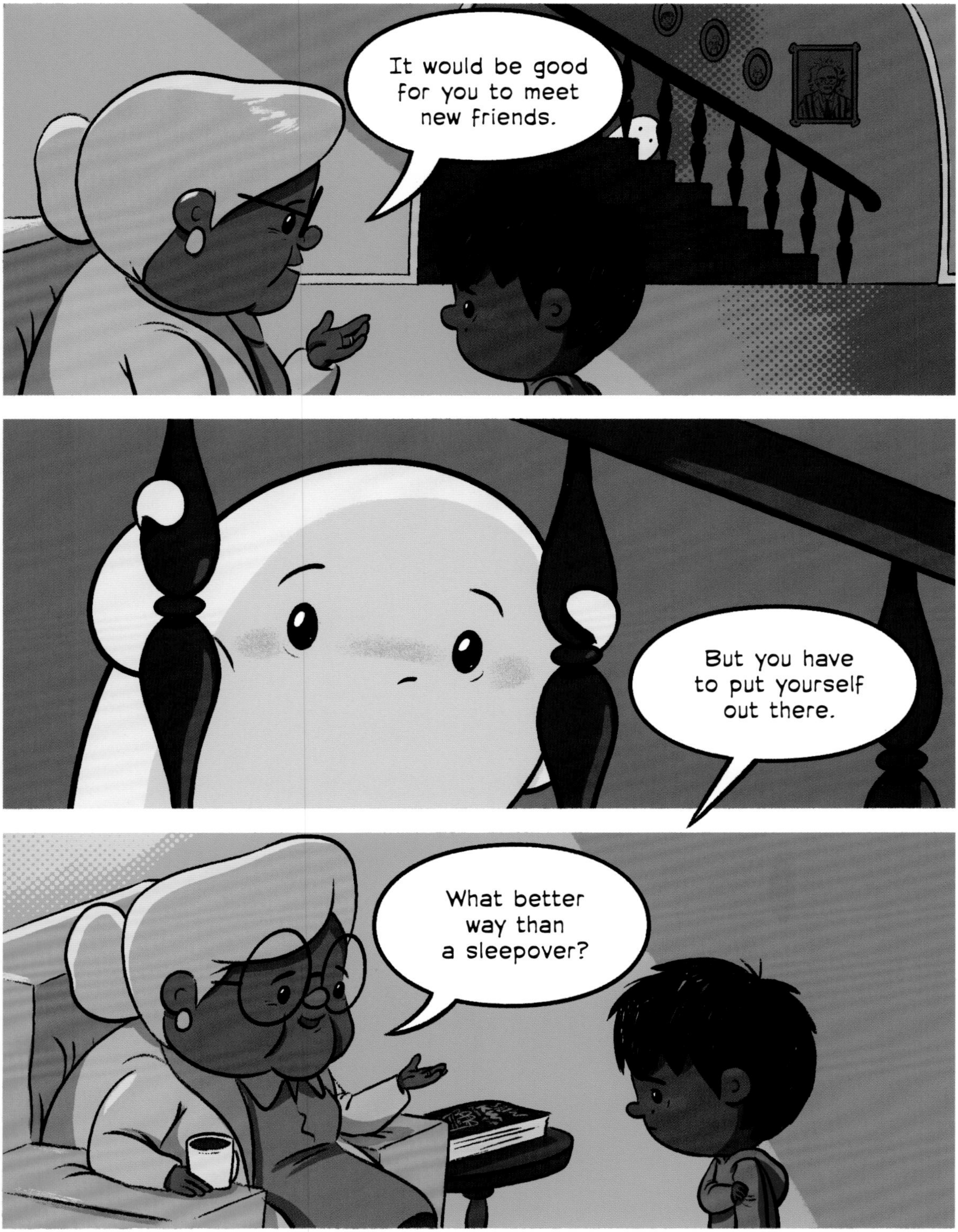
It would be good for you to meet new friends.
But you have to put yourself out there.
What better way than a sleepover?

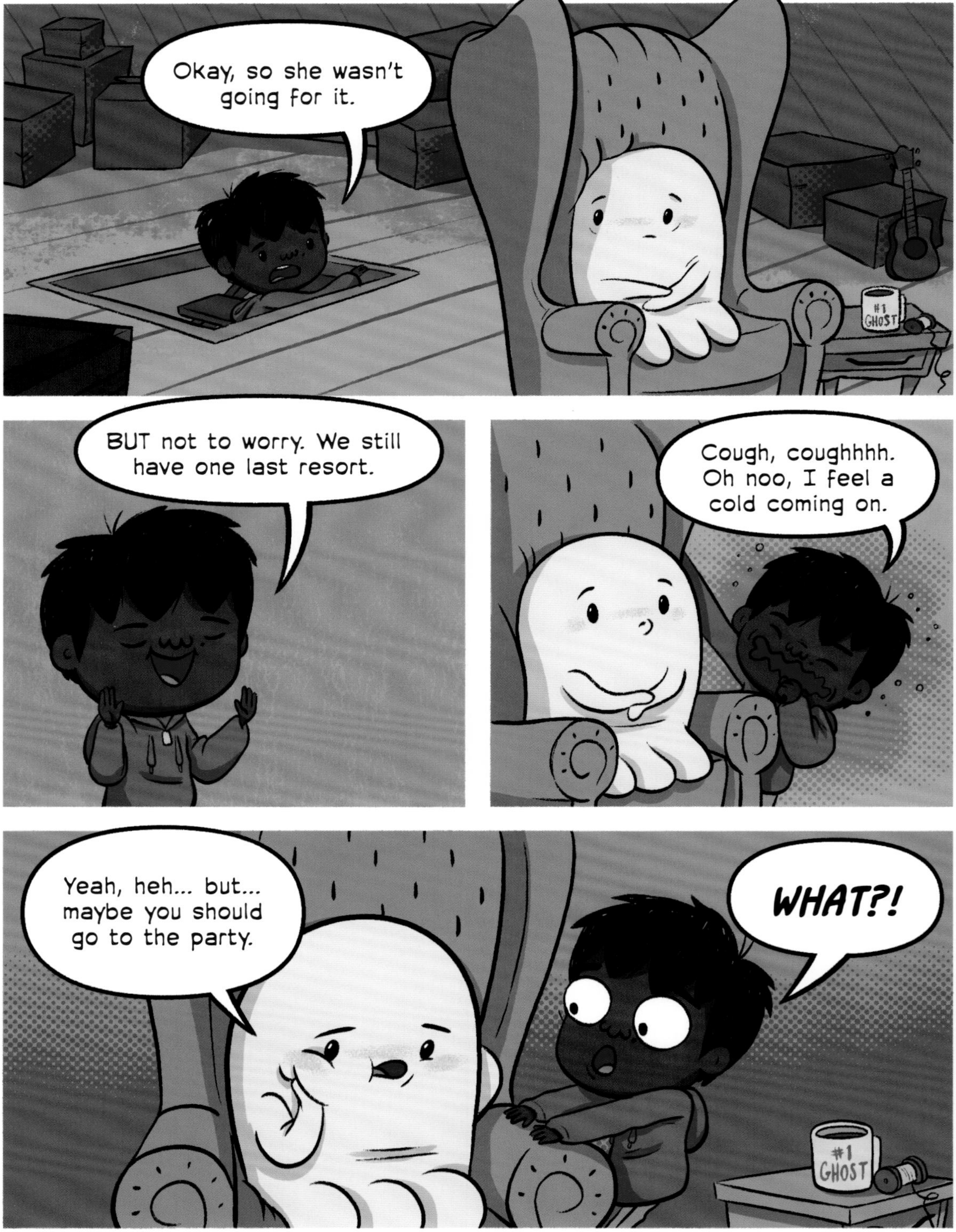
Okay, so she wasn't going for it.
#1 GHOST
BUT not to worry. We still have one last resort.
Cough, coughhhh. Oh noo, I feel a cold coming on.
Yeah, heh... but... maybe you should go to the party.
WHAT?!
#1 GHOST

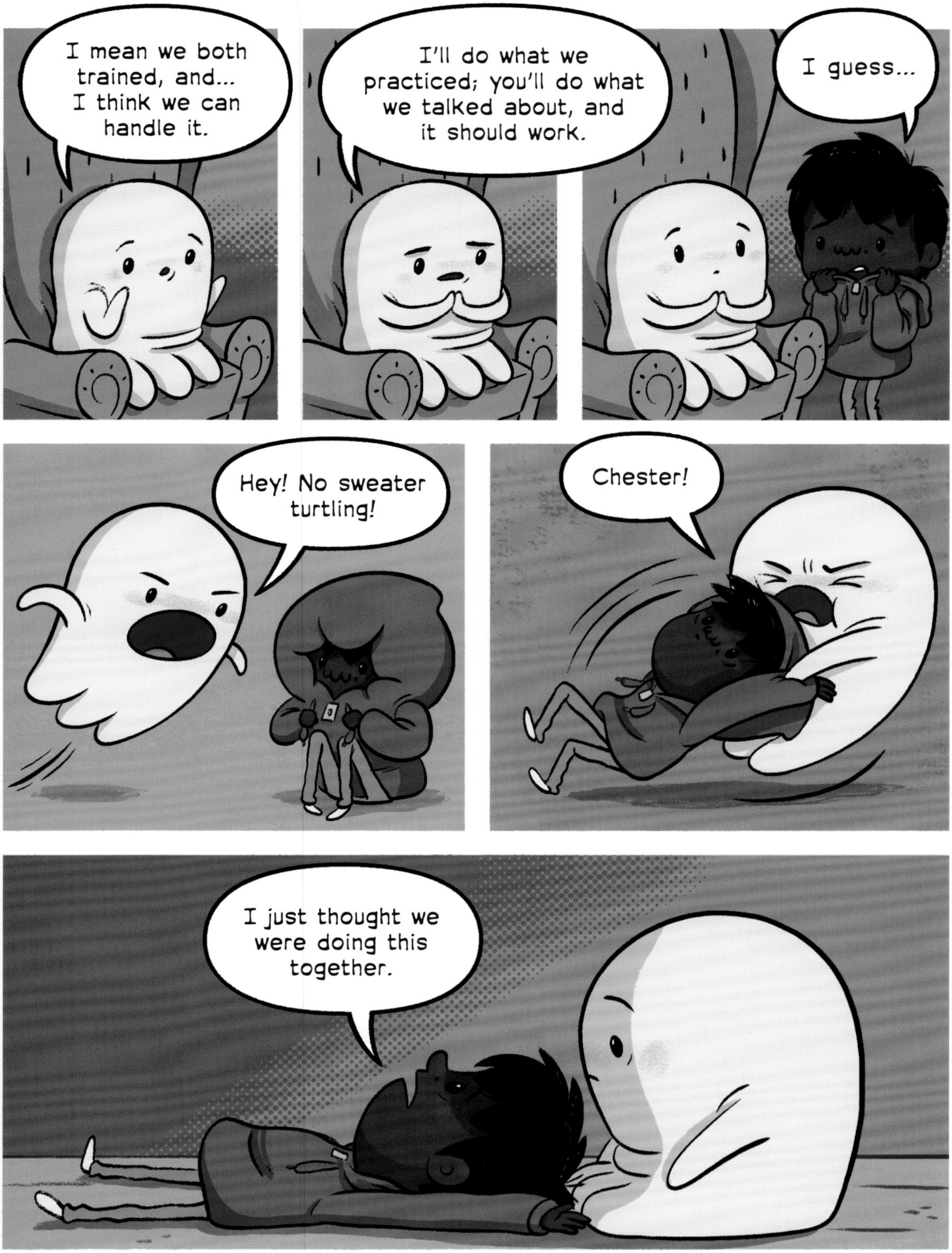
I mean we both trained, and... I think we can handle it.
I'll do what we practiced; you'll do what we talked about, and it should work.
I guess...
Hey! No sweater turtling!
Chester!
I just thought we were doing this together.

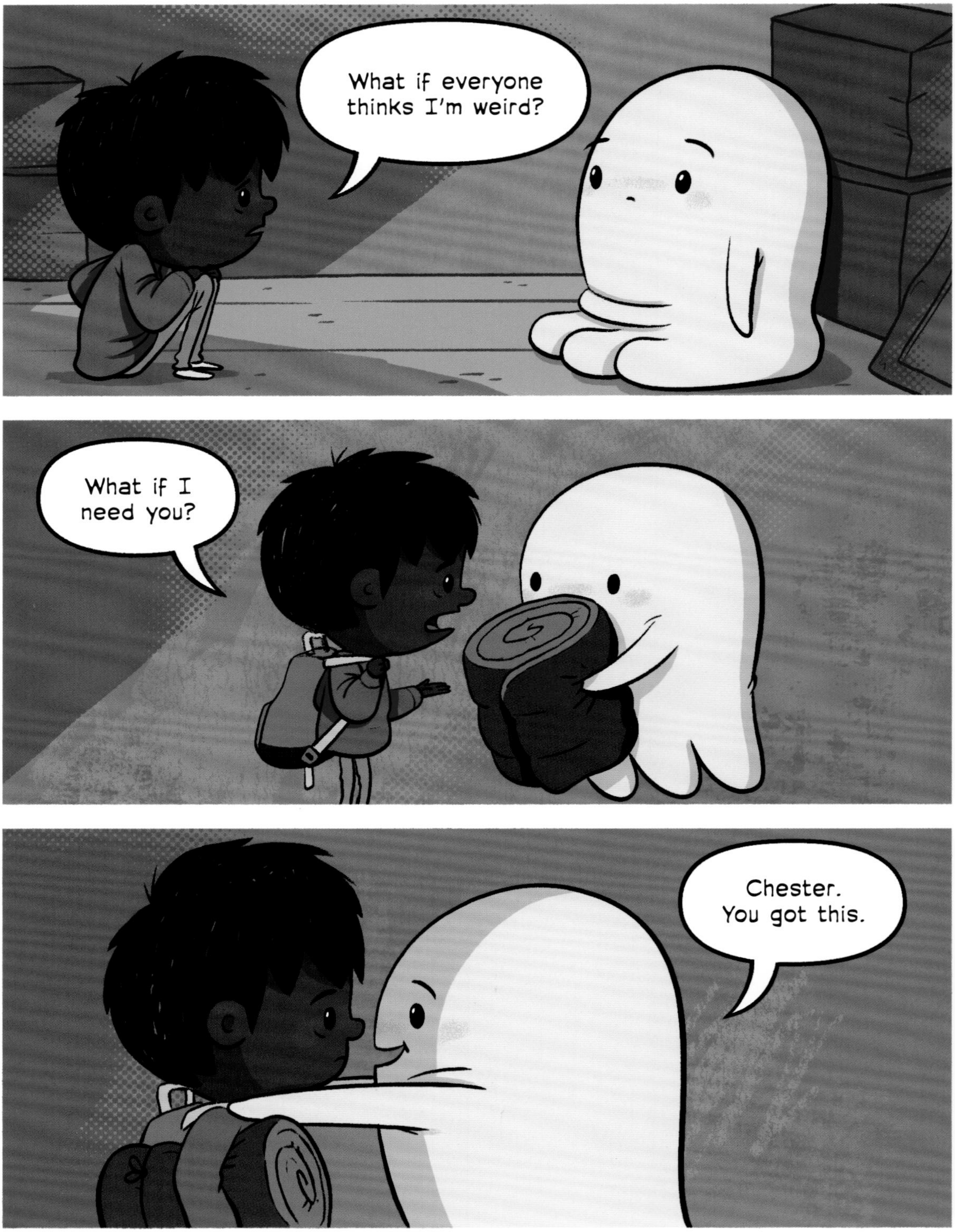
What if everyone thinks I'm weird?
What if I need you?
Chester. You got this.

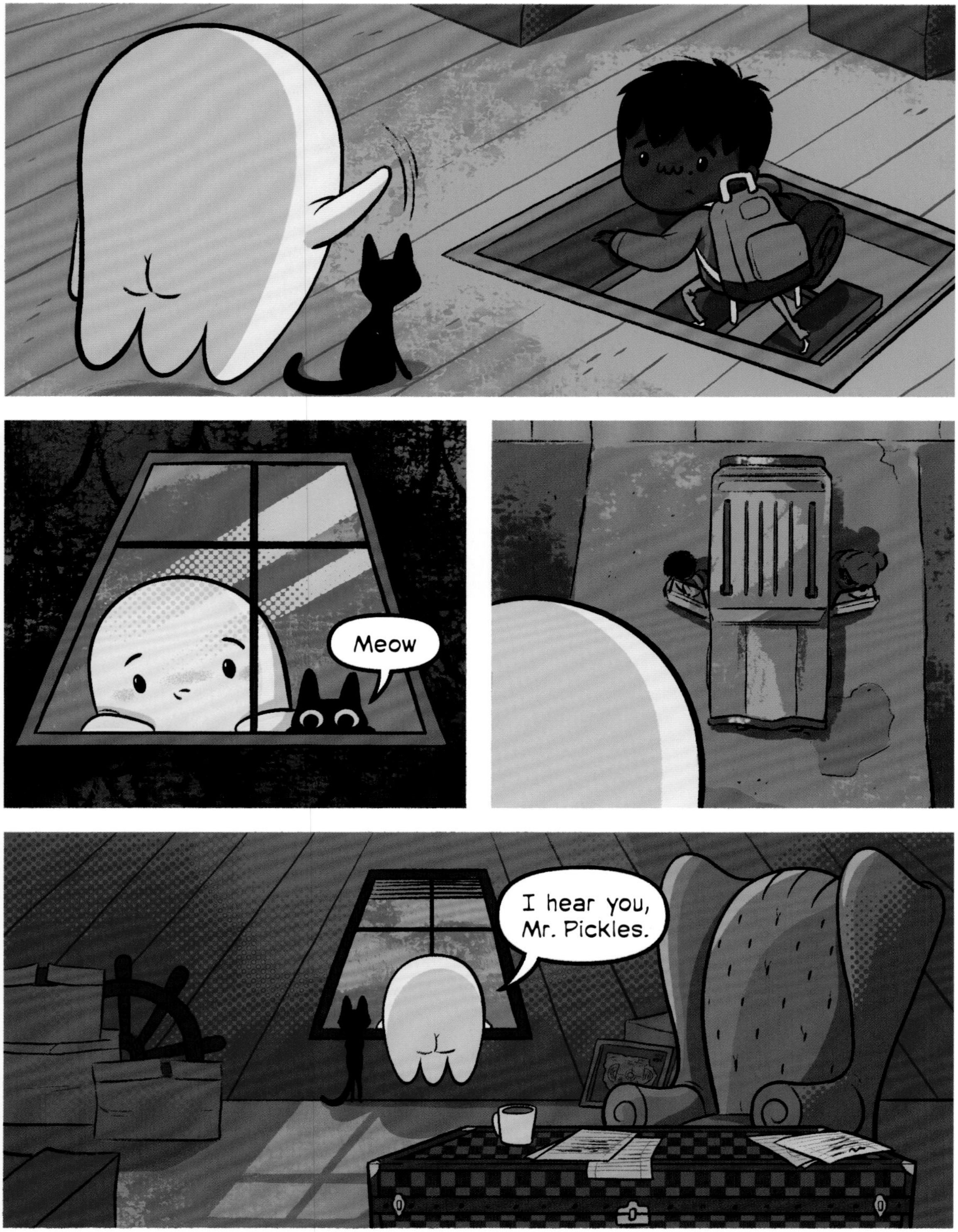
Meow
I hear you, Mr. Pickles.

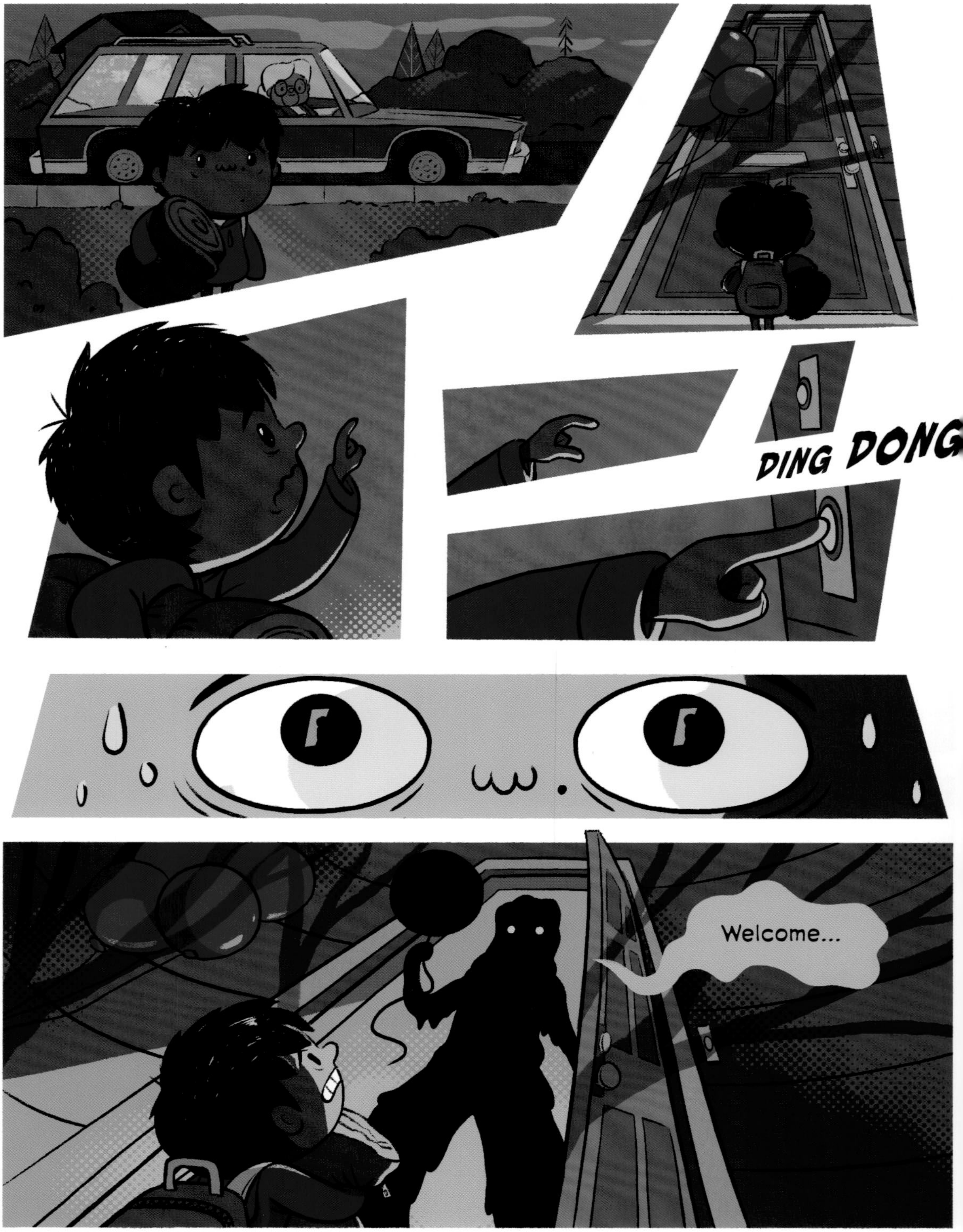
DING DONG
Welcome...

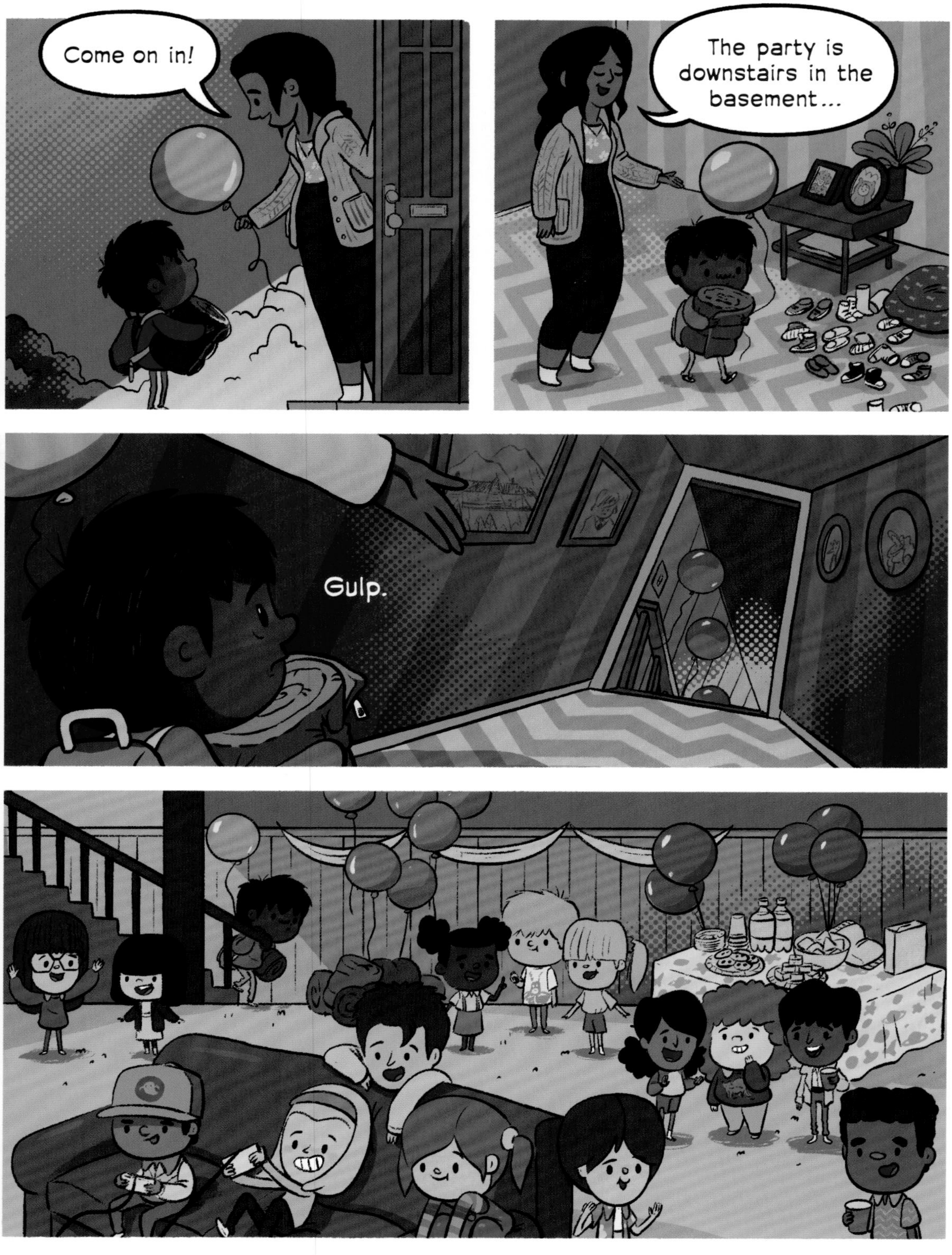
Come on in!
The party is downstairs in the basement...
Gulp.

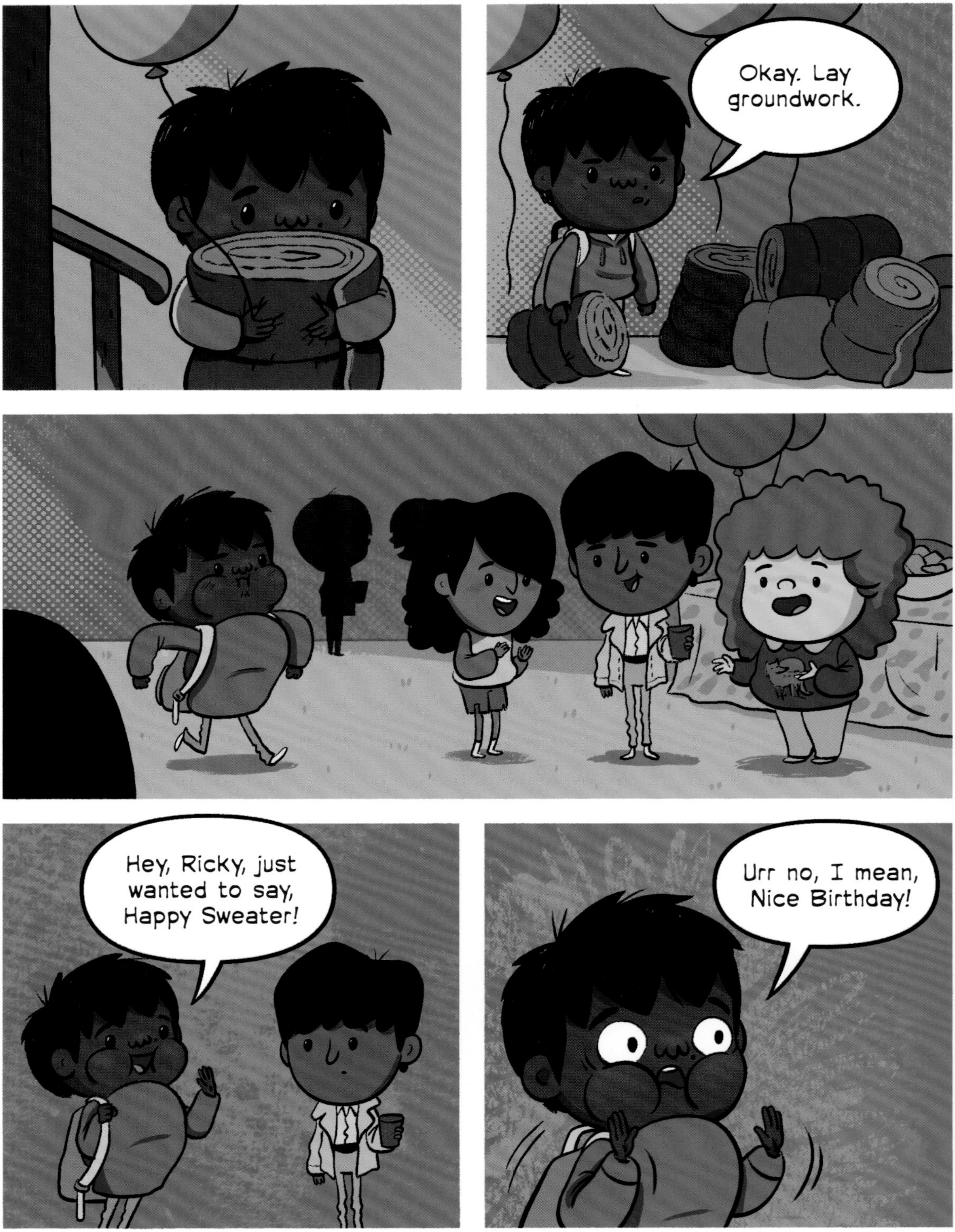
Okay. Lay groundwork.
Hey, Ricky, just wanted to say, Happy Sweater!
Urr no, I mean, Nice Birthday!

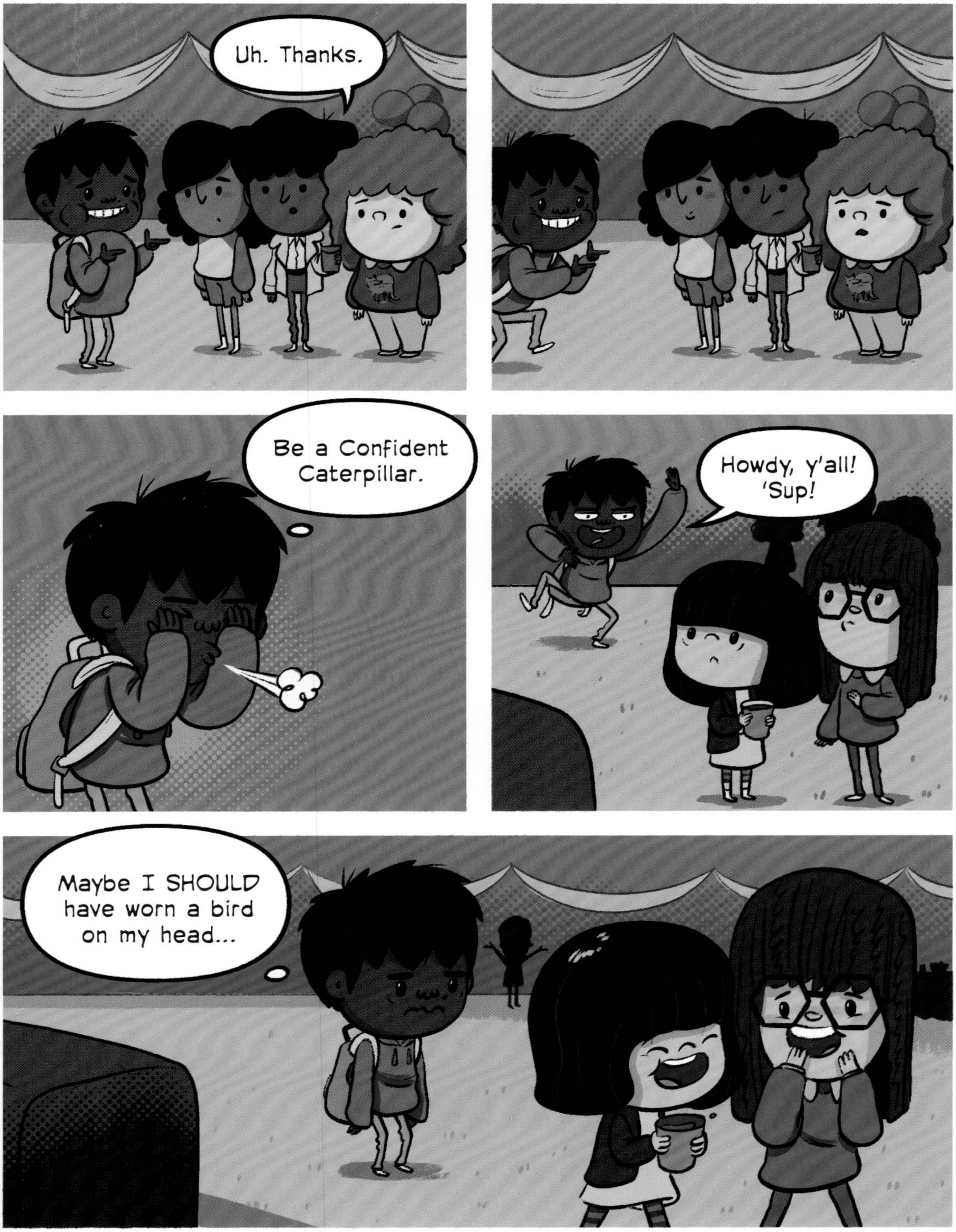
Uh. Thanks.
Be a Confident Caterpillar.
Howdy, y'all! 'Sup!
Maybe I SHOULD have worn a bird on my head...

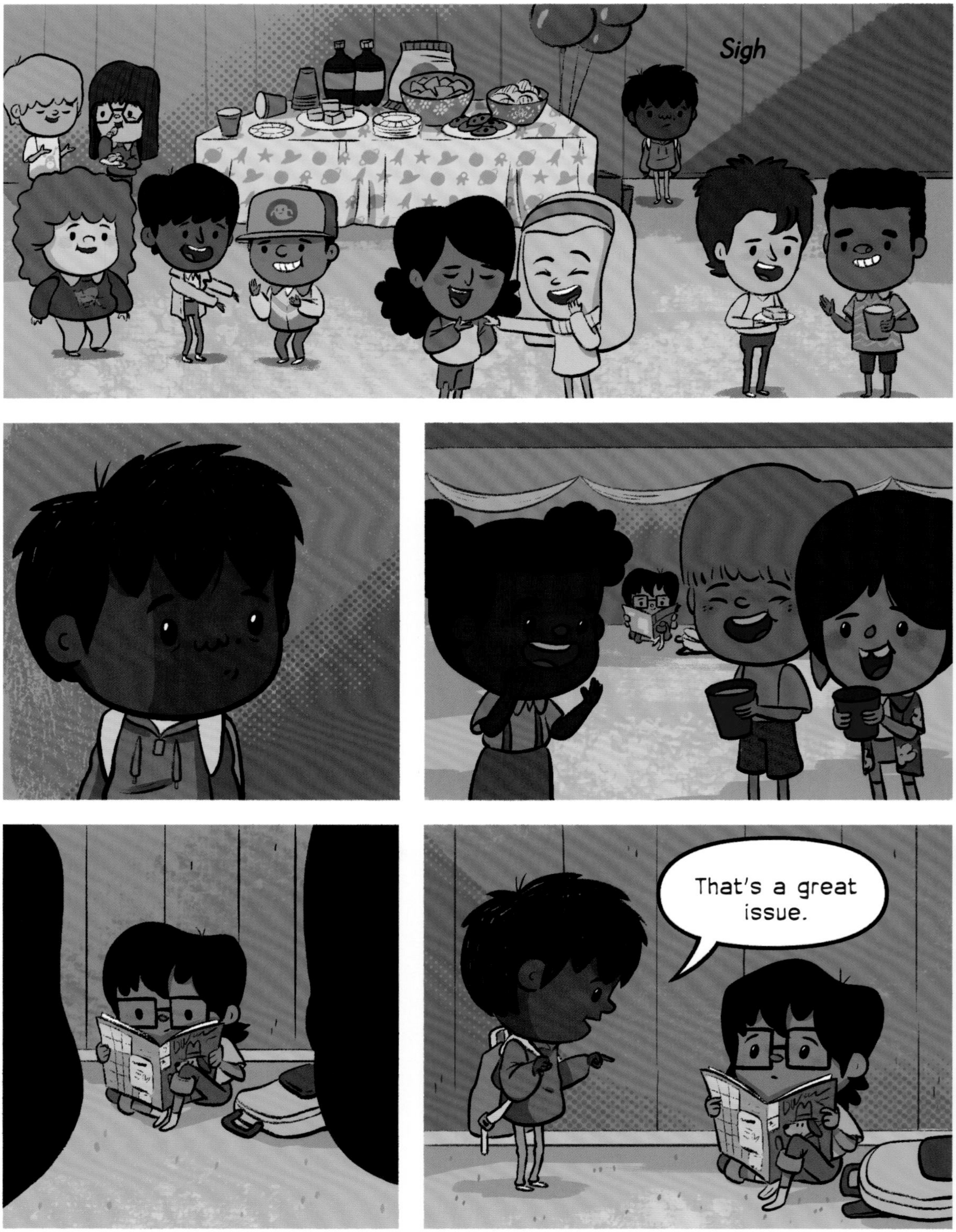
Sigh
That's a great issue.

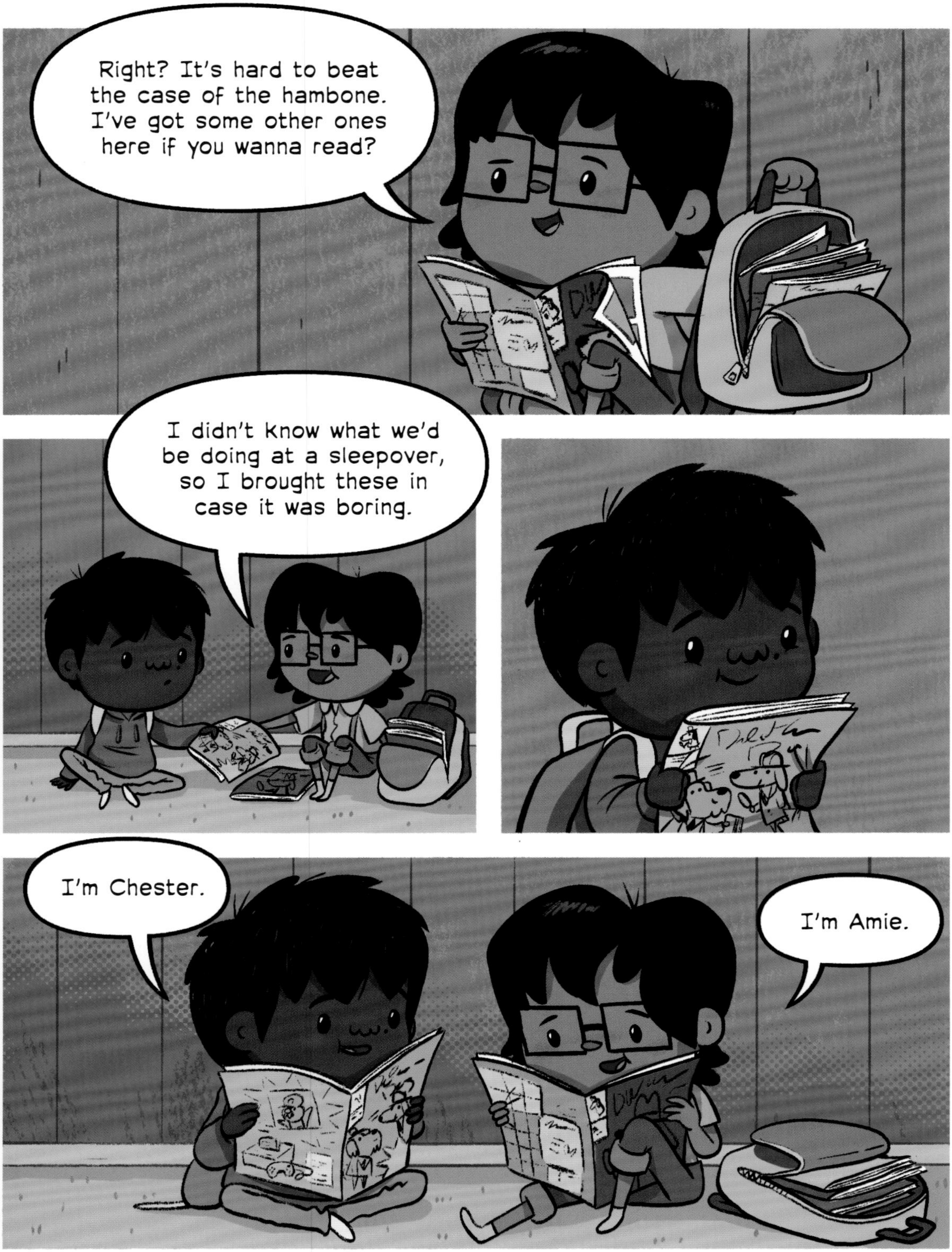
Right? It's hard to beat the case of the hambone. I've got some other ones here if you wanna read?
I didn't know what we'd be doing at a sleepover, so I brought these in case it was boring.
I'm Chester.
I'm Amie.

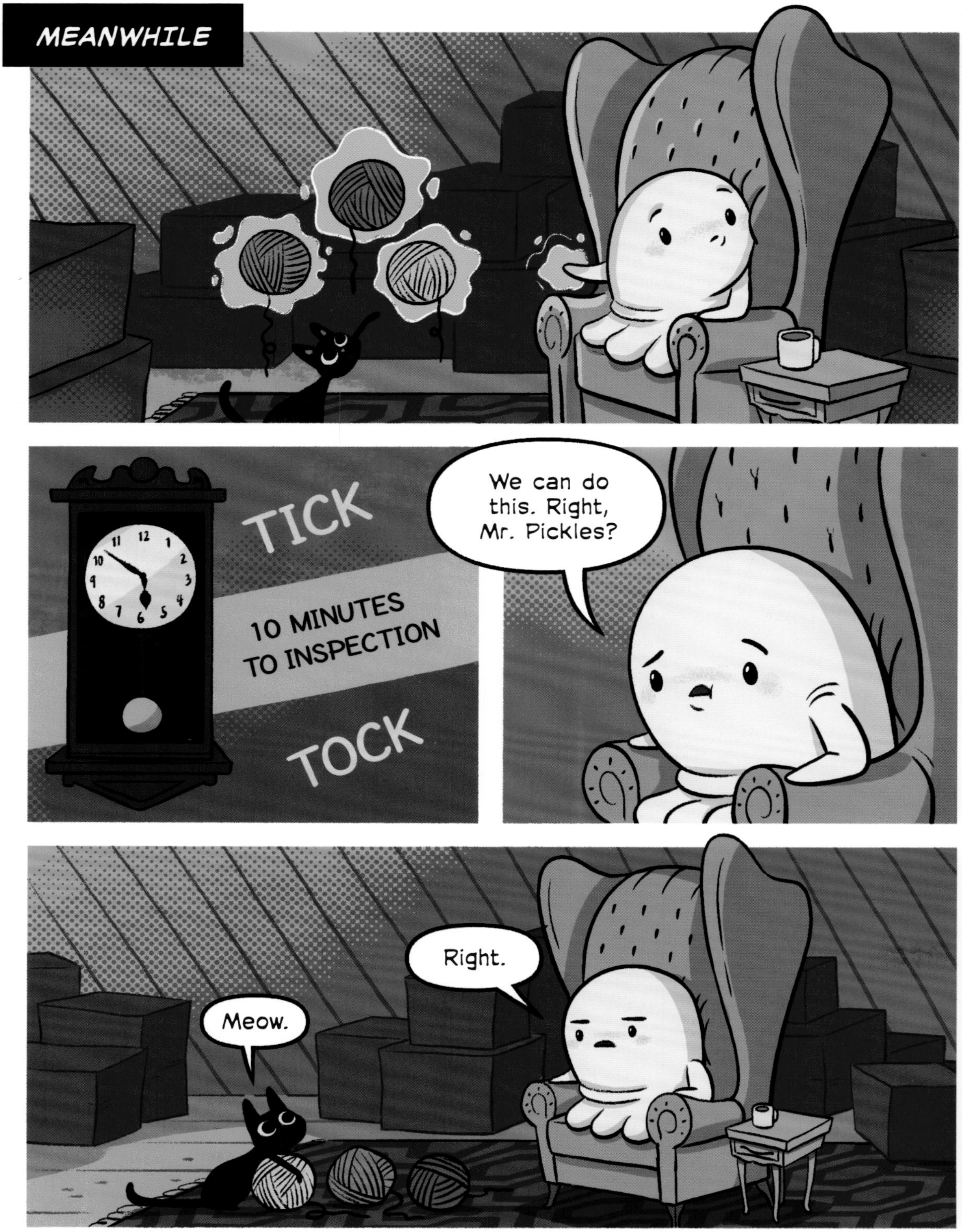
MEANWHILE
TICK
10 MINUTES
TO INSPECTION
TOCK
We can do this. Right, Mr. Pickles?
Meow.
Right.

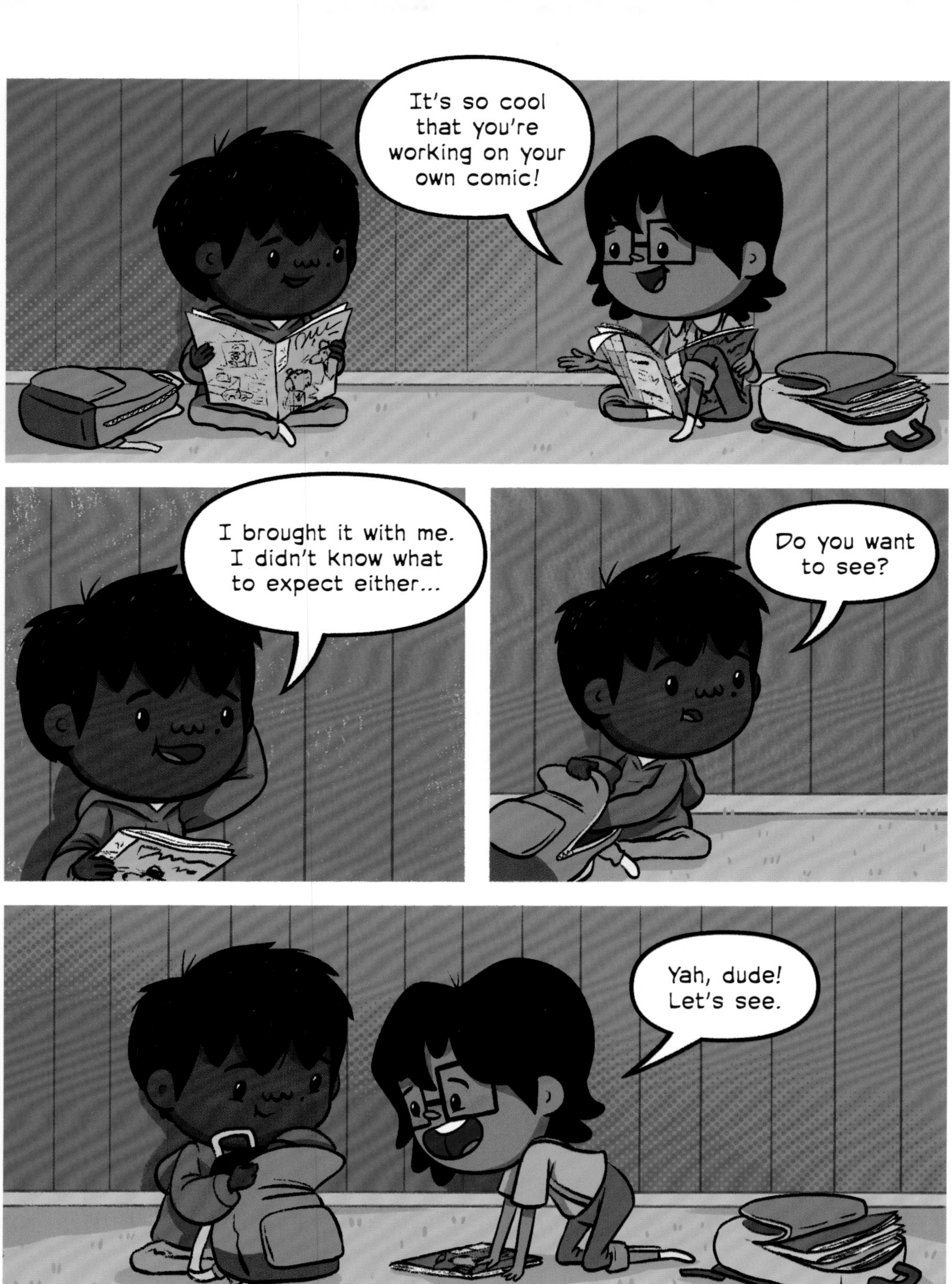
It's so cool that you're working on your own comic!
I brought it with me. I didn't know what to expect either...
Do you want to see?
Yah, dude! Let's see.

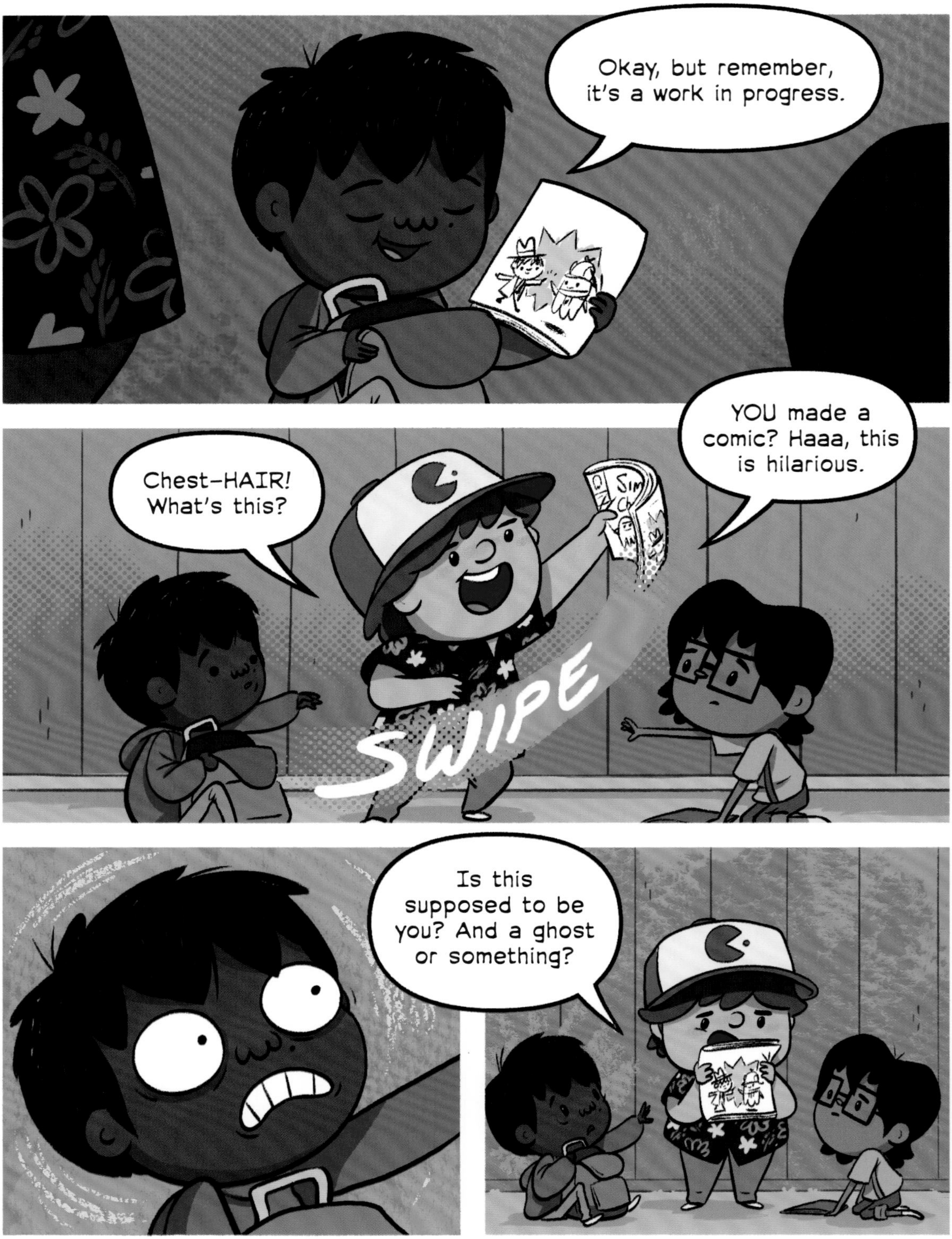
Okay, but remember, it's a work in progress.
Chest-HAIR! What's this?
YOU made a comic? Haaa, this is hilarious.
SWIPE
Is this supposed to be you? And a ghost or something?

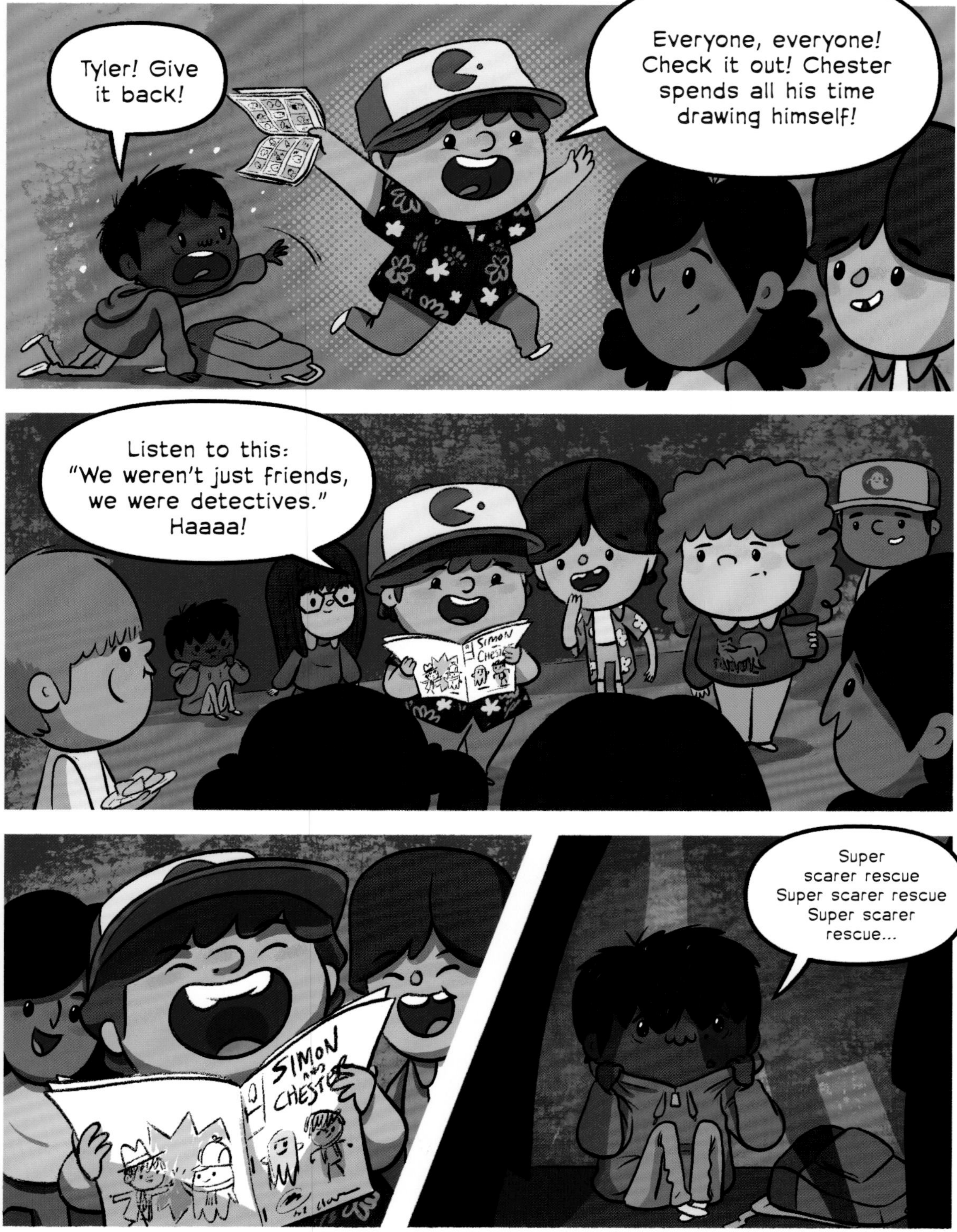
Tyler! Give it back!
Everyone, everyone! Check it out! Chester spends all his time drawing himself!
Listen to this: "We weren't just friends, we were detectives." Haaaa!
SIMON AND CHESTER
Super scarer rescue Super scarer rescue Super scarer rescue...

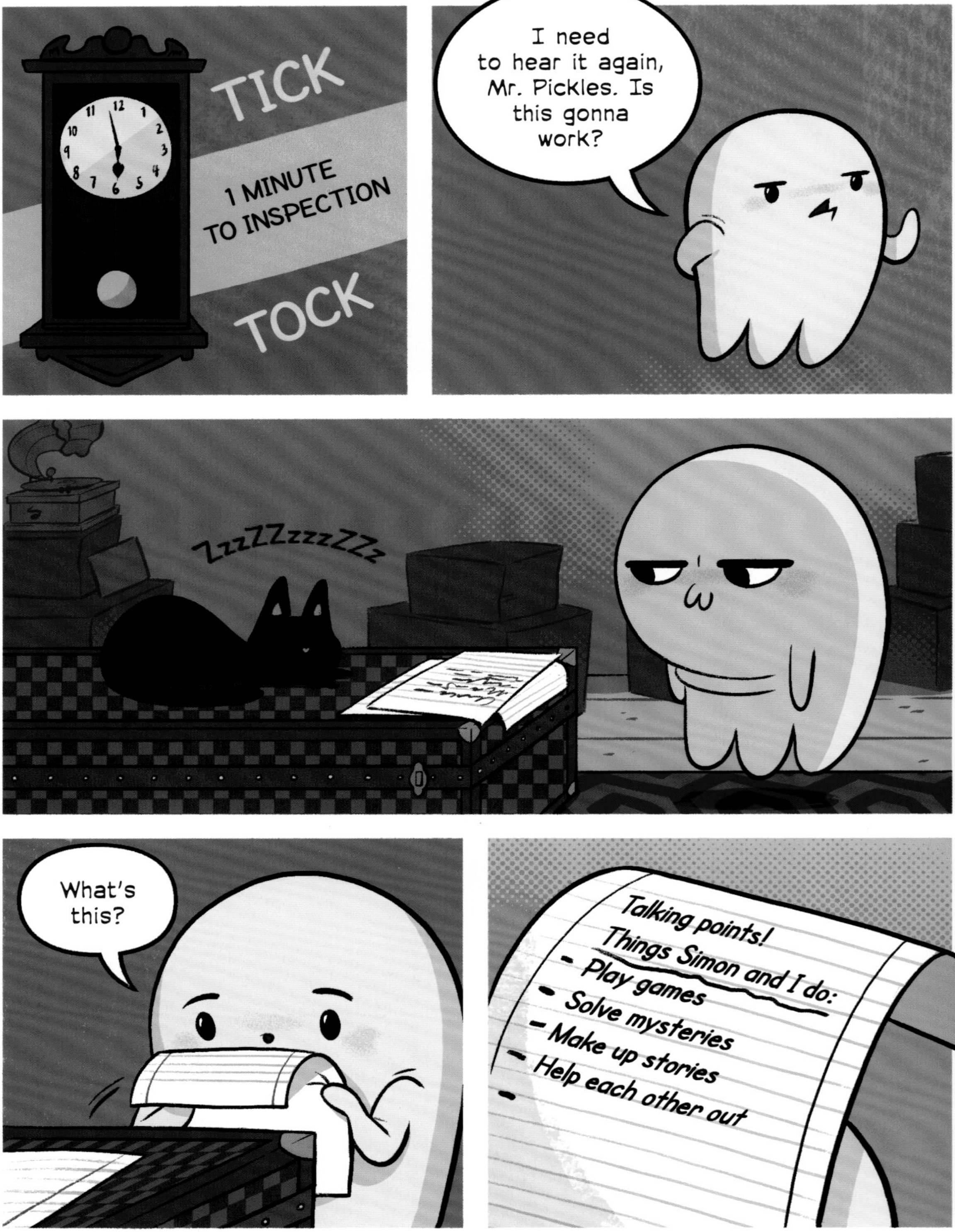
TICK
1 MINUTE TO INSPECTION
TOCK
I need to hear it again, Mr. Pickles. Is this gonna work?
ZzzZZzzzZZz
What's this?
Talking points!
Things Simon and I do:
- Play games
- Solve mysteries
- Make up stories
- Help each other out
-

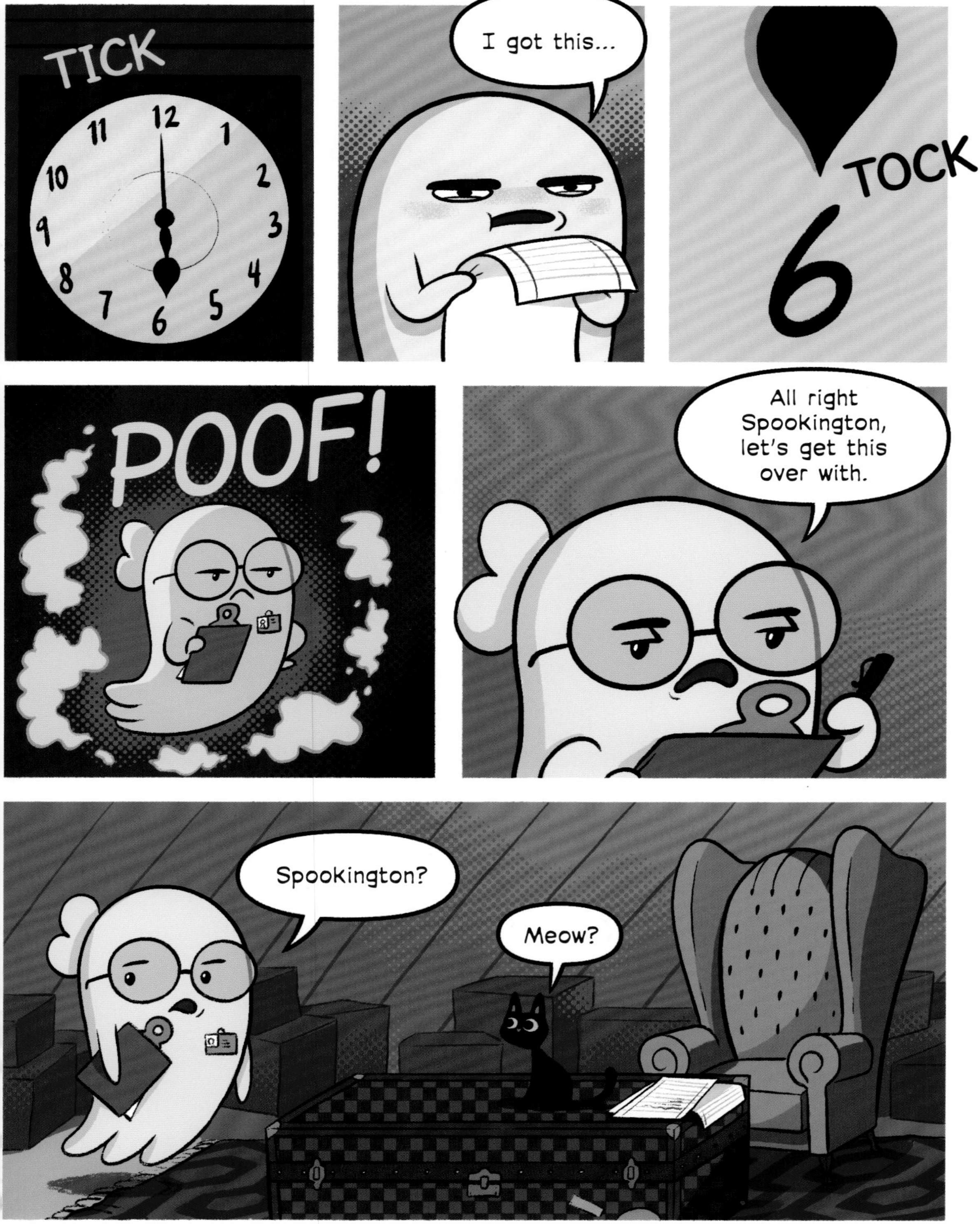
TICK
I got this...
TOCK
POOF!
All right Spookington, let's get this over with.
Spookington?
Meow?

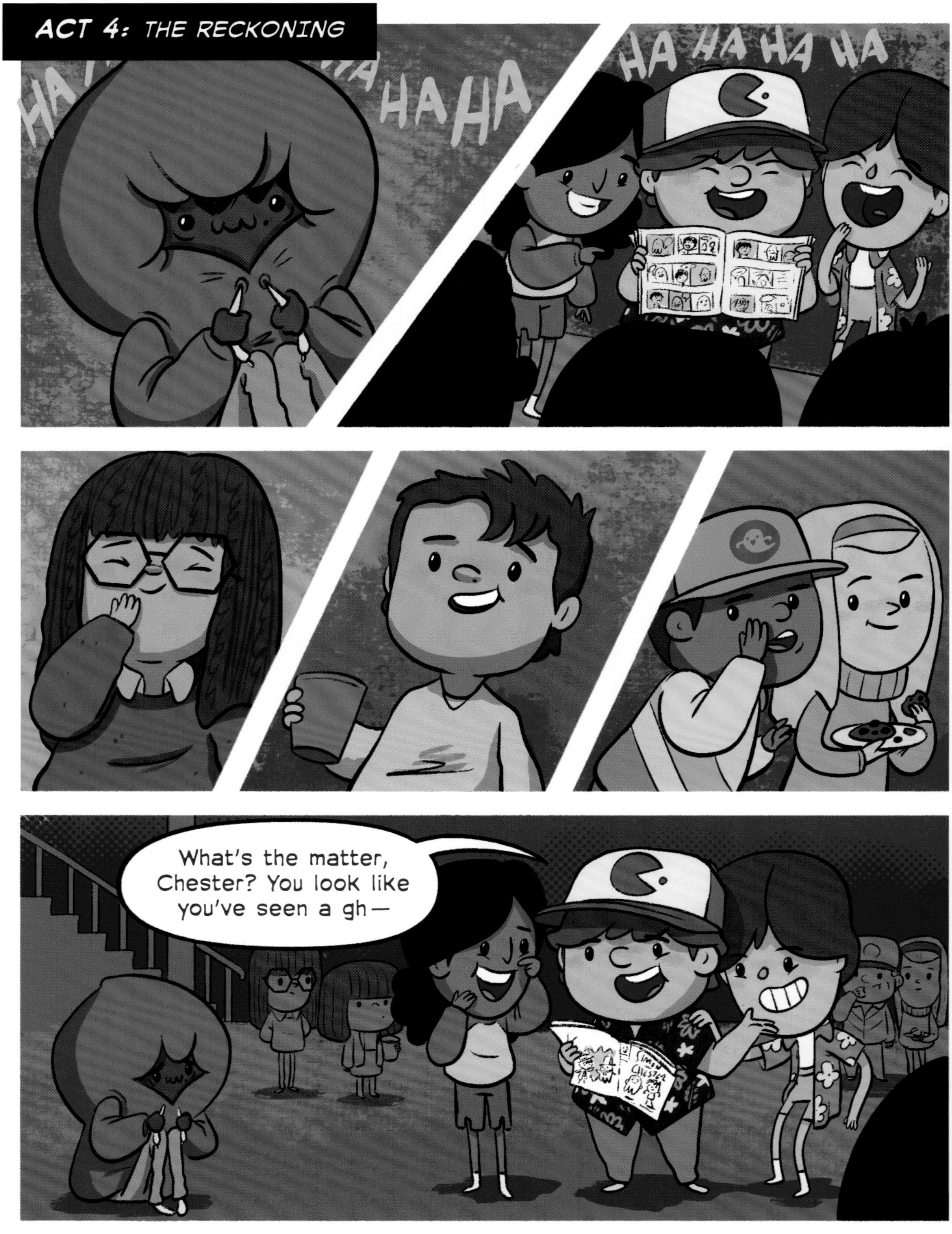
ACT 4: THE RECKONING
HA HA HA HA
HA HA HA HA
What's the matter, Chester? You look like you've seen a gh—
SIMON CHESTER

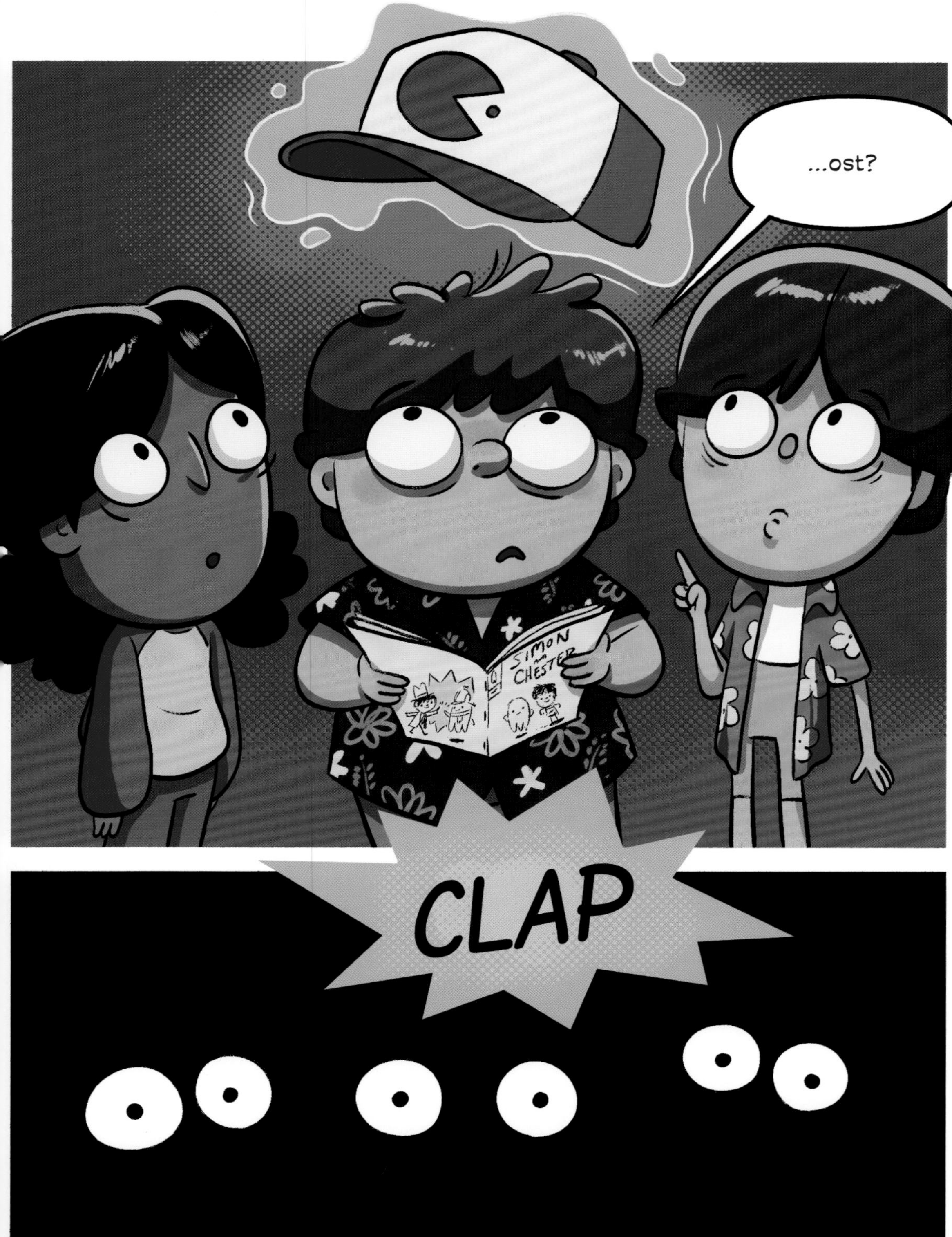
...ost?
SIMON AND CHESTER
CLAP

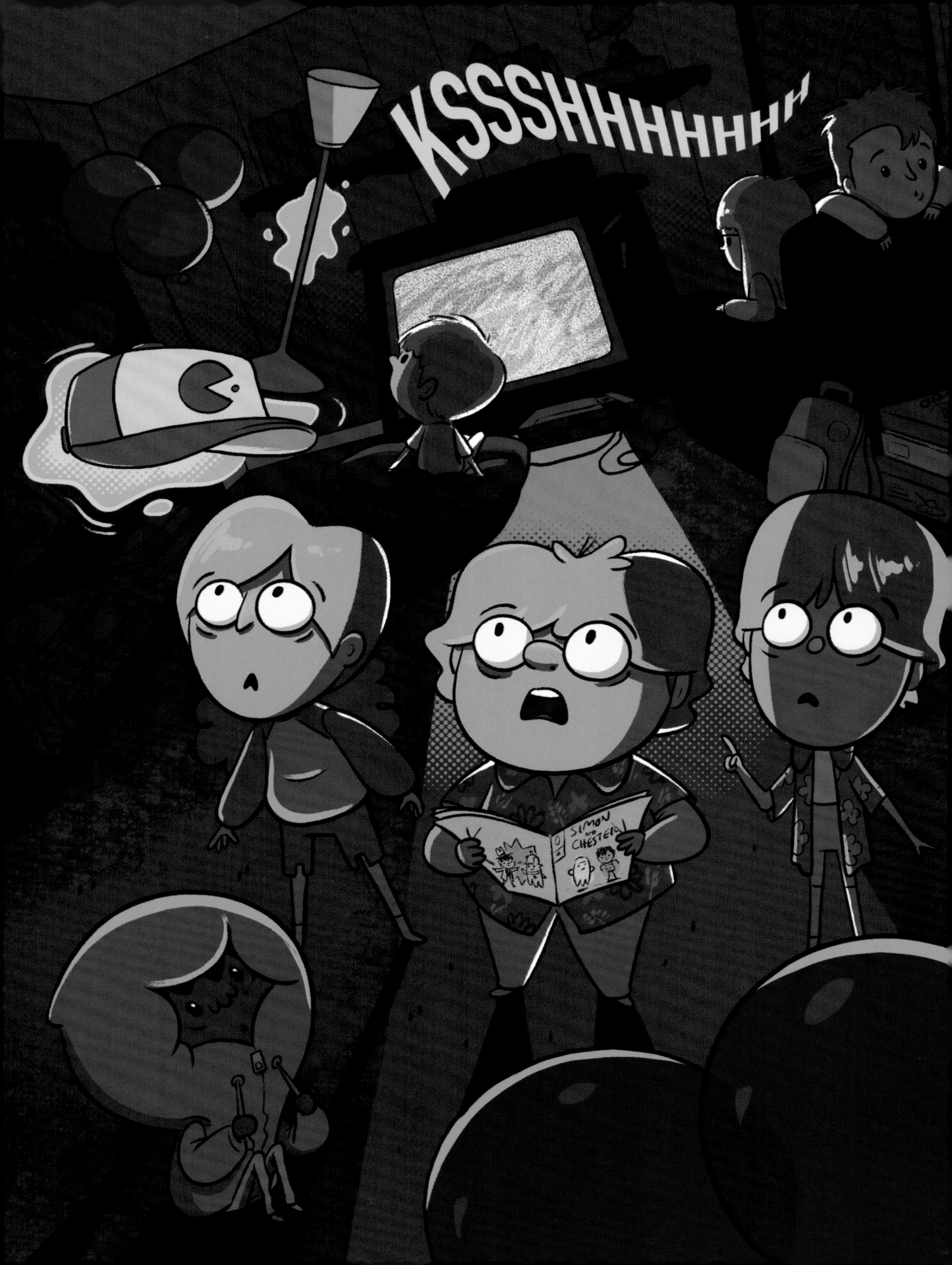
KSSSHHHHHHH
SIMON
CHESTER

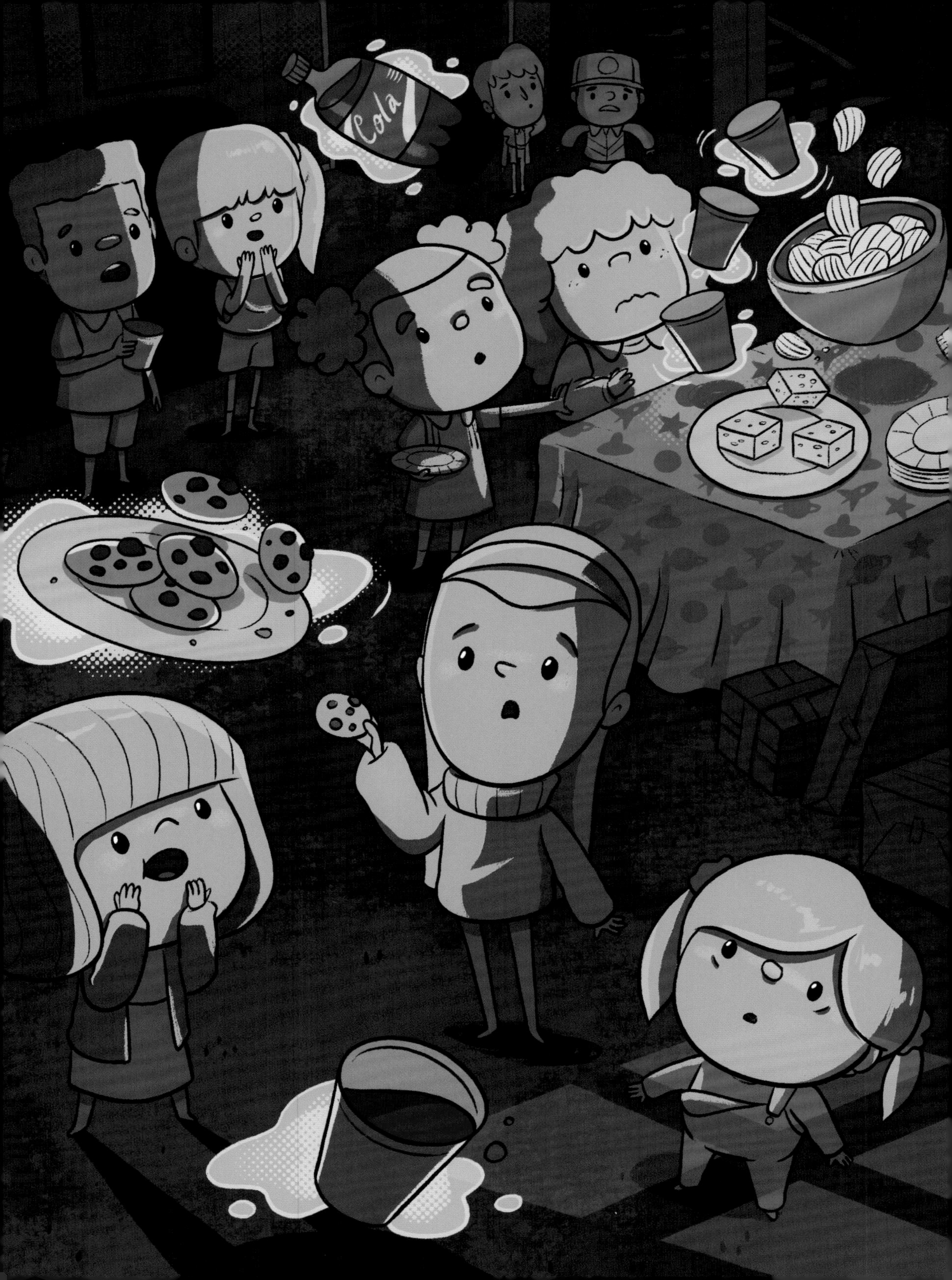
Cola

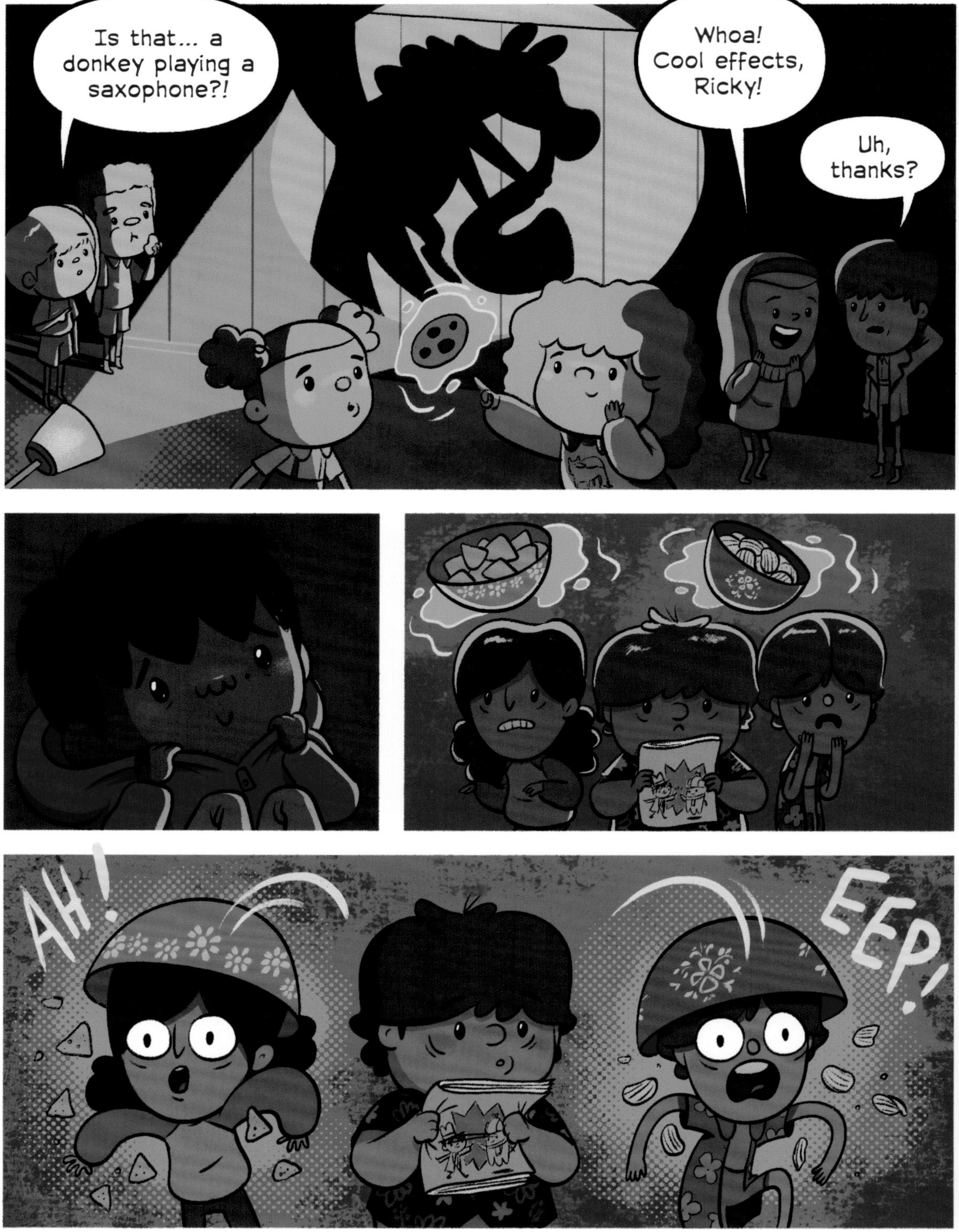
Is that... a donkey playing a saxophone?!
Whoa! Cool effects, Ricky!
Uh, thanks?
AH!
EEP!

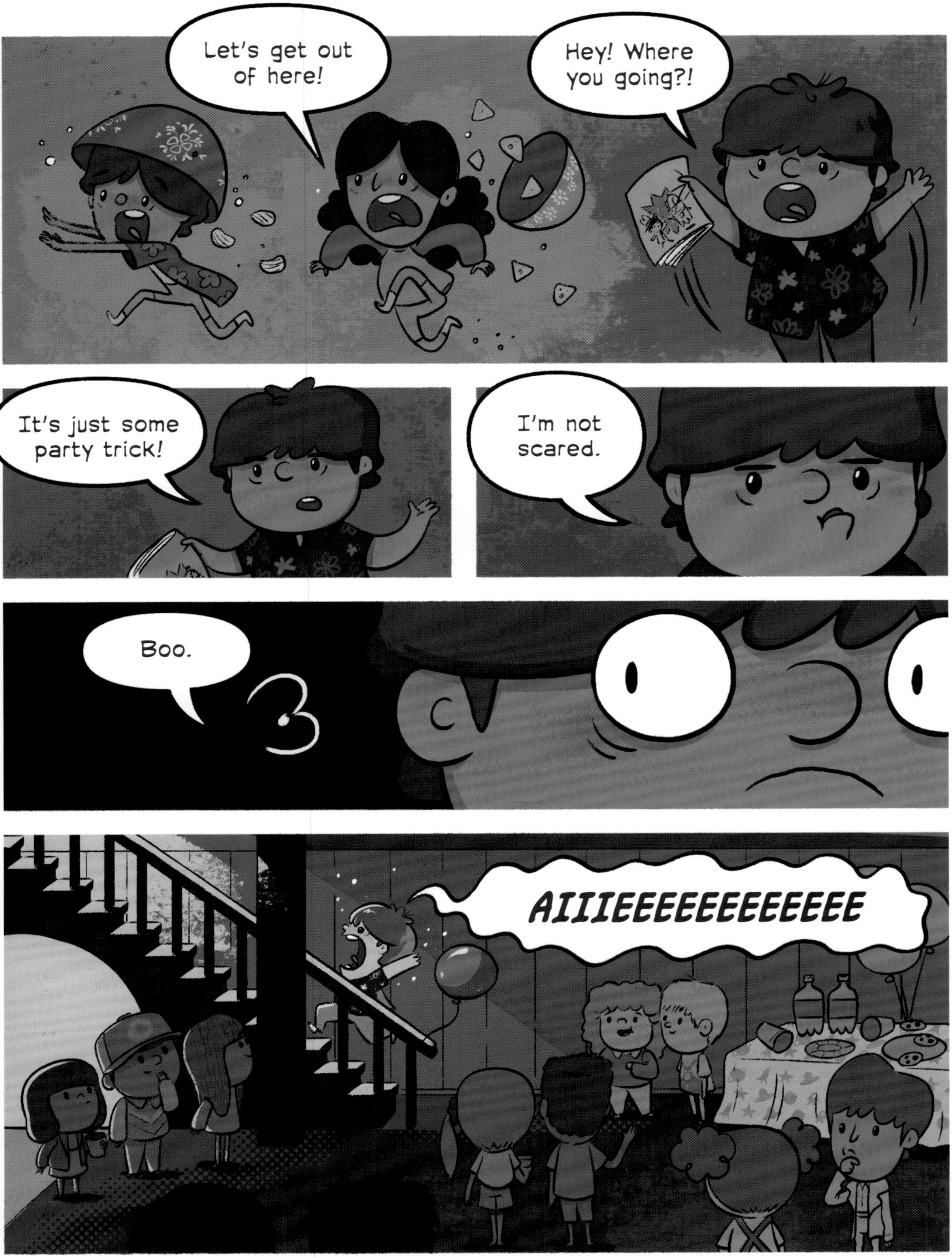
Let's get out of here!
Hey! Where you going?!
It's just some party trick!
I'm not scared.
Boo.
AIIIEEEEEEEEEEEEE

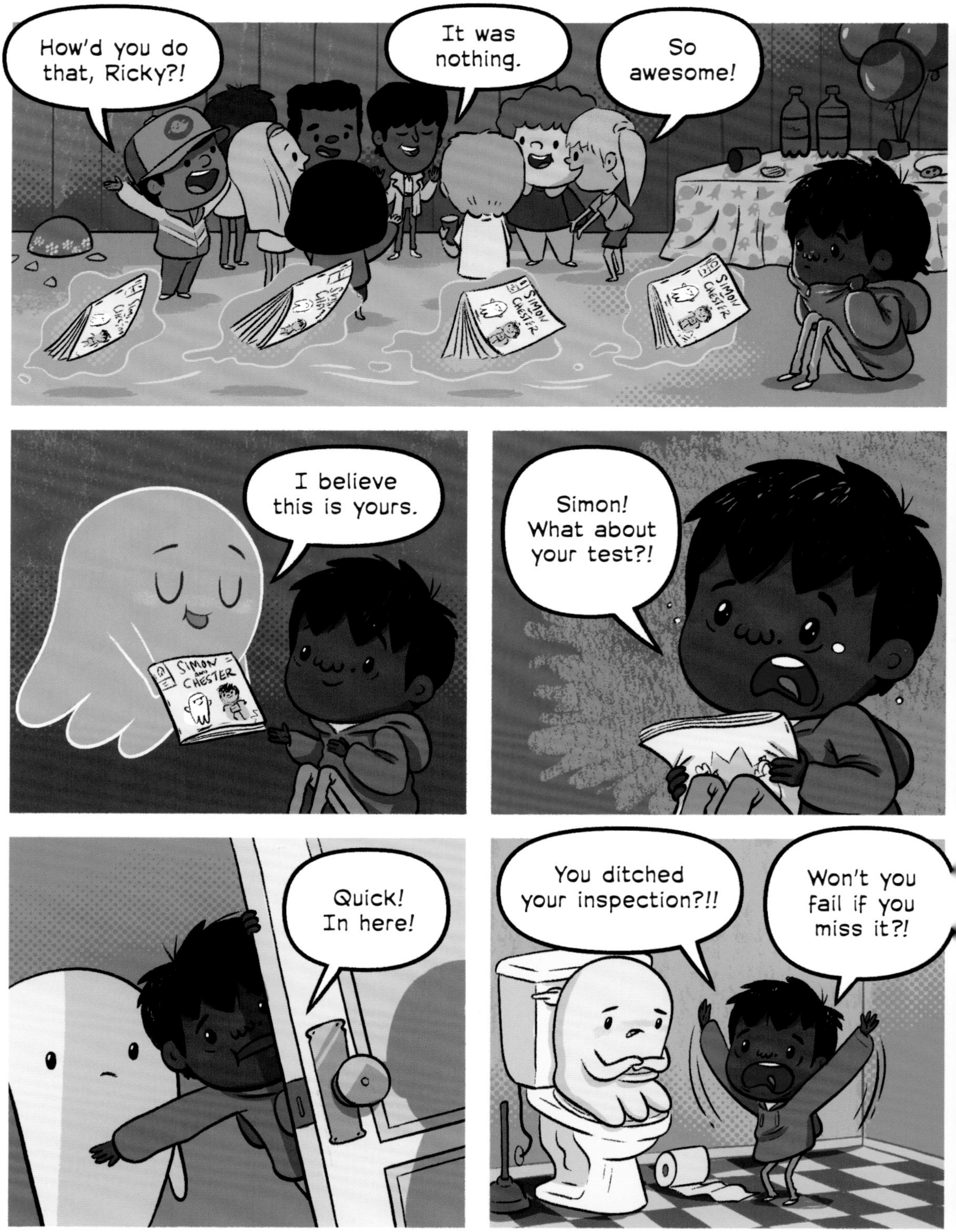
How'd you do that, Ricky?!
It was nothing.
So awesome!
SIMON CHESTER
I believe this is yours.
SIMON AND CHESTER
Simon! What about your test?!
Quick! In here!
You ditched your inspection?!!
Won't you fail if you miss it?!

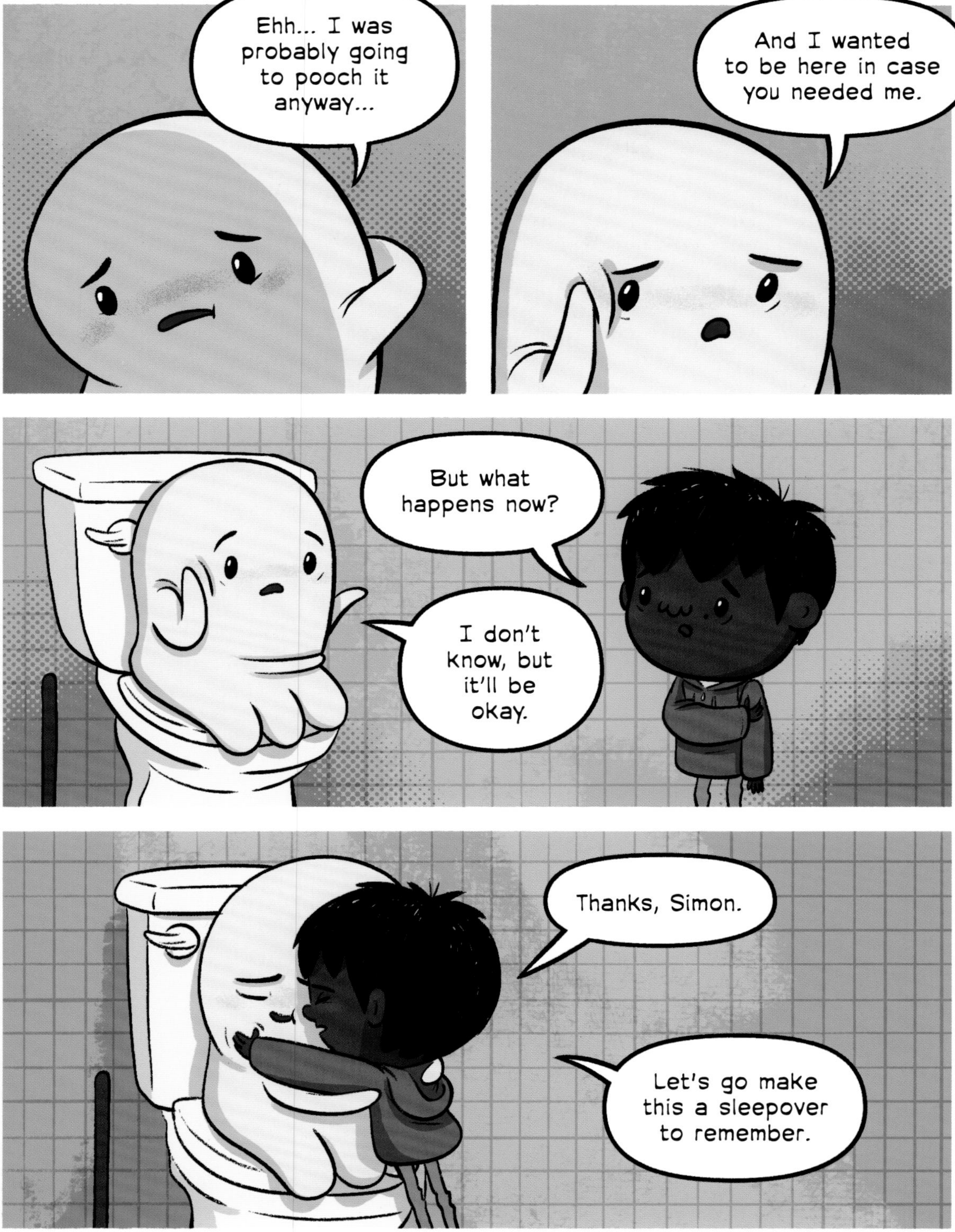
Ehh... I was probably going to pooch it anyway...
And I wanted to be here in case you needed me.
But what happens now?
I don't know, but it'll be okay.
Thanks, Simon.
Let's go make this a sleepover to remember.

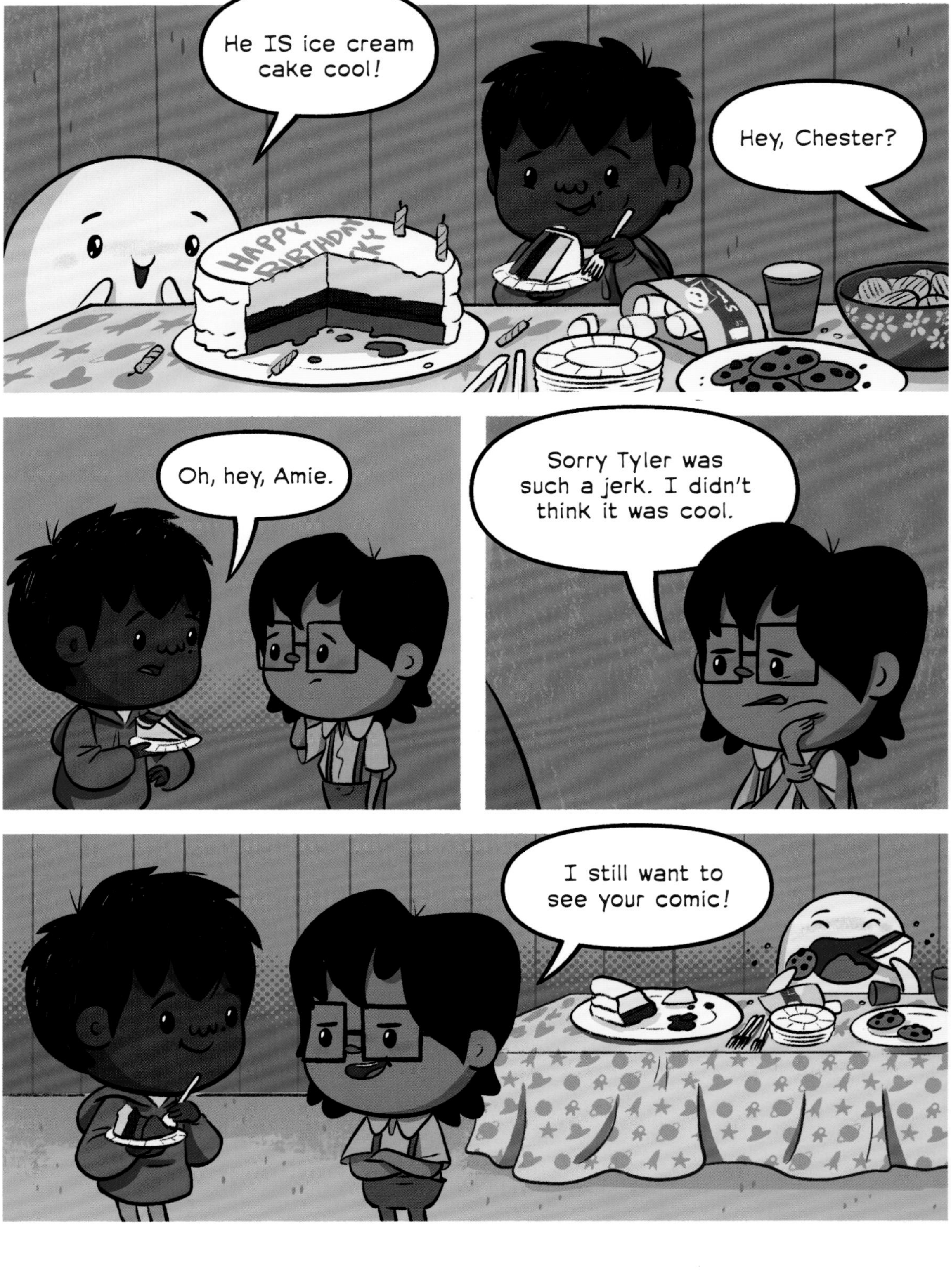
He IS ice cream cake cool!
Hey, Chester?
Oh, hey, Amie.
Sorry Tyler was such a jerk. I didn't think it was cool.
I still want to see your comic!

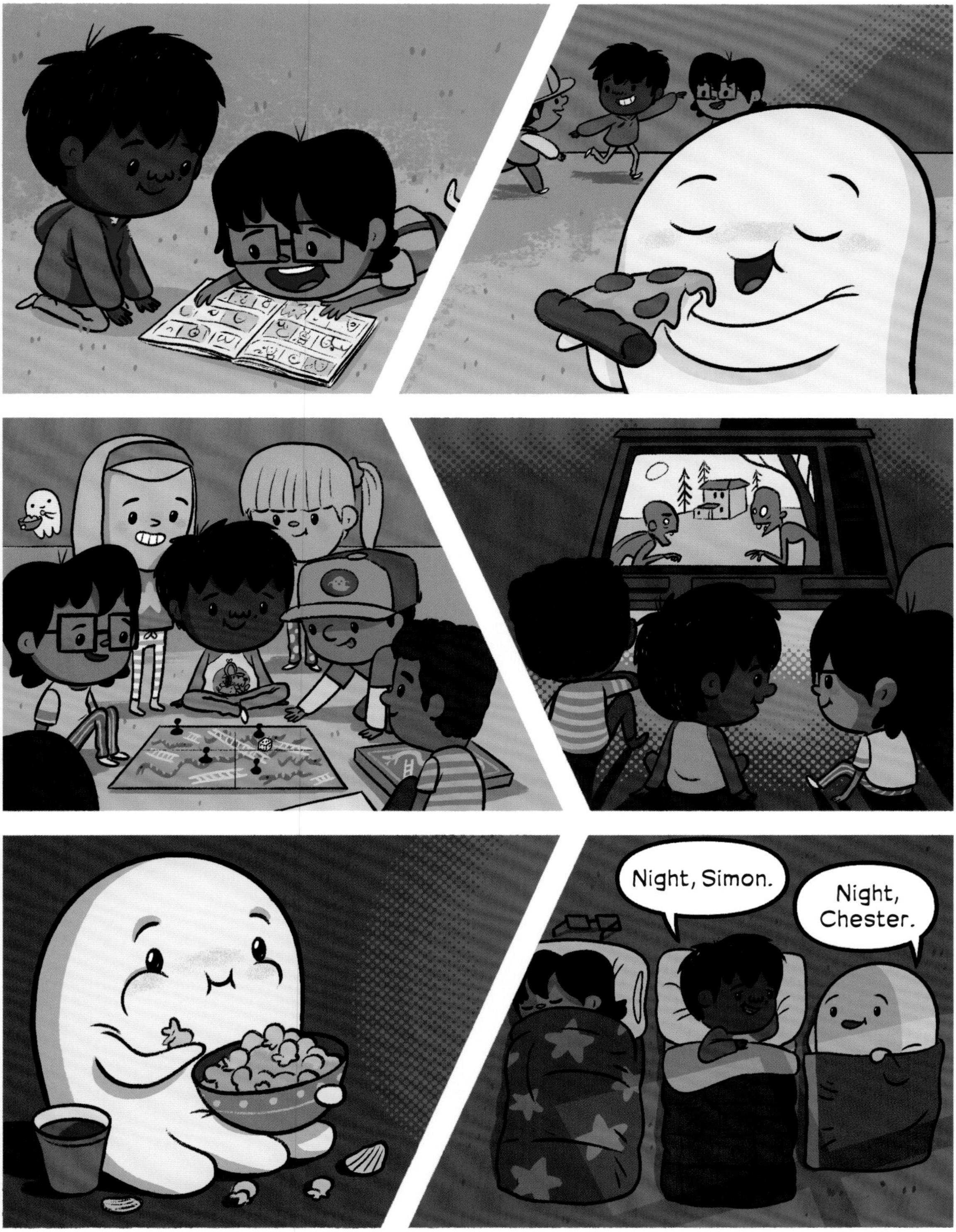
Night, Simon.
Night, Chester.

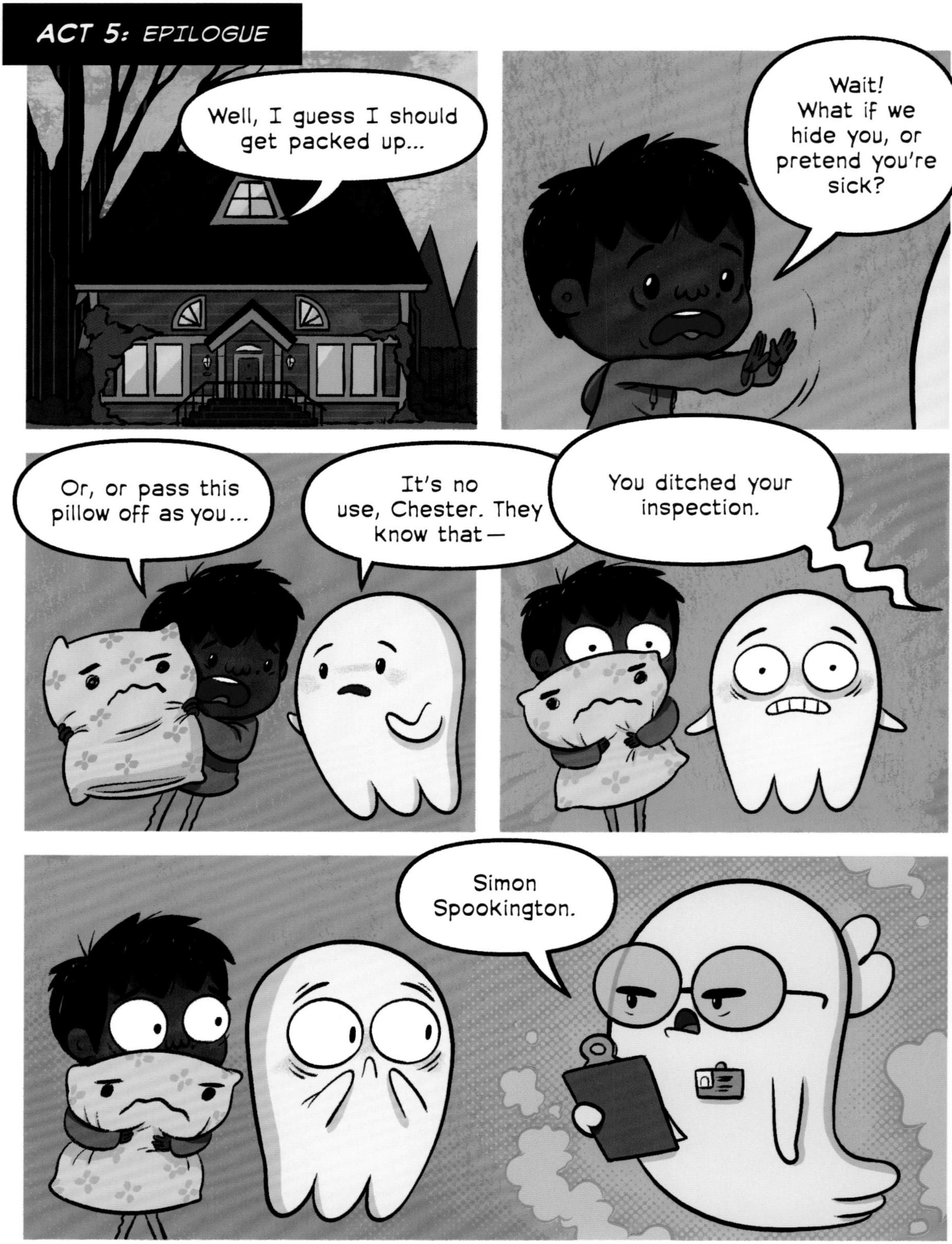
ACT 5: EPILOGUE
Well, I guess I should get packed up...
Wait! What if we hide you, or pretend you're sick?
Or, or pass this pillow off as you...
It's no use, Chester. They know that—
You ditched your inspection.
Simon Spookington.

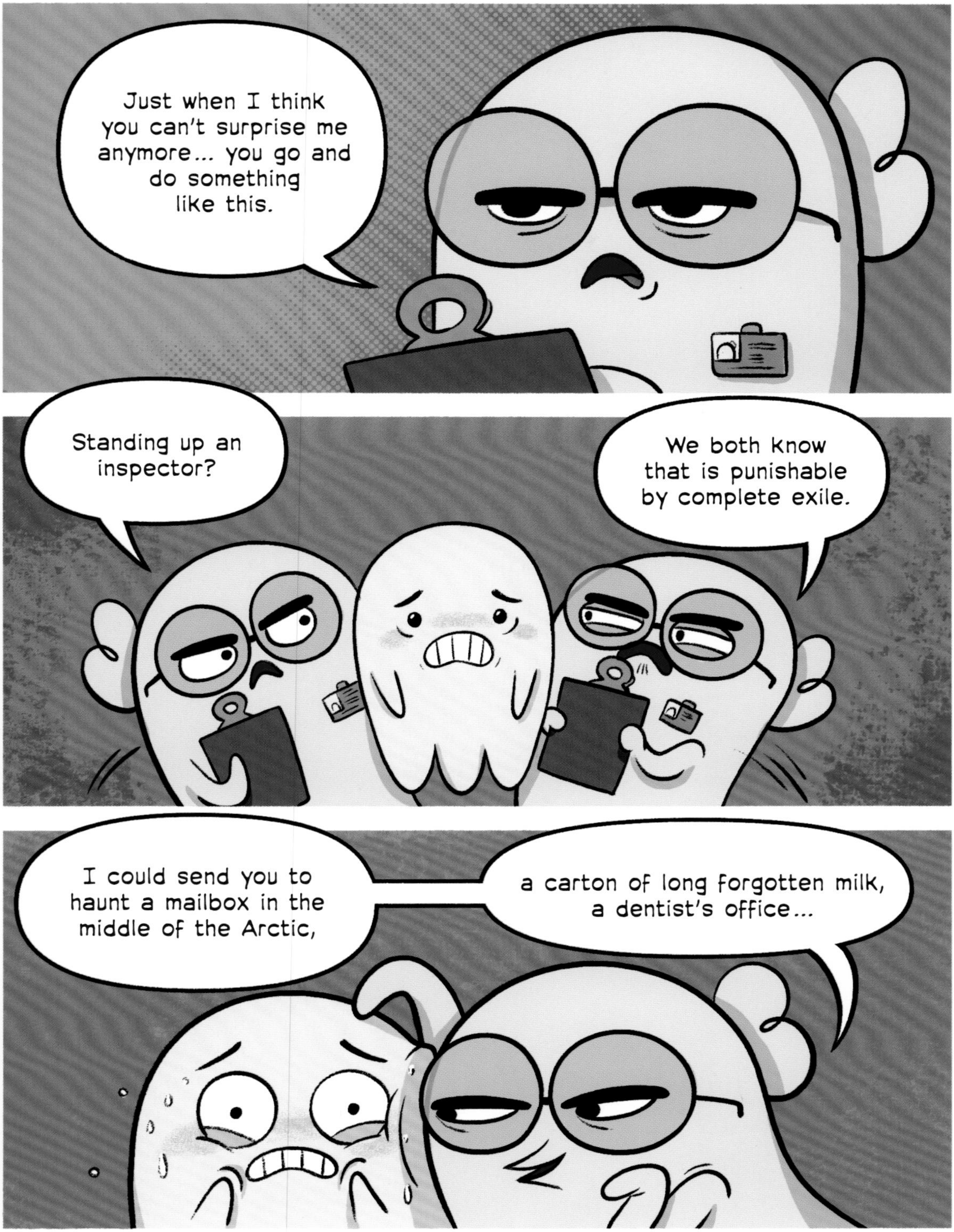
Just when I think you can't surprise me anymore... you go and do something like this.
Standing up an inspector?
We both know that is punishable by complete exile.
I could send you to haunt a mailbox in the middle of the Arctic,
a carton of long forgotten milk, a dentist's office...

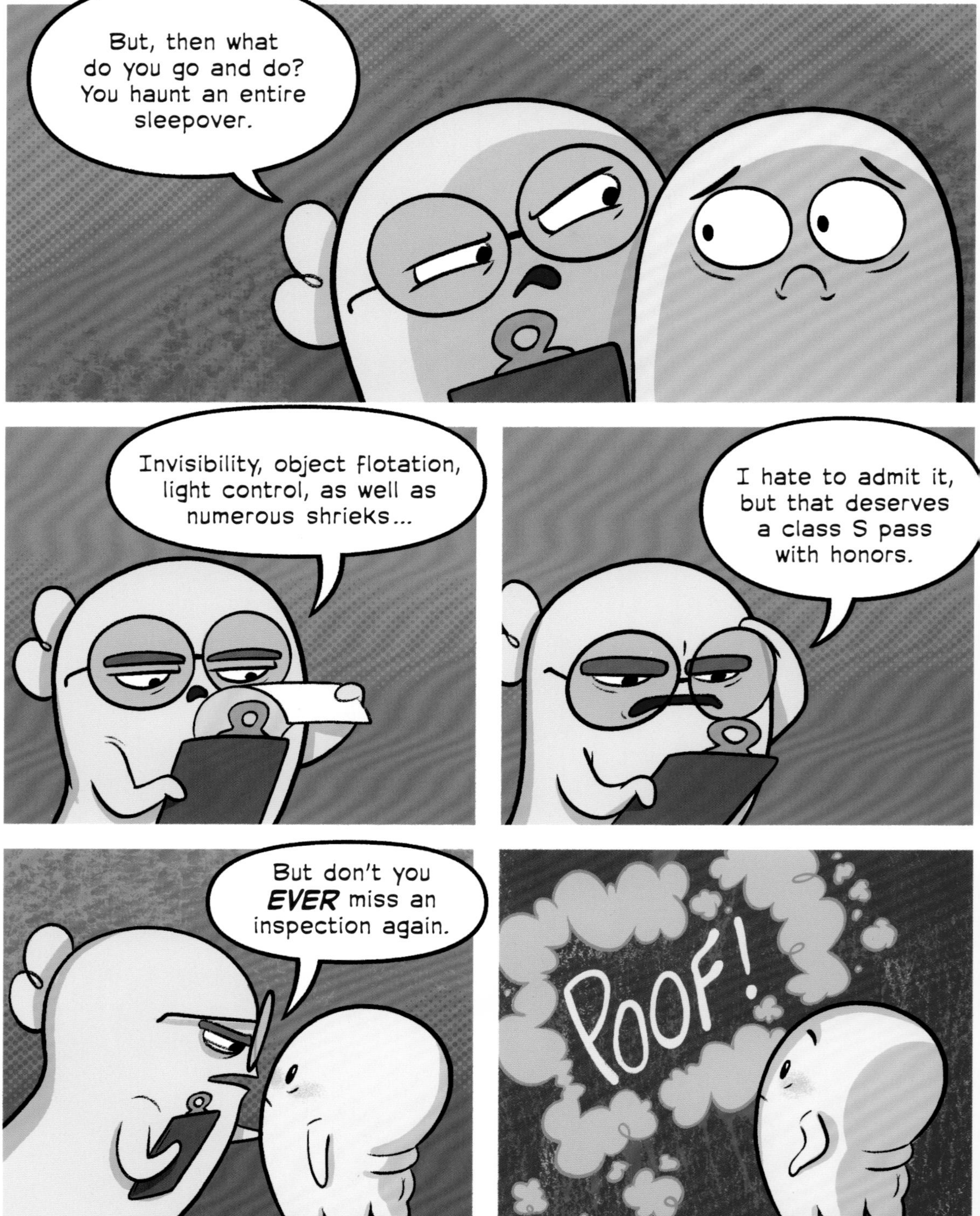
But, then what do you go and do? You haunt an entire sleepover.
Invisibility, object flotation, light control, as well as numerous shrieks...
I hate to admit it, but that deserves a class S pass with honors.
But don't you **EVER** miss an inspection again.
POOF!

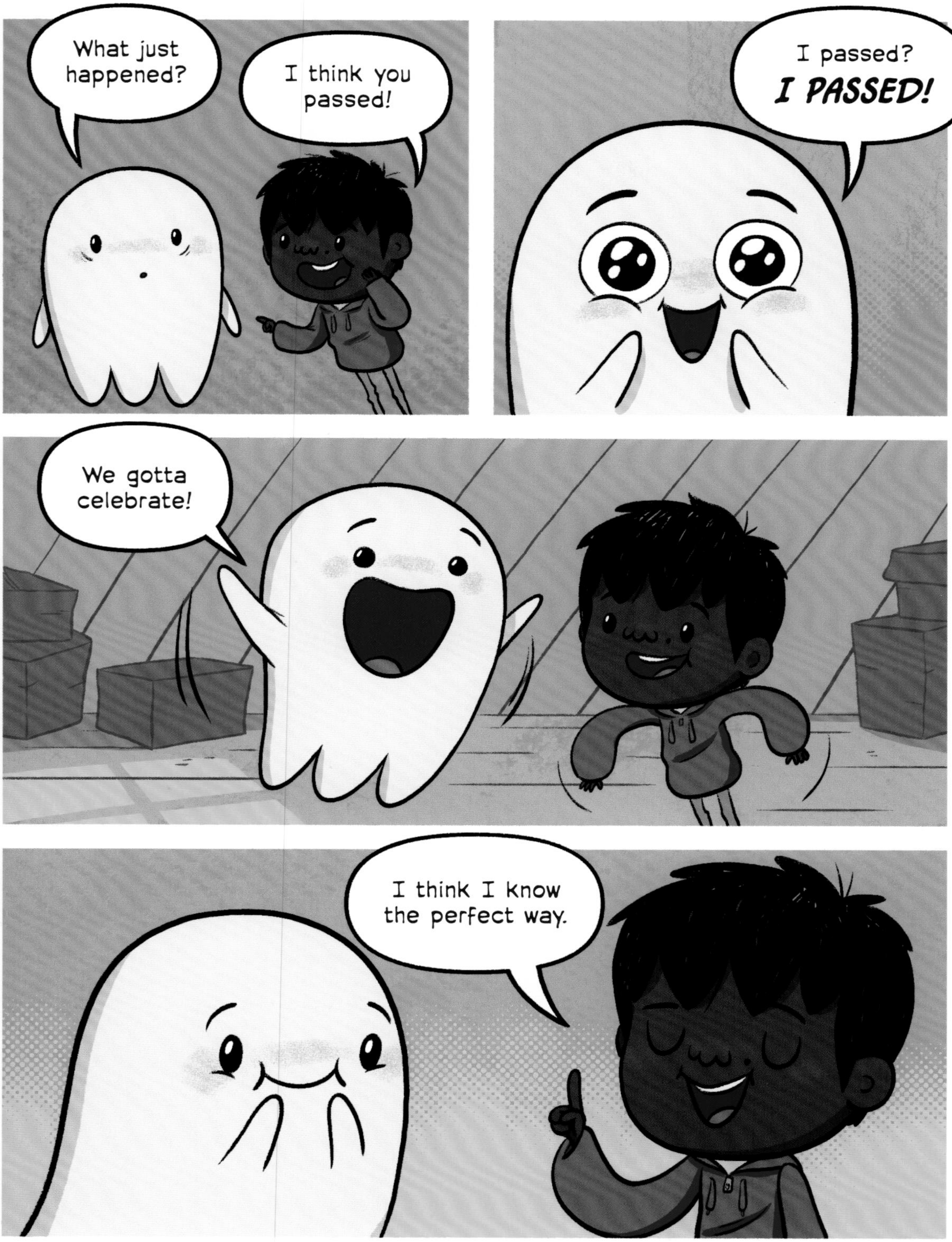
What just happened?
I think you passed!
I passed? I PASSED!
We gotta celebrate!
I think I know the perfect way.

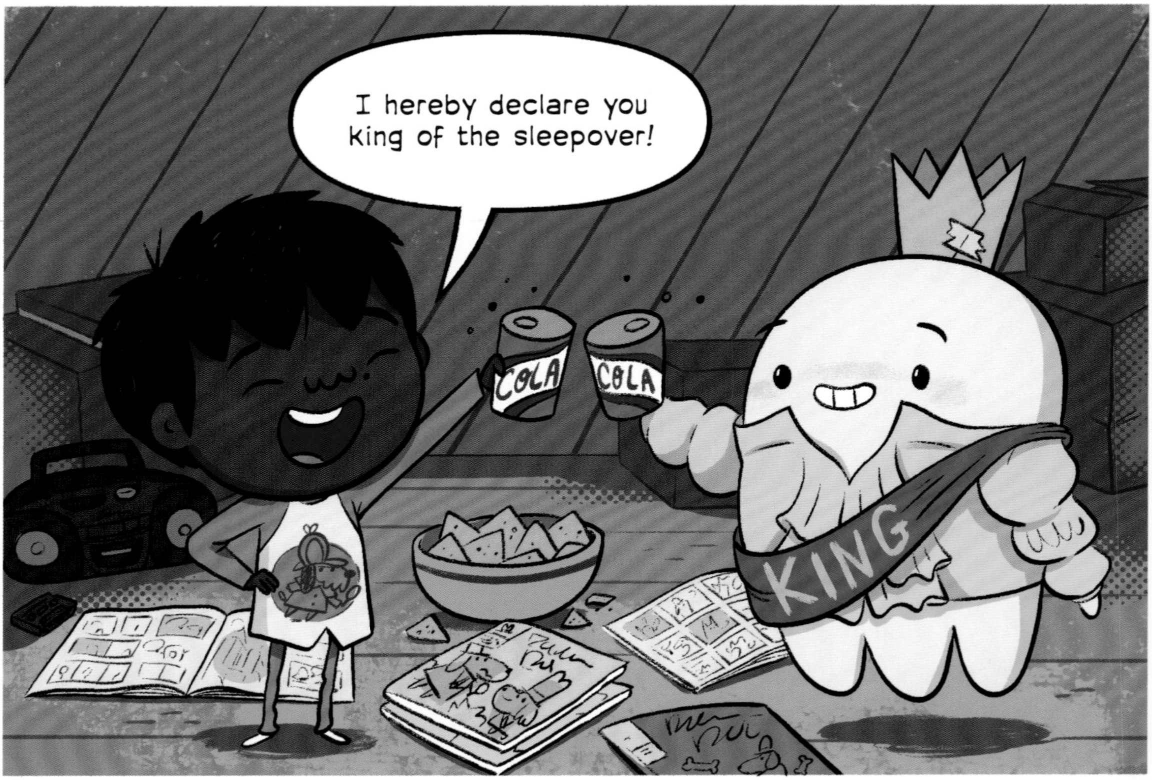
I hereby declare you king of the sleepover!
COLA
COLA
KING

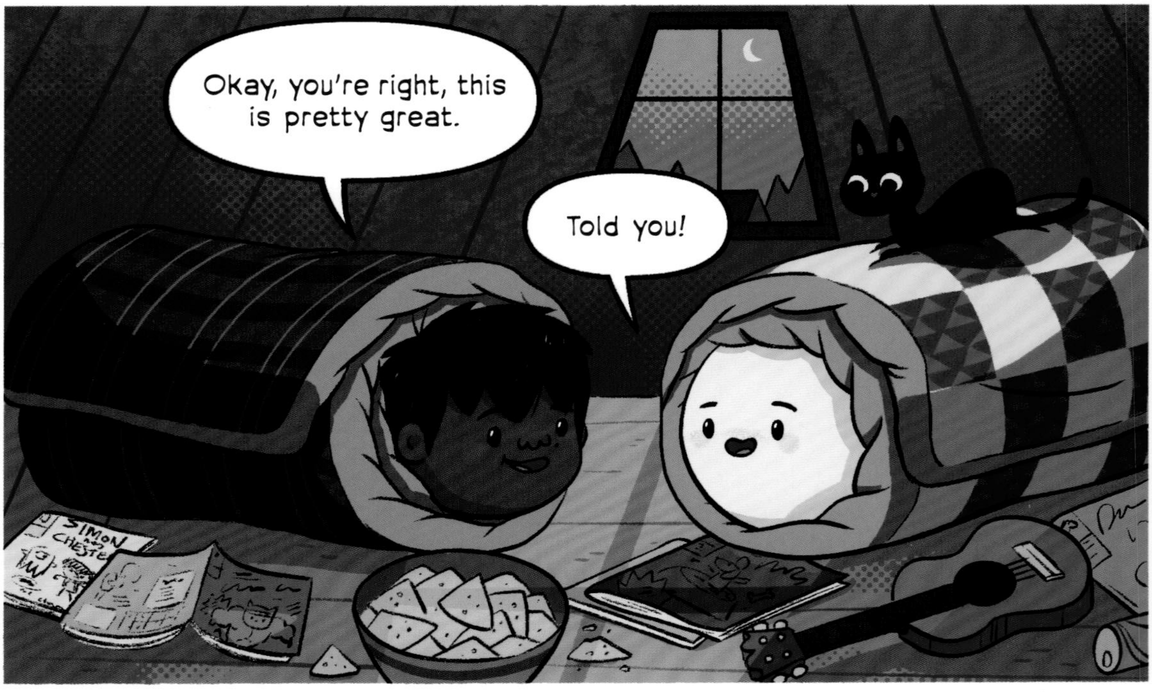
Okay, you're right, this is pretty great.
Told you!
SIMON

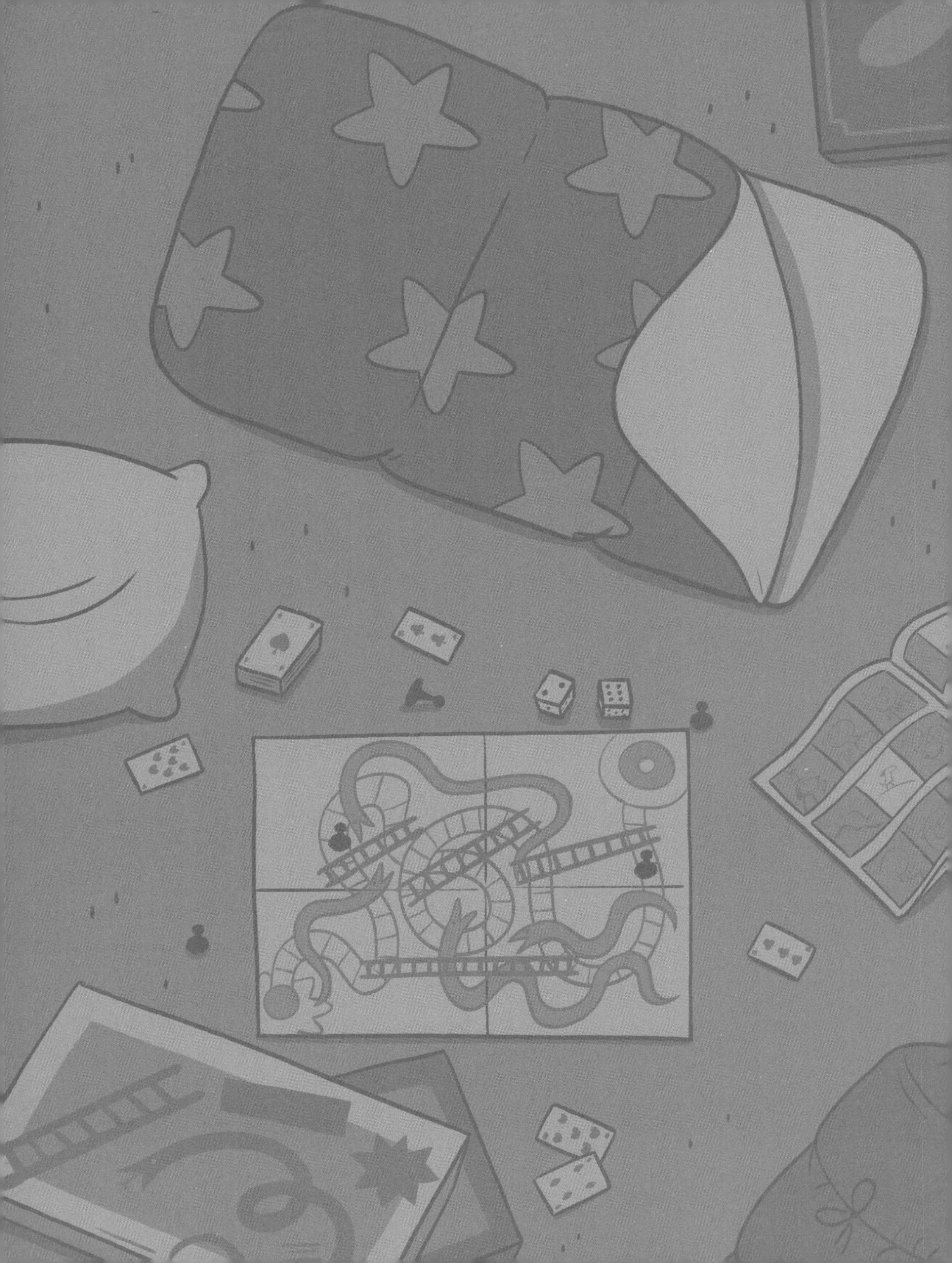